Praise for TOXIC WATERS

By David G. Ferguson

"Take an Ontario conservation officer and put him on a sailboat on Lake Huron. Mix in the crooked owner of a waste management company who is secretly dumping barrels of toxic material in the lake. Add a beautiful environmental activist and her father, the judge.

Now you have the makings for a fast-paced tale of suspense and adventure. In his first novel, Ferguson, a retired conservation officer, delivers the goods."

Shawn Perich – Northern Wilds Magazine, Minnesota, USA

"Congratulations. I just finished reading Toxic Waters. What a great read. Good story, complicated plot, interesting characters. At one point I thought it was turning into an Errol Flynn film. Well done. I will recommend it."

Murray Finn, Elliot Lake, Ontario

"Dave: I just wanted to drop you a line to say how much I enjoyed your book, Toxic Waters ... I look forward to your next novel. And thanks for presenting our ministry as 'the good guys'!"

Bill Thornton, Deputy Minister (Ret'd.) Ontario MNRF

Praise for BEAR RUNNERS

By David G. Ferguson

"Looking for an **absolute thriller** that combines your love of the outdoors with great story telling? Then pick up a copy of David Ferguson's *Bear Runners*. When you start to read this story, you will find it impossible to put it down."

Gord Pyzer – Outdoor Canada Magazine

"A young conservation officer takes a posting in Ontario's far north where he meets a young and beautiful bush pilot and encounters an elusive polar bear poacher.

... A great bedtime read, although the story moves so quickly you might not want to put it down...."

Shawn Perich – Northern Wilds Magazine, Minnesota, USA

"I picked it up in the morning and never put it down until I finished reading it at midnight. **That's what makes a great story.**"

Gary Jolicour, Stratton, Ontario

"Just got back from a remote cabin in the Yukon where I finished Bear Runners. Loved it! A bit freaky reading about the murder in the remote cabin when I was sitting alone in a remote cabin in the middle of a cold winter...."

Greg Derbyshire, Brantford, Ontario

Praise for UP HALFWAY CREEK

By David G. Ferguson

"**A darned good read.** The details woven into this novel brought many memories of places and events from my five years as a Conservation Officer at Moosonee. Believe me, the settings, people and happenings are authentic. At the same time, the topics dealt with are right out of today's news. You won't be disappointed."

Pat Brown, Retired Ontario Conservation Officer

"**Another entertaining and action-packed wilderness crime adventure** with the duo Rob McNabb and Samantha Williams; but it's also a standalone story if you haven't read Bear Runners yet.

I enjoyed the survival-in-the-wilderness aspects of the book and the thorough descriptions of the Ontario landscape and various equipment (airplanes, boats, ATVs) instrumental to the excitement in the story. The story flows very well and the various storylines are woven together nicely."

J.E. Schwartz, P.Eng. San Diego, California

"**Good read! Kept me up half the night to finish it!** Well written. Characters and plot rich in interesting detail and well developed. Nice for us northerners to be in familiar territory. Sensitive treatment of difficult issues involving abuse of children.

Roland H. Aube, Elliot Lake, Ontario

Praise for DOUBLE BACK FUR RUN

By David G. Ferguson

"**Best book yet**. This was a great read!! I had a hard time putting this down so I could go to work. Everyone should read this one. I'm looking forward to his next one."

J. Magill, Lethbridge, Alberta

"**Another exciting yarn**. A simple assignment to retrieve a truckload of illegally exported fur turns into a wild chase back and forth across northern Ontario, Manitoba and Saskatchewan. Throughout, the COs team up with other enforcement agencies as the story unfolds. The situations are realistic, as are the characters. The attention to detail is there whether it is tactics, equipment or technology. The author's experience and love of the profession of resource law enforcement shine through. Once you start, it is hard to put down."

Pat Brown, Sault Ste. Marie, Ontario

"**A great read.** It brought back memories how unexpected situations could develop when I was still working. It caught my attention in the very beginning, and I had a hard time putting it down but it always made me want to read more. Congratulations, another great novel."

Don Weltz, Retired Conservation Officer

Moose Down

David G. Ferguson

Published by
North Channel Novels
705-849-8238

Published in Canada by North Channel Novels
705-849-8238
Toxicwaters001@gmail.com

ISBN: 978-0-9939522-5-8

Aside from the factual information contained in the Ministry of Natural Resources and Forestry news release leading Chapter 1, this book is entirely a work of fiction. Names, characters and incidents are either the product of the author's imagination or are used fictionally. Any resemblance to actual events or persons, living or dead is entirely coincidental.

This story uses a mixture of metric and imperial units of measure — that's just the way it is here in Canada.

Cover by the author.

To conservation officers, game wardens — world-wide protectors of our wildlife and natural resources, by whatever title is printed on your badge and shoulder flashes.

As much as it may feel that we are continually swimming against the current, ours is an honourable profession. Don't ever give up.

Acknowledgements

My continuing thanks to Marnie Ferguson for her evaluation, editing and helpful encouragement, as she steered me, once again, from raw manuscript to finished story. This book is our fifth such collaborative project.

I wouldn't be comfortable putting my book on the market without first submitting it to several folks for pre-reading. My humble thanks to Joanne Marck and Norm Brown for their enthusiastic approval of this novel. Joanne's comment: "Great story. I just couldn't put it down." And from Norm: "A thrilling novel from beginning to end….4 wheel drive fully engaged and under power throughout!"

Novels by David G. Ferguson

Toxic Waters

Rob McNabb and Samantha Williams Wildlife Crime Series:

Bear Runners
Up Halfway Creek
Double Back Fur Run
Moose Down

Excerpts from original Natural Resources news release:

BULLETIN

Ontario Protecting Moose From Illegal Harvesting

May 10 2024

Ministry of Natural Resources and Forestry

The Ontario Court of Justice in Red Lake fined 20 defendants a total of $178,400 and ordered them to pay $44,525 in surcharges for a variety of moose hunting violations. In addition, the court issued a total of 59 years of hunting licence suspensions.

Bob Green's Fly-in Camps Ltd. and Green Airways pleaded guilty to hunting moose without a licence, discharging a firearm from a motorboat, possessing wildlife illegally killed, making a false statement in a document and obstructing a conservation officer.

Fourteen other individuals, including eight United States residents were fined varying amounts and given hunting licence suspensions ranging from one to twelve years.

Part 1

Chapter 1

Monday, October 3, 0245 – Over the North Channel, Lake Huron

With navigation and landing lights turned on, the De Havilland Beaver floatplane came from the north and descended toward the Cockburn Island air strip. The Beaver wasn't equipped with wheels. When it was just above the treetops, the aircraft went dark and banked right, turning west on its final approach for a moonlit landing on the calm waters of False Detour Passage. It was headed for the beach on the uninhabited eastern shore of Drummond Island, Michigan. Neither the pilot nor his passengers had any intention of notifying US Customs and Border Protection of their arrival.

Using just enough power to keep the plane airborne, the pilot stayed low over the water to avoid American radar. According to his contact on Drummond, he had only a twenty-minute window before the next Homeland Security drone eyeballed that section of the international border. Everything had to happen quickly. It usually did.

The pilot cut the power at the last possible instant. The wings lost their lift, and the floats kissed the water almost immediately. He killed the engine and the Beaver's momentum allowed it to coast the remaining short distance toward the beach. His island contact, wearing chest waders, entered the cold water and caught the nearest float. He pivoted the Beaver to face the open water. His helper joined him, and they backed the plane up to the beach until the floats grounded gently on the gravel bottom.

The pilot was already out and standing on the float. He directed his four poaching passengers to begin unloading. They'd done this before. It went like clockwork. One passenger handed baggage, rifles and sacks of deboned moose meat to another passenger on the float. That man passed the goods to the island contact and his assistant who set the load on the beach. The whole load, including a decent set of moose antlers, was discharged in less than three minutes. Without pausing to chat, the pilot passed an envelope to his contact — cash payment for services rendered. Then the contact and his helper gave the Beaver a shove clear of the beach. The passengers loaded everything into a pair of 6-seater side-by-side ATVs. Their trucks were parked in a discreet location at the head of the trail several miles away.

Another moose successfully harvested and delivered — two weeks before moose season opened. Money in the bank for the fly-in outfitter. The whole operation gave truth to the term, moonlighting.

The pilot fired up the Beaver's engine and departed the same way he had arrived, just above the water of the passage. He hugged the trees of Cockburn Island until he turned on his navigation lights and simulated a departure from the island air strip.

—

Saturday, October 8, 1535 – private dock, on Long Lake, near Sudbury, Ontario

"It's the going rate, mister … exactly what I quoted you last week. You won't get moose from anyone else for anything less. If you could buy it at the grocery store, I wouldn't be doing this.

But you know they can't sell it, and I've got big overhead … big risks, what with the plane and all. So if you still want to hold your fancy wild game dinner and show off for your big investors, it's like I said … you pay me the price we agreed on, or the meat stays on the plane and I'm outa here."

The customer, a self-important property developer, handed the pilot an envelope with the previously agreed on cash. Had tried to negotiate a better deal but hadn't really expected to win. Ten minutes later, the empty float plane was airborne and headed home.

It's been a profitable month up 'til now, the pilot thought to himself. Two Michigan groups and three domestic sales. Couldn't ask for much better. But the new game warden starts on Monday. I'll have to be a whole lot more careful … at least until I get a feel for how the guy works. Fuckin' bush cops. Maybe he won't be any more effective than the last guy, but there's that one wild card that might be a problem. Guess I'll find out, soon enough.

Chapter 2

Saturday, October 15, 0845

It was the opening day of the moose hunt, and it was pouring rain — just like it had been for the last three days. At least it was a warm rain. But an enforcement flight was out of the question. Again.

Conservation Officer Rob McNabb was in a foul mood as he drove out of Blind River. The day's destination was over forty kilometres north of Elliot Lake. Mission: check road access moose hunters for compliance with the hunting regulations. Fat chance they'll even be out if the rain doesn't let up.

McNabb had been transferred into the district just five days before to fill a CO position left vacant for almost two years. His marching orders were spelled out, loud and clear. "You are being provided an aircraft and pilot for one simple reason: Fly-in poachers have gone rogue and taken over the remote parts of the district. Bring *them* to their knees and the road access outlaws should fade away, either out of fear or respect for your airborne accomplishments. Seize any aircraft used in violations regardless of potential influence of their owners. We'll handle the complaints." McNabb had already seized three aircraft in his brief five-year career — more than any other CO in the province — so that requirement didn't worry him. Rich, arrogant bush plane owners didn't worry him, either.

What did worry him, was that Blind River District had always been protected by four COs. In recent years, however, three officers had transferred out, and one had retired. None of them had been replaced until McNabb's recent arrival.

Poachers *were* having a field day, and law-abiding folks had raised hell with politicians for leaving local natural resources unprotected for so long. Hence McNabb's recent reluctant transfer.

His wife, Samantha Williams, was a pilot and a Deputy CO. She flew bush planes for the Ontario Provincial Air Service and was the pilot assigned to McNabb. They would fly around the district trying to provide the level of resource protection that had traditionally been handled by four COs.

Neither Rob nor Sam had asked for the transfer. In fact, they both resented having to leave Moosonee and the James Bay frontier, their home and work area for the past five years. They had first met while Rob was investigating the case of a polar bear poacher and Sam had been assigned to fly him around Ontario's arctic frontier.

For Rob, meeting Sam had been love at first sight. For Sam, it was a little more complicated than that, but a bond had soon formed, and they were every bit as much in love now as they were back then.

On this miserable autumn morning, Deputy CO Eric Snyder was riding in the truck with McNabb. Snyder had retired from the job eleven years earlier, but with no active officers left in the district, he'd taken up a deputy's badge to help the new guy find his way around. The sixty-seven-year-old retiree had a wiry build and was maybe five foot-eight. His curly black hair had gone mostly to grey. Unlike McNabb, Snyder was unpaid, a volunteer. He was not issued a uniform and he carried no sidearm. Aside from a Kevlar vest he'd resurrected from his days on the job, he carried no defensive equipment. But he could still handle himself if push came to shove.

McNabb drove, squinting through the rain-streaked windshield. Even doing 10 km/h below the 90 km/h speed limit, he was driving white-knuckled. He had already added windshield wiper blades to the mental list of upgrades for his eight-year-old enforcement truck.

The government Ford F150 crew cab, called a High Visibility Enforcement Vehicle, or HVEV, had been a good truck for the job, once upon a time. But with more than 300 k on the odometer, it was on its last legs. It had already broken down once and had to be towed on his second day in the district.

"Ease up, Rob. Emergency lights ahead." Eric Snyder was the first to see them. Through the rain blurred windshield, McNabb just saw the combined purplish glow of the red, blue and white flashing lights of the police vehicle.

"Yeah, I've got it now … sort of." He slowed right down to creep past a police SUV that was parked behind a transport truck. And as they passed the rig, they saw a lone constable standing on the roadside in the pouring rain. He was facing three men. Three big dangerous looking men wearing sleeveless jean jackets and tattooed from their knuckles to their hairy shoulders. The constable looked to be an ordinary sized guy, maybe close to McNabb's six-foot height.

"Oh boy," Snyder said. "That looks like trouble right there. We should make ourselves useful, Rob. Pull up in front of the rig and turn on your light-bar … if it works. The police here helped me out enough times over the years … just by showing up."

The emergency light bar did work, and it drew the attention of two of the three heavies confronting the cop. The presumed driver of the transport continued mouthing off to the constable as McNabb and Snyder walked toward the group.

Snyder approached while McNabb held back a few metres and made sure they saw him rest his hand on his pistol grip. He had forgotten his hat in the truck and his sandy brown hair was already rain-slicked to his scalp. It wasn't the most professional image, but it gave him a look of desperation — a man not to be messed with.

Snyder spoke to the driver's two buddies. "I think you fellows would be more comfortable waiting in the cab. When your driver and the constable have finished their business, you'll be welcome to move on … if that's what he has in mind."

The heavies looked at each other, tried to stare down the old guy, but that wasn't working. They weighed their odds against an apparent civilian — older but speaking with authority, a fish cop, armed and in uniform looking like he just wanted to shoot someone, and of course, the constable. Finally, one of them shrugged. They chose to stand down. One climbed back into the cab and the other sat on the tractor's running board. Snyder and McNabb stood in place until the truck driver climbed aboard and started the diesel. The transport pulled away, the driver now in possession of a speeding ticket and an order to attend the nearest weigh scale for a complete commercial vehicle inspection.

The constable, rain dripping off his hat and coat, turned to McNabb and Snyder. "Hey, Eric. I appreciate you guys stopping by. Wasn't sure what was going down when I first saw the two guys sneaking forward on the other side of the cab. It was too late to back down. The driver was getting mouthy, but the silent goons with him felt like the greater threat."

Turning to McNabb he said, "You, I don't know, but thanks for showing the colours."

"Darren, this is Rob McNabb. He's our new game warden."

"Oh, the guy with the airplane. I'm Darren Brown."

McNabb smiled and shook the constable's hand. "You know that the aircraft is a secret, eh, Constable Brown?"

"Oh, don't worry, McNabb. Since *everybody* in the district already knows about it, your secret can't go any farther. But I'll pass the word along anyhow," Brown finished with a grin. He was about to say something else, but a silver Honda Civic with a loud sport exhaust ripped past them ignoring the flashing emergency lights, the wet road and the crappy visibility. It was headed eastbound, accompanied by the sonic booms from its cranked sound system. "Nice meeting you … gotta go." Back in his cruiser, lights and siren on, Constable Brown took off after the speeder. McNabb and Snyder returned to the CO truck and tried to shake off some of the rainwater before climbing back in.

Chapter 3

McNabb put the truck in drive, got back on the highway and continued toward their destination. He wasn't sure if they would get there or be delayed by a breakdown or redirected to another complaint. He'd been racing from one occurrence to the next on every shift since he had arrived in the district. Doing that for the past three days with an unmarked pool car while the HVEV was in the shop, hadn't been great for his morale.

"Darren's got an affinity for aircraft too," Snyder said. "Used to fly for the police, but eventually he took a demotion so he could spend more time with his young family."

"Flew police choppers?"

"He started out flying their fixed wing traffic planes down south. Cessnas. Up and down the freeways, clocking speeders for the ground troops. Then he moved on to rotary birds, but with only two fling-wings in their provincial fleet at the time, he found he was away more than at home. It put a strain on his marriage, so he did something about it. He's a real stand-up guy."

"I hesitate to ask, Eric, because every time I have tried in the last couple of days we've been called to deal with another occurrence." He reached over and turned down the volume on the Motorola two-way radio. "But, having been assigned the task of bringing fly-in poaching in the area to an end, can you give me any idea how big the problem here really is?"

"They gave you an impossible assignment, Rob. Reminds me of a CO down in Minden who was told by the minister's office to move all the bears out of Haliburton village before Halloween. Didn't want any kiddies attacked by bears. There had been a lot of bear sightings that year."

"Did it happen? The removal?"

"No. It didn't happen. I was that CO. I spent every shift in the village for a week and never saw, caught or tranquilized a single bear before the deadline. But then, not one trick-or-treater got eaten by bears either. Can't say the result will be as good, here though … some of these fly-in poachers are very efficient predators.

"Anyhow, to answer your question, some of the players here have probably changed since I was on the job. There used to be about fifteen or twenty guys with private planes who would fly in for the hunt from Sudbury, Sault Ste. Marie, and some local. Also a few came from farther south.

"And I think there are still four commercial outfitters working the district. The one commercial guy that most concerned me got old and sold the business. There were several others we suspected of opportunistic poaching too, but without the ability to access an aircraft of our own at a moment's notice, we never caught anyone. And the witnesses … usually pissed off hunters … seemed they could never provide enough detail for us to lay any charges. But now, having a dedicated aircraft, we'll have a better chance of meeting some of these guys. Once we get some flying weather, we can start to get a feel for who needs to be watched."

—

Thirty-five minutes north of Elliot Lake, McNabb turned onto the Kindiogami Lake road, a gravel surfaced forest access road, and followed Snyder's directions toward their first destination.

With the rain pouring down, most hunters would be waiting in their camps, impatient, hoping for the rain to stop.

The camp where they were headed now was one that Snyder had always suspected of taking moose before the season opened.

"Maybe it's not even the same crew there anymore," Snyder said. "A lot can change in eleven years … old guys give up hunting, get sick or die off, new guys get invited into the group … who knows. But just once I'd like to snag someone at that camp with a preseason moose. I always had the feeling I was missing something there."

"Well, we'll give them a good look over, Eric." Despite his cloudy mood, McNabb liked his new partner and didn't want to tarnish their working relationship.

"I'm guessing they'll be in camp like everyone else," Snyder continued. "So, why don't you go on in and keep them occupied while I scout around outside. Used to be that they always kept me occupied, so I never really got to explore the adjacent bush. There was never a game pole in the door yard. Had to be one somewhere nearby, but I never found it. And yet they always got moose. Every year."

McNabb drove a little farther up the forest road until Snyder had him turn off and follow a two-track trail.

"Okay, stop. Let me out here, Rob. The camp's just over the top of this hill. You go in as if you are on your own, and I'll circle around on foot … see what I can find. Give me a shout on the radio if you need me."

"Ditto, Eric. See you in a bit." As soon as Snyder pulled up his rain hood and closed the passenger door, McNabb started to ease the truck up the hill. The trail was growing in with birch saplings that were catching on the mirrors and thumping against the side panels of the patrol truck — not that anyone would notice the new scuff marks. If someone was outside, they would probably hear him coming, but inside, the rain drumming on the roof would drown out his approach until he was in the yard.

When it came into view, the place looked like a real rat's nest of old ramshackle buildings. There was a main cabin, a woodshed, an outhouse, and a generator lean-to. They were all in the same state of disrepair. Most of the siding material appeared to have been salvaged from snowmobile shipping crates that bore the Ski-Doo logo, now badly faded. McNabb understood why Eric suspected the occupants of illegal hunting activities. The place gave him that feeling too. And there was a lot of garbage lying around — something he never tolerated.

He parked in the midst of half a dozen vehicles — a recent model Lincoln Navigator and five pickups, ranging from a flashy new Chevy 4X4 to a thoroughly used Dodge that was apparently still on the road.

The camp door swung open as McNabb approached. But the person who emerged was not the official greeter. He simply unzipped his fly and preceded to urinate off the front step. Then again, maybe that *was* his official greeting. Rob had to wait until the guy finished before there was room on the narrow step to get to the door. He had already seen some real dumps for hunt camps in his short career, but this one took first prize.

He stepped inside. "Good morning campers. I'm Conservation Officer McNabb, doing my rounds. How come you guys aren't out beating the bush for your moose?" he said, trying for a bit of levity. By the looks of them, they could have used a rain shower, but he refrained from mentioning that — maybe they forgot to bring soap — and there were six of them. The place reeked of body odour, stale food, beer farts and God only knew what else.

"Thought we'd wait a bit." The giant who spoke approached McNabb, one hand coming forward. Rob wasn't sure he wanted to shake the grime encrusted paw. Not because of the germs it was likely breeding, but because it was the size of a baseball catcher's mitt. If the guy chose to, he could crush every bone in Rob's primary shooting hand.

But the big man leaned past him. The outstretched hand was reaching for a bottle of Black Velvet whiskey on the kitchen counter, not for a handshake. The guy poured himself a generous mugful of firewater and returned to sit at the grubby table.

"How did you fellows make out in the moose tag draw?"

"Heh, the usual," came from another inmate.

Not a very chatty bunch. "Well, seeing as how you are all together, may I check your licences please." Nobody moved.

"Okay, no problem. You aren't out hunting right now. Don't need licences to sit here in this … ah … cabin." He caught himself just in time — almost said "filth."

"I'll be running the roads with the police for the rest of the hunt," he improvised. "We'll stop in each time we're by here until we've verified everyone's paperwork."

After that announcement, it took no time at all for one guy to dig the wallet out of his pocket. He pulled out his licence and handed it over. Another stood up and headed over to one of the bunks lining the back wall and returned a moment later with his.

Gradually, everyone except one man produced a valid moose licence. One cow tag and one bull, the rest had calf tags. The last guy claimed to be the cook, not a hunter. McNabb didn't know whether to feel sorry for him or to gag at the thought, but he accepted his explanation. He kept the licences in his hand for the time being, hoping to hear from Snyder before too long.

Chapter 4

Eric Snyder was zigzagging his way through the bush several hundred metres behind the hunt camp. As he pushed through an extra thick patch of brush, it felt as if his rain suit was as wet inside as it was on the outside. It seemed that the better some rain gear was at keeping the rain out, the more likely it was to retain body heat and sweat. And now, his efforts had worked up a major sweat.

He was beginning to wonder if maybe he'd guessed wrong about these guys. Hadn't seen any sign of human activity back here yet. No trails through the bush — nothing.

Then he caught a sound that wasn't consistent with rain falling in the forest. He pulled his hood back to hear it better, and to gauge the direction. Got it. With his hood back up, he turned to the right and walked another fifty metres. The sound of rain drumming on a plastic tarp led him to a large tarp stretched across the elusive game pole.

"Ha! Gotcha, boys."

—

In the camp, McNabb asked, "If I go out there and check, will I find any loaded firearms in your vehicles?"

"No sir. We keep 'em all in here." The giant reached behind his chair and pulled back a blanket that hung like a curtain on the wall between two rows of bunks. Five rifles rested on a rack. Not locked, but out of sight. He let the blanket fall back in place. "Once we arrive, all our huntin' is done on foot.

No four-wheelers either. Movin' around with machines just drives the moose off into someone else's area. We stay quiet and all the other camps drive them our way."

"Makes sense," McNabb conceded. "You guys have been hunting the area for a few years, I take it."

"Started here in the eighties, before the mines closed down in Elliot Lake," the giant said.

"Only half of us is from the original gang," came from the cook. How could he stay with it for so long, McNabb wondered. I guess they're well suited to each other.

Just then, his radio squawked.

"Go ahead, Eric."

"Got cold cuts out here, Rob. Bring your kit. I'm straight south of the camp about two hundred metres."

"Ten-four. Be there shortly." He looked at the group gathered around the table. "Okay, gents, my partner has found your preseason moose. Does anyone wish to own up?"

No one volunteered. No surprise. But more importantly, no one denied that there was a preseason moose hanging behind their camp. No one thought to say: "That's not ours." A tactical error on their part. Not that that excuse would ever stand up in court, but a good defence lawyer could make an issue of it.

"That's not a problem, fellas. We'll get all the charges sorted out after we do the forensics on whatever Officer Snyder has found out there."

The giant: "Snyder? … fuck. I thought he retired. That asshole pestered us for years."

McNabb: "He said he missed you guys. Came out of retirement, just for old time's sake." That drew a few chuckles. Good to keep the mood light as much as possible. Less chance of tempers flaring. "Okay, boys. Who's coming for a walk? And remember, anyone who stays back in camp won't know what his buddies have told us." Everyone but the cook pushed away from the table and got into some sort of rain gear.

Five minutes later they arrived at a game pole sagging under the weight of twelve quarters of moose. The pole was an eight-inch diameter spruce with the bark removed. It was suspended horizontally, almost sixteen feet above the ground between two poplar trees that grew about twenty feet apart. Hanging the meat well above the ground allowed the cooling process to begin and kept it above the reach of foxes, wolves and most bears.

Eric Snyder had placed a wobbly ladder at one end of the row of hanging quarters.

"Got your thermometer handy, Rob? Just by feel, I can't detect any warmth in these quarters. Had to have been shot at least a day before season opening."

"Thermometer coming right up." As he opened his CSI kit he said, "Before we go to the trouble of taking temperatures of each carcass, maybe you guys would like to tell us when these moose were actually shot?" No one spoke up.

"Okay, here's the way this works. The guilty person or persons speak up now and only they will be charged with preseason hunting. But if no one wants to confess, we'll do the whole forensics thing, seize all the firearms and anything else we figure constitutes evidence of the crime. And since we won't know *who* is responsible, you will all be charged as parties to the offence."

"How much is the fine?" the giant asked.

"That's out of my hands. An offence this serious goes to court. Cooperate from now on and that *will* go in your favour. Dig in your heels and the local judge will likely up the ante." The last justice of the peace for the area had retired, so the local provincial court judge was now covering for the lower-level court as well as her own criminal court.

"This is my first year here, but I hear she's tough. Maximum fine under the Fish and Wildlife Conservation Act is twenty-five thousand."

"Less if we come clean?" he asked.

"Generally, much less. Right, Eric?" His deputy nodded yes.

"Well," the guy paused, looked at his companions then continued. "We got here before lunch two days ago. Heard there was weather comin' in … it was already raining some. We thought we'd scout around … just checkin' out the prospects." The giant stopped and looked at one of the other men. "Les, you want to do this? Some of us'll help with the fine … I will, anyways." He looked at the others and several heads nodded in agreement.

"My wife'll skin me alive, guys. She don't even like eating moose." The scrawny guy named Les stood there looking absolutely miserable.

"We'll all chip in, Les," one of the others spoke up. "I might have to borrow some, depending on how much the fine is, but I vote we split it five ways. We all took part one way or another."

"Okay, let's hear it, Les," McNabb urged.

"Well, it wasn't all that complicated, Officer. Uh … Tony," he nodded toward the giant, "he told me to walk the path to the old dried-up beaver pond. It's just another couple hundred yards down that way from here and it ain't dried up no more. When I got there, a cow and two calves was feedin' on pond weeds. So I up an' dusted the cow … one shot … and the calves never moved more'n a few yards. So I shot them too. I know it weren't right, but what difference would two days make, eh?"

"We all heard the shots," Tony wrapped up the story, "and we went down and drug them out of the water and helped him gut and quarter them and get them hung up here."

"So, I have to ask," Snyder said. "You understand that there's a two-year statute of limitations on offences under the Act, so you can't be charged for things you did back when I was working, but I'm curious. Were you doing this back then, too?"

"Yeah, some years we did." Tony admitted. "Wouldn't be right to lie about it. Not now, anyways."

McNabb pulled out his notebook. "Okay guys, we are seizing the moose, but I'll keep my word. Les is the only one being charged. And we'll cancel the cow licence and two calves. You are down to the two remaining licences for the rest of your hunt. Don't screw it up.

"And there's something else I noticed. While your camp is leased on a land use permit, it is still considered Crown land. I want all the garbage cleaned up and carted off to the landfill … not chucked farther back in the bush. And I want it done by the time I come back through here a week from today. Otherwise, I'll be handing out a bunch of paper for littering, and that's not cheap, either."

Snyder took over again. "You've seen the fair treatment Officer McNabb has given you today. But he'll sure be upset to find out if you repeat this kind of shit in the future. He'll come down hard on you … no breaks. And I *do* know the local judge. If you go to her court a second time, she *will* hand down the maximum fine. I guarantee it.

"Now, while Les and Officer McNabb take care of the paperwork, you guys start taking down the quarters. We'll take some temperatures to add to our time-of-kill log. That'll be your contribution to wildlife forensic research. Then we'll hike the meat out to our truck. If we can borrow your rain tarp, we'll be able to protect the meat on the way to the cooler."

"What happens to it after that?" Tony asked.

"The tarp?"

"Funny guy. No, the meat."

"Donated to needy folks."

"We might qualify after we pay the fine."

McNabb chuckled, "Guys who drive new pickups and Lincoln Navigators don't generally make the cut." The chuckle spread through the group. He was relieved that the hunters had come around to cooperating without a major hassle. His first impressions had led him to expect a tense interaction. Five or six pissed off, grubby hunters against him and Snyder….

Chapter 5

1450 – Southbound on highway 108

With the meat of three seized moose weighing down the HVEV pickup, McNabb and Snyder headed back to the office to process the seizures and write up the charges. The rain had almost quit, the sky was looking brighter, and McNabb's mood had brightened as well. They talked about their success at the filthy moose camp as they rolled down the highway.

"A good day's work, Rob," Snyder said. "One camp checked, and three moose seized. First day of the hunt and you hit a three-run homer."

"You were the one at bat, Eric. I was just there as the cleanup man. The inning was over before I got to bat. It's just too bad we didn't get to check any other camps before you won the game."

"It doesn't matter who scored, Rob. It was a team effort. And the word will be out in that corner of the district pretty quickly: 'the new game warden means business.' I'll bet we won't be able to buy a charge in that corner for the rest of this season."

As McNabb crested the next hill on the winding, roller coaster highway, he saw the road ahead blocked by traffic. A police cruiser was on the scene, all lights flashing, and a dump truck with damaged grillwork was parked on the northbound shoulder. Wrecked radiator, judging from the coolant pooled under the truck. Rob coasted to a stop behind the last vehicle in the line. "Wonder what's going on down there."

"Road wreck of some sort, I'd guess," Eric replied. "I see people standing in the middle of the highway, up past the police cruiser. Pinned occupant, or a fatality? Maybe we'd better see if we can help with anything."

McNabb activated the four-way flashers, and they got out of the truck. Walking down the centre line he could already see more than he had from inside the cab. A deer was lying on the road, legs thrashing. Obviously injured.

They walked past the dozen vehicles that were backed up behind the police SUV. A young female constable was trying to keep the bystanders away from the terrified animal, and at the same time deal with an agitated woman.

"You've got to take her to a veterinarian," the civilian insisted in a shrill, grating voice. "I moved up here from the city because I was told northern people were kind and caring. Leaving that poor animal there without medical treatment is cruel and inhumane."

McNabb wedged himself through the small crowd. "Excuse me, Constable. I'm Rob McNabb, the new conservation officer in Blind. Do you need a hand here?"

"Hi, I'm Mary Miller. McNabb, eh? The guys were talking about you at the shop. The guy with the airplane." While they talked, the agitated woman became even more so, and Constable Miller returned to the matter at hand.

"Maybe you *can* help. I don't know what to do about this deer. Thrashing around like that, the poor thing is suffering for sure, but someone is going to get hurt if they get too close. Everyone else on my shift is tied up with a domestic in town, so I'm on my own and this is my first month going solo."

"Okay, Mary. Baptism by fire, huh? Let's try this." He looked up and raised his voice to address the gathered crowd. "I'm Conservation Officer McNabb. We need all of you to return to your vehicles. We are going to put the deer out of its misery, and I'm sure that may be upsetting to some of you. It will be easier for all of us if you don't have to watch." The last part was directed primarily at the agitated bystander.

Constable Miller didn't look all that comfortable about performing euthanasia on the deer, and the concerned citizen was totally against it.

"*You can't do that!*" she screamed. "Take her to the vet. *Right now*!"

McNabb tried to explain the situation to the distraught woman. "Ma'am, it's a him, not a her," he said, realizing as he spoke, that the gender of the poor beast didn't much matter. But he went on. "And this poor buck has a broken back and badly smashed hind legs. He's probably got internal injuries as well. He was hit by a dump truck, after all. Even if deer did respond well to veterinary medicine, which they generally don't, this fellow still wouldn't have any chance of surviving. And finally, anyone trying to lift him into a truck to transport him to a vet could get badly slashed by those flailing front hooves. Now please return to your vehicle."

"Well, if you are going to kill it, then are you going to give it a decent burial?"

"Ma'am, even if there *was* a pet cemetery around here, no government agency is going to spend *your* tax dollars on a burial. Now, if someone wants to salvage any meat, they are entitled to take the carcass away. If not, then we'll move him into the bush where he will provide food for a wide variety of other wildlife."

"But…."

Eric Snyder appeared at the woman's side just as McNabb's patience was on the verge of running out. The deputy's timing was impeccable. "Excuse me, ma'am, I'm Deputy Conservation Officer Snyder. I'm with Officer McNabb. Been on the job a long time and I've seen these situations too many times before. There's nothing we can do to help the deer. Let me take you to your car. Which one is yours?" Finally lost for words, and feeling a little woozy, the woman pointed and let Eric lead her away.

Constable Miller turned to face McNabb. "I'm not comfortable about doing this either. I never shot a helpless animal before."

"I'll take care of it this time. But you need to see how it's done … I guarantee you, there will be others. Don't feel bad. It isn't something I enjoy doing either. I botched it badly the first time I had to do it."

McNabb drew his 9 mm pistol, bent down behind the deer and quickly fired a single round. With its spinal cord severed at the base of its skull, the animal instantly went limp — vital signs absent. It was no longer suffering. At that point, a man who was waiting by one of the pickups parked behind the cruiser walked up and asked if he could claim the deer. McNabb helped him drag the carcass off the road near his truck and then walked back to join Snyder at the HVEV. "Thanks Eric."

"I figured she might be getting on your nerves."

"You read me like a book, partner."

"In large print, my friend."

By the time they were on highway 17 driving west out of Spragge, the sun was shining. First sunshine he'd seen in a week and McNabb was beginning to enjoy himself. He decided maybe it was not such a bad district after all. He'd met two of the local police constables today and paid forward, never knowing when he might need their assistance in the future. And then his cell phone rang.

Chapter 6

1545 – Westbound on Hwy 17

The truck's Bluetooth system didn't work — another defect to report — so Rob pulled off the road and took the phone from his pocket. Call display said Comm Centre, and he knew which operator was on today. He connected the call and put it on speaker mode. "McNabb here. Hi, Mary Ellen."

"*Hi Rob. Would you please turn your radio back up? We've been trying to reach you. We got a careless hunting complaint in Algoma Mills. Are you in a position to respond?*"

"We're about fifteen minutes away, I'd guess."

"Less than ten from here, Rob," Eric said, and McNabb nodded.

"Details, M.E.?"

"*Someone's shooting at the spawning salmon from the highway 538 bridge over Lauzon Creek. Folks fishing along the creek bank are plenty upset.*"

"Okay, we're on it. Deputy Snyder says ETA is less than ten minutes from here." He disconnected the call and pushed the old F150 hard — light bar flashing. If the guy kept on shooting around a busy fishing hole, someone could get shot.

Seven minutes later he turned down highway 538 and drove under the railroad overpass at the bottom of the hill. Right ahead of them, one man stood at the railing of the road bridge over the creek. He was shooting at salmon in the water below with a .22 calibre rifle.

Irate anglers were yelling up at him from where they were fishing along the creek banks. McNabb parked on the bridge and approached the shooter unnoticed from behind. Snyder headed across the bridge to move the anglers out of the line of fire. They should have been smart enough to do that without an invitation.

McNabb watched while the guy fired another shot into the creek forty or fifty feet downstream. At such a shallow angle to the water surface, it was quite possible that bullets could ricochet. With no control over where the shots went, someone could easily get hit.

McNabb waited until the man opened the bolt action to eject the empty brass, then tapped him on the shoulder and announced himself: "Conservation officer." If that move startled the guy, the gun couldn't be accidentally fired — the rifle's action was still open. No risk to the creek bank anglers.

And the guy *was* startled — and swung the rifle around.

"Whoa there, fellow. Where did you take your hunter safety training?" McNabb demanded as he grabbed hold of the rifle barrel with his left hand and held it high. He kept his right hand in reserve for blocking any fists headed his way, or, in the worst-case scenario, for drawing his pistol. Initially, nothing happened. The man, dirty, unshaven and probably in his forties, was about the same height as McNabb, and he stood there, straining to take back control of the gun.

"Stand still. Stop struggling. I asked you where you took your firearms training?"

The struggling eased for a moment. But the shooter still held a firm grip on his rifle. "Learned myself. No government is going to tell me what I can or can't do, or how to do it. I'm a sovereign citizen, livin' off the grid, so you've got no authority over me. Ain't no harm shooting the fish, since they die after they spawn anyhow."

"Sorry to burst your bubble, pal, but I'm charging you with careless hunting for starters. Now, let go of the rifle. And I need to see your identification."

"You can't have my fuckin' rifle, and if I'd known I was going be hassled by a fuckin' game warden, I'd a used the bigger one."

"What's your name?"

"Fuck you."

There was little point asking any more questions. Out of the corner of his eye, McNabb could see that a few of the creek bank anglers had moved up to the other end of the bridge, less than twenty metres away. And somehow, the guy had managed to get the bolt closed again. The gun was loaded, cocked and the guy's finger was inside the trigger guard. On the trigger. Someone really could get hurt.

"Let go of this rifle *right now*," McNabb ordered. "You are under arrest for obstructing an officer," he grunted. The guy was strong. And he wasn't letting go. Now Rob had both of his hands on the rifle and had to struggle just to keep it pointed away from the spectators.

In McNabb's self defense training, the teaching was, when there was a threat to your life, or the lives of others, there are no Queensberry rules. You do whatever it takes to gain control of the situation. In this case, there was only one move that would disable the guy and relieve him of the rifle without getting into a major brawl.

As McNabb twisted the muzzle straight up in the air, the shooter fought to improve his balance and set his feet in a wider stance. Exactly the move McNabb hoped for. He kneed the guy in the groin. Kneed him hard. And the guy went down, curled into the fetal position even before he hit the pavement. Of course, that was going to make it difficult to get handcuffs on him, his hands being clenched tight between his thighs. But he let go of the rifle and that gave McNabb time to open the bolt and unload it. Snyder appeared from nowhere and took control of the rifle.

"We called 911 and the cops are on the way," one of the bystanders said as he walked toward McNabb and the fallen shooter. Rob noticed that one of the others had his cell phone up and pointed his way. Videoing the action. Crap. We're going to be on YouTube or the TV news before the end of the day. The look on Rob's face must have telegraphed his concern to the guy because he spoke up without lowering the phone.

"Not what you think. This is for the cops. You got that guy dead to rights. The son of a bitch put a bullet into my wife's car over there. If the police weren't coming, I was going to offer to throw him off the bridge for you … onto the rocks below. And us four are all going to swear out statements against this asshole."

McNabb thanked him, then bent down to put cuffs on the prisoner. "You are under arrest, for resisting arrest, assaulting a peace officer, taking fish by means other than angling and dangerous use of a firearm. And there's bound to be a few more I'll think of before we are done. Do you wish to say anything in answer to the charges," and he recited the official police caution from memory as he cuffed the man's wrists behind his back. He was searching the man for other weapons when the first police cruiser arrived. Constable Mary Miller stepped out and walked over.

"Officer McNabb, I didn't expect I'd get to repay you so soon for this afternoon's favour."

"Oh, no need to put a 9-mil round into the back of his head. Maybe a few minutes ago … oh shit." He looked at the guy taking videos with his phone. "Are you still recording?"

"No, my wife just called me back. I was on the phone. Did I miss something?"

"Not that needed recording, no." A wave of relief washed over him. Cameras were everywhere these days. You were *supposed* to keep that in mind when you did or said anything on the job.

"Okay, Constable, he's been cautioned. The specific wildlife charges against him are careless hunting and taking fish by means other than angling. But I think the criminal obstruction, assault and firearms charges will take priority. He disavows organized government. Says he's a sovereign citizen living off the grid and claims we have no jurisdiction over him."

"They used to call themselves preppers, didn't they?"

"They've evolved … uh, bad choice of words. Devolved, maybe. They're showing up videoing themselves in police confrontations on Facebook and YouTube. Anyhow, my guess is that he has no firearms acquisition or possession permit either. And, during the struggle, in a spontaneous utterance, he admitted to having a larger rifle. I found these in his pocket when I searched him." He held up a set of car keys without an electronic fob. "I'm guessing they'll fit that old Crown Vic parked over by the outhouses. Bet there's no insurance or recent registration either."

"Let's get him into my cage first, Rob. Then we'll take a look at the rolling rust can."

"You guys got no right. That's my property."

"By your actions sir," Miller said, "you gave us all the authority we need."

He resisted being moved toward the police vehicle, but Miller and McNabb half dragged him there, wrestled him through the back door with Miller pushing the guy's head down to clear the door opening. Another police SUV rolled to a stop just as they got the door closed.

A tall, stocky, middle-aged sergeant got out of the passenger side and approached. "Rob McNabb? I'm Harry Mitchell. Good to finally meet you," he said and shook McNabb's hand. "Keeping him in line, Eric?" Snyder and Mitchell were next door neighbours.

Eric smiled and gave him a thumbs up. "He's pretty good at taking care of himself, Harry."

"Good to meet you too, Sergeant."

Before the sergeant had a chance to continue, his driver stepped out of the police vehicle, laughing. "Officer McNabb, are you trying to put us out of a job?" Constable Brown quipped.

"Hey, if we could beat you here, driving our old rolling wreck, it's pretty obvious you weren't interested in this bust. But if you want to wade around in the creek separating the dead salmon that were shot from the ones that died of natural causes, go for it. Pretty hard to charge the guy for fishing by means other than angling if we don't have any evidence."

"Constable Miller, do you have enough from McNabb to get this started?" Sergeant Mitchell asked.

"I do, Sarge. But he might want to join us when we search the Crown Vic over there."

While McNabb and the police searched the car, Eric Snyder waded through the shallows in the creek and found several salmon that were obvious shooting victims. He picked the smallest two and left the others on the creek bank to feed the seagulls and bald eagles. The car search turned up little of interest for the COs, but the police were going to be tied up for hours documenting the worldly chattels of the sovereign citizen. They called to have the vehicle towed to the detachment.

Chapter 7

Ministry of Natural Resources office, Blind River

It took the rest of the shift for McNabb and Snyder to catalogue the moose seizures from their morning bust and the bridge shooter's salmon with the bullet holes. The moose got locked in the walk-in evidence cooler and the fish in a chest freezer. The officers still had to go back to the police detachment and give their statements on the latter case.

When they were done, McNabb dropped Snyder at his place, then drove his own truck the twelve kilometres home. The house was a thousand square foot bungalow on Centre Street in Algoma Mills. It had been the only house he and Sam could find in their price range on short notice. Built on a poured concrete basement, the house had good bones, but it needed some major TLC. It still had its original clapboard siding, and the white paint was due for a major redo, or better still, be replaced with modern siding. And there was a mouse infestation indoors that their big orange tabby cat was trying to bring under control — the hardware store was out of mouse traps.

The house faced south and was located between two vacant, treed lots. All three lots were large properties laid out in the 1950s. The front lawn was in rough shape — would never be featured in *Better Homes and Gardens*. The gravel driveway was a single lane over the culvert, but widened out to double, with one lane going into the garage and the other passing between the house and garage, leading to the back yard. The gravel surface supported a healthy display of autumn wildflowers — commonly referred to as weeds. The deep back yard was half lawn, over the septic field bed and the rest was bush lot. The garage matched the house for siding and overall condition.

McNabb drove up the street — almost home after an eventful day.

"Well, shit." The driveway was blocked by two big terracotta planters that came with the house. When he left for work in the morning, the big pots had been stationed on either side of the front doorstep — where they belonged — where they'd been since before they bought the house. He pulled to the side of the street and got out of the truck. This was the third incident of mischief they'd experienced since moving in. Someone didn't like game wardens, he assumed.

The first time, someone had simply moved his boat, on its trailer, from the side yard to the front of the garage. The second incident found their garden furniture moved from the back yard and stacked on the side doorstep.

This was a definite escalation — still mischief, not yet vandalism. But it was a concerning trend just the same. The planters, full of earth and last summer's dead azaleas, were heavy — Rob figured close to a hundred pounds each. He tilted the first planter partway on its side and began to roll it, on its bottom rim, across the yard, back toward the front step where it belonged.

Sam came out of the house wearing unlaced work boots and no jacket. "Assholes are at it again, eh? This must have just happened in the last half hour, Rob. Mae Ling and I were in the basement doing the laundry and scrubbing grungy stains off the concrete floor when Lottie saw you drive up." Sixteen-year-old Mae Ling was their adopted daughter and Charlotte Jean was a busy four-year-old of their own creation. She was in the living room, playing dress-up with the cat when she saw her father rolling the planter across the front yard.

Sam went to the end of the driveway and struggled to get the second planter tilted. Despite standing only five-foot-four, the fiery redhead was halfway to the step with that one when Rob offered to take over. She declined his help.

"I've wrestled four-hundred-pound drums of aviation fuel around in the bush, McNabb. I can sure as hell manage this little flower pot." Rob was not about to argue with his wife. Her fiery attitude was one of the things that he loved about her. That and her trim, but muscular figure.

He was examining the yard while Sam manoeuvred her planter toward the steps. "Did you notice there are no roll marks like what we just left on the ground? None from when the pots were moved down there. Someone carried those suckers. Awkward load with the weight all out front. Take a strong man to do that."

"Or more than one guy. I don't like the way this bullshit is escalating, Rob." Sam wiggled the planter into position. "Did you borrow a trail camera from the office?" That had been an idea they had agreed on after the second incident.

"I phoned the wildlife tech, and she said the biologist has all their cameras out on a bear survey. Maybe we can afford to order one of our own." He headed across the road to bring the truck in.

"A cheap one maybe," Sam called back as she headed for the house. "After payday … after we stock up on mouse traps. See how much they cost first."

When he got inside the house, he could smell something with cheese and garlic cooking. Sam was doing a macaroni casserole in the oven. Simple, but substantial. Lottie was busy pouring three cups of cat kibble into a one cup cat dish. The eighteen-pound tabby was hoovering up the overflowing kibble with little regard for the pink doll's skirt Lottie had dressed him in and Mae Ling was on the couch doing homework on her laptop.

"How was your day, Flyboy?" Sam asked as she gave him a loving hug. She'd given him the nickname early in their relationship, after he had successfully flown a stroke victim — an older pilot — more than two hundred miles out of the bush in an Otter which McNabb, a student pilot with only eighteen hours of total flight time, wasn't licensed to fly.

"Started out crappy but improved after that. Eric is a great guy to work with. Too bad he's retired. We seized three moose; met three cops I hadn't met before, and I took down a gun-toting 'sovereign citizen' idiot with a knee to his balls when he wouldn't let go of his rifle. He'd been shooting salmon here in the creek, with no regard for the folks fishing from the shore. He's in jail at least until Monday. No bail court tomorrow.

"How was your day off, Sweetie? … stranded here on the homestead with no transportation at hand."

"Yeah, life without wheels is the pits, Robbie. Shouldn't have sold my old Sunbird before we left Moosonee. We've gotta look for a decent used car soon … but only after a few more paydays. So, anyhow, the girls and I walked up to Wilson's store for some supplies … and they have your favourite rum there.

"Some guy in there was complaining about somebody flying circles over where he plans to hunt moose. I asked where, but he said that was a secret. Suggested somewhere east of Elliot Lake. Said he couldn't see the plane to identify it and had no idea if it was big or small or anything about what type of engine. Not much help."

"I guess it's time we shake some trees then, Sam. Weather's supposed to be perfect tomorrow … finally. And Eric's willing to come along. Says he doesn't do church. Maybe we will get to check some of the local fly-in operators if we see any of them buzzing about."

"Or just go high and watch for a bit," Sam suggested.

"Some of each, maybe. We've got to get the word out that the new game warden kicks ass. Only way to do that is land at some fly-in camps and find a few asses to kick."

"Mae Ling," Sam called out to the living room.

"What, Mom?" the pretty Asian teen set her laptop aside and came to the kitchen.

"Can you watch Lottie tomorrow? Mrs. Snyder is helping at a church tea and rummage sale all afternoon." Eric's wife Nancy, a retired school teacher, had insisted on providing day care for the family when she and Lottie had bonded over the course of an evening together.

"Sure, Mom. She keeps asking to explore the jungle behind the house. We'll do that after we tidy her room."

"Can Tigger be a tiger in the jungle, Mae Ling?" Lottie asked.

"Only on his leash, Lottie."

"Oh goody!" The little one ran to the cat and took off the pink skirt and dressed him in a lion's mane she'd found on a trip to Value Village. Lion — tiger, close enough.

Rob and Sam were proud of Mae Ling. They had been working on a big poaching case that crossed paths with a sex trafficking ring and they'd taken part in the dangerous rescue of Mae Ling from one of her abusers. Three years ago, she was a tiny, scared thirteen-year-old illegal immigrant. Now she was taller than Sam and had become a self-confident young woman. Wanted to save the world. And she loved taking care of her little sister on the odd occasion when childcare wasn't available.

Chapter 8

Sunday, October 16 – Elliot Lake

It had started to rain again last evening around supper time, but stopped during the night and now the sky was clear. A great day for their first moose hunt flight. Except their day got off to an inauspicious start.

Rob and Sam picked up Eric Snyder early, as planned, but halfway to Elliot Lake, the water pump on the enforcement truck broke, and they had to get it towed. And they had to get a ride back to the office. And someone had locked the cabinet where the pool vehicle keys were kept. The key to the cabinet wasn't where it used to be when Eric was still working years earlier, and it wasn't in any other logical hiding place around the front office.

Rather than squandering any more time looking for it, they put the family crew cab on mileage for the drive to Elliot Lake. They needed to salvage something of the day.

As soon as they arrived at the airport, Sam began a thorough pre-flight inspection of the government Turbo Beaver. Her uniform included a Provincial Air Service blue ball cap and a blue insulated jumpsuit. The latter was simply a fancy coverall with lots of pockets and provincial air service shoulder flashes.

The ball cap struggled to contain the tight red curls that framed her round, freckled face and accentuated her youthful appearance. Anyone who didn't know her, might have wondered when the government started hiring teenagers to fly their million-dollar bush planes. In fact, at thirty-one years, she was three days older than Rob.

While Sam checked over the aircraft, Rob rolled open the hangar doors and Eric loaded their daypacks and other gear into the plane. The Elliot Lake airport was the nearest commercial facility to their office in Blind River. As secure as their rented hangar was supposed to be, McNabb had already beefed up the locks, and he'd asked the ministry to install motion activated floodlights and security cameras. He wanted to make sure Sam's plane would not make an inviting target for any outlaws planning revenge.

The bright yellow Turbo Beaver had been modified by Viking Air, in British Columbia, to become an eight-seat variant of its original six-seat configuration and was mounted on amphibious floats.

The powerful bush plane was built for short takeoffs and landings, and at 10:45, Sam turned the Beaver onto the single paved runway and advanced the power. The yellow bird was airborne after only a brief takeoff run. She banked the plane to turn east toward their first aircraft-related complaint where some action might be found.

As they flew over the vast wilderness east of the city, brilliant fall colours painted the rolling Penokean Hills. Sam was impressed by the abundance of lakes and spectacular rock faces. Between every range of hills there was either a lake, river or stream. The water in some lakes was tinted brown by tannins but still clear enough to spot rocks and shallows — the no-go places that could destroy a float plane trying to land.

She flew in a wide zigzag pattern to enlarge their search area, but they saw no aircraft all the way to the eastern limit of Blind River District, so they headed north, and landed at several lakeside camps to check the hunters there. At the first camp, everyone was out hunting but the cook. He hurried to tuck his skin magazines out of the way when he saw the female pilot walking up the path with the others. He invited them in for a coffee.

"No, thanks," Rob said after he introduced himself and his deputies. "We got off to a late start this morning. We're trying to make up time. How is your group making out?"

"Rained half the day yesterday, then when it quit, some idiot made a bunch of low passes with a float plane right over the hill our guys planned to hunt. Pissed everyone off … sorry miss," — he had no idea Sam could out-curse a sailor.

"Can you describe the plane?" McNabb asked.

"It was too far away to see the registration or any details, but it was just a little fellow … two seats, one behind the other. One of those, you know?"

"Yeah, okay. Colour?"

"Light, with some green trim."

"Well, if you get any better sightings, we'd appreciate a call." He gave the man a business card.

"There's no cell signal here, you know. Gotta hike up that hill just to get a weak one-bar. Can probably text you, though."

"That would be great. Any sightings would be appreciated."

—

At the next camp the whole gang was there. Five happy campers were in the process of hanging a cow moose. The carcass was properly tagged. The meat was still warm — shot that morning as they described, and everyone was properly licenced.

The officers had only been airborne again for fifteen minutes when Eric asked Sam to circle a camp he saw on River Lake. "Strange," he said over the intercom. "There's a lot of gear in front of that camp. Must be planning a long hunt with a big gang. Don't see anyone around, though. No smoke coming out the chimney, either."

"Sam, let's drop in and check the place out." McNabb was curious too. A lot of supplies but no sign of life. Something seemed off about that.

Five minutes later, Sam taxied the Turbo Beaver toward the camp. She pivoted the plane at the last minute, raised the water rudders and applied reverse thrust to back up to the sand beach. The three of them got out and jumped the short span of water between the floats and the dry sand. They tied the plane to nearby trees and headed up to the camp.

A plywood-sided cabin sat in a clearing in the jack pine forest. It had been stained brown some time ago and was now in need of a fresh coat. The covered front porch was no more than forty feet from the water's edge, and it was piled with supplies.

Stacked four high along the outside wall to the left of the door was a collection of plastic and metal-clad coolers bearing a variety of names and other personalized markings. Most were sealed with duct tape. They opened a few to find they contained canned goods and non-perishable foods — nothing open that would attract bears.

"When we're finished, I'll get the duct tape from the plane and reseal them," Sam volunteered.

Gasoline jugs of various sizes were lined up on the other side of the door and hemmed in by a dozen propane cylinders. Those too, bore the names or marks of different owners.

"There's enough stuff to supply a small army for weeks," McNabb said.

"That does appear to be somebody's plan," Snyder confirmed.

"Must be supplies from over a dozen camps here," Sam said.

"They're not just ripping off camps," McNabb said, "the government is taking a hit too." He pointed at a red gas jug with *MNR* stencilled in black paint.

"I wonder whose camp this is?"

"Can't remember, off hand," Snyder said. "Let's see the map, Rob."

From his jacket pocket, McNabb pulled a worn area map. "Hmm. It just shows it as a Land Use Permit, an LUP, but no name. I can find out who it is registered to at the office tomorrow.

"Let's take a look inside." The door wasn't locked, and on entering the camp, they found seven outboard motors of all makes and ages, ranging from four to fifteen horsepower, two gasoline-powered generators and a propane cookstove which sat in the middle of the room — the camp's gas stove was still in place at the end of the counter. There were also blankets and mattresses, camp cookware and more boxes of food.

"This can't be anything but a cache of stolen goods, Rob," Snyder suggested. "Let's get serial numbers from the motorized stuff, and you can turn them over to the police."

McNabb started recording serial numbers from the outboard motors and Snyder returned to the porch and recorded names found on items that had been marked by the original owners.

When she finished taping the coolers shut, Sam Williams went exploring. Behind the camp, she found a trail that wound up a steep rocky outcrop. In places that were sheltered from the rain by overhanging branches, there was evidence of recent foot traffic. Looking back from the top, she could just see part of the camp roof through the treetops sixty or seventy feet below. The trail was faint where it crossed a stretch of bare bedrock, but she followed it until she came to something hidden in a cedar thicket. It was covered by a camouflaged tarpaulin.

She released several bungee cords and uncovered what she had suspected when she first spotted the tarp. It was a recent model Polaris ATV. Tires were hardly worn.

She returned to the edge of the rock outcrop and looked down on the camp. "Hey guys," she called, hands cupped beside her mouth to amplify her voice. "Come look at this."

Snyder stepped off the end of the porch and looked up in the direction of her voice. He called into the camp to get McNabb's attention.

"Rob, your pilot is onto something up the hill behind us." By the time they climbed to the spot, Sam had the tarp off the machine and was scouting around the edges of the clearing, looking for a trail.

"How did that get in here?" McNabb wondered, aloud. "Sure didn't come up the path from the camp. Do you see a trail leading off from here, Sam?"

"Still looking."

McNabb circled the Polaris. "No licence plate on it." He located the serial number and added it to his list. "We'll run it by the police with the other numbers when we get back to the shop."

Snyder called over his shoulder as he headed in a different direction into the bush, "Here's the trail." Something had jogged his memory. "We're up on a long ridge here and if I recall correctly, the only way an ATV could come and go is this way out to the road. It'd be a couple of kilometres from here."

They returned to the camp and took pictures of the presumed pirate's booty. "Let's get airborne again, Sam," McNabb said. "See if we can hit a few more active camps while we have time." After their morning delays, McNabb wanted to cover as much of the district as possible in the time left.

Snyder started down toward the aircraft. "Yeah, we've got a lot of country to cover. Let's head for Bark Lake then work our way west."

Chapter 9

1530 – In the Turbo Beaver over Bark Lake

Sam was about to circle a camp at the west end of the lake before landing when a white piston engine Beaver with blue markings flew past. It was well below them and several miles to the east.

"I'm not sure if they've seen us. They'd be looking into the glare of the sun," McNabb said over the intercom. "But let's follow them Sam."

"We won't have been in the sun the whole time, Rob. Unless he's got his eyes glued to his cell phone screen, he'll likely know we're here." She turned and climbed another thousand feet to begin following the older Beaver.

Eric Snyder focussed his binoculars on the plane as they caught up with it. He could clearly read the wing-top registration — CF-OMG. "That looks like North Shore Air Service. He's one of the four operators in the area. Always had the feeling the guy was doing shifty stuff, but any time I checked him, he was clean. Mind you, I never once got the chance to follow him like this."

"He's the one from Elliot Lake, right?" McNabb asked.

"Yeah. He's also got a pale blue Super Cub. The guy from Chapleau … ah, True North Adventures if I remember right, also flies a Beaver. White base colour, but I've forgotten what colour trim. They were always hard to tell apart from a distance."

"And the guy from Webbwood?"

"Cessna 185 with flaming red trim. No mistaking him, but there's another Beaver, light coloured again, flying out of Massey … off the Spanish River. They started up after I retired, so I've got no history with them."

The Beaver ahead of them was flying arrow straight, on a course that would take it to Elliot Lake. Sam looked at her husband. "He's got to know we're following, Rob. Do you want to stay with him? Or check some more camps?"

McNabb looked at his watch. "Follow him in. Maybe he's got meat on board. We can introduce ourselves and check him out. Good PR. Then we'll head for home. Even if he's doing nothing wrong when we check him, it'll be after five by the time we refuel and put the yellow bird back in its cage.

"Haven't covered as much ground today as I'd hoped, but we can chalk most of that up to a clapped-out High *Maintenance* Enforcement Vehicle. Second tow job in a week. I don't know how they expect peak performance from us if we're left with expired equipment. Good thing the air service is a different branch." Some of the government fleet planes were over sixty years old, but every bit as fit as the day they came off the line.

—

The Beaver they were following landed on Elliot Lake and taxied to a dock next to what Snyder said was called the North Industrial Area. It was a hodgepodge of businesses — some no longer operating — anchored by a Ford dealership closest to the highway entrance. Sam set the Turbo Beaver down right after the other plane landed and followed it in. There was just enough space left on the dock to tie up the government plane. The North Shore Air Service pilot was a tough-looking guy about McNabb's height. His dirty-blond hair hung in loose curls down over his ears. He had just finished cleating his bow line when McNabb and Snyder approached.

"Mr. Ritchie, I'm Conservation Officer Rob McNabb. How are you today?"

"Oh, the game warden with his own plane." He looked over at the Turbo Beaver docked nose to tail behind his own weather-beaten bird. "Nice wings. Heard you were coming. Good to know who I'll be watchin' for," Ritchie said, grinning. "But you won't catch *me* doin' anything wrong."

Ritchie held out his hand to shake Rob's — squeezed hard — a power play. McNabb held his own grip with just as much strength. Didn't let go until Ritchie loosened his grip.

"So, are you here to bother me … like this guy always did?" the outfitter asked. He seemed somewhat surprised to see the retired CO with McNabb. "What *are* you doing here, Snyder? I thought you pulled the plug."

"What can I say Reggie … I plugged back in for a bit. Something to fill my idle hours."

"Well, I don't get no idle hours, so unless you guys have got business with me, I've got work to do."

"Just a quick chat and a quick check, Reg," McNabb said. "For starters, how are your outpost camps doing?"

"That's what I'm busy doin' … checkin' my camps. One cow so far is all. Tracks for some camps no tracks for others. Just bringin' the cow in now, before heading out to finish my camp checks. My dock hand should be here anytime now to drive it to the cooler."

"Okay, we'll take a look."

"She's legal. I checked their licences before leaving the guys in there. Don't want no hassles with the government."

McNabb already had the back door open and was climbing into the plane. He took Reggie's comment to be his okay to enter the Beaver — not that he needed permission. COs' authority to inspect vehicles, vessels and aircraft came under the heading: *Inspection of conveyance.*

Four quarters of moose lay on the deck, covered by a tarp. When he folded back the tarp, the hunter's validation tag was attached as required, and so was the cow's vulva patch — still attached by the cow's own connective tissue to one of the hind quarters. This was necessary to verify the gender of the critter. When hunters failed to leave the external sex organs attached, COs across the province often referred to it — amongst themselves — as a sex offence.

"One more thing to check." The season had opened only yesterday. If the moose was truly shot after season opening, the meat should still be a trifle warm. McNabb inserted a thermometer probe into a meaty part of a hind quarter. After a moment, he called out the temperature.

"Fifteen degrees Celsius, Eric."

"Considering the average daytime and overnight temperatures …" Snyder ran his finger across a time of death chart for moose, "T.O.D. between eighteen and twenty-four hours, Rob."

"In that case, you're good to go, Reg," he said as he climbed down to the dock.

Without replying, Ritchie turned and walked up the dock, short on patience as he waited for his dock hand to show up.

"Introductions are over I guess," McNabb said to his team. "Might as well get going." And to Ritchie, he called, "You'll remember that you can't use your planes to spot moose, right?"

"I know that, damn it!" he yelled back. "Snide Snyder, there, reminded me every damned year … seemed like for an eternity. Jeez." He turned, walked on up the dock and disappeared into what appeared to be his office.

"Nice touch with the reminder, Rob," Snyder said. "Like he said, I did it just about every year. If we ever do catch him dirty, he won't be able to claim in court that no one ever told him. Not that it's needed."

"Yeah, I figured it's the kind of thing the court would like to hear. Absolutely no ambiguity on the part of the arresting officer."

"I think you'll get along just fine with our judge. It's that extra mile stuff she likes. She's big on summations like, 'Well, Mr. Doe, the officer gave you plenty of warning the first time he saw you. So, you have no one to blame but yourself. I'm assessing double the fine recommended by the prosecutor.'"

McNabb said, "I didn't see anything to suggest any problems with Ritchie today, but I got the feeling that he'd bend the rules if the opportunity came along. 'Won't catch me doing anything wrong.' It was just the way he said it."

"Him and his asshole kid. Has Mae Ling said anything yet about the school bully? That's Ritchie's son. Lives in Blind, with his mother, but works for his father on occasion. He's a classic redneck. Failed several grades, big ape of a kid. I think he's already had a few run-ins with the police, too."

"No, she hasn't mentioned him. Where is the meat locker Reggie uses, Eric?"

"Local butcher, up near the first set of lights, has a separate shop in a refrigerated shipping container behind his regular store. He cuts big game in the evenings."

"Well, let's get back to the airport. We still need to stop at the Blind River detachment and give the police our list of serial numbers from the River Lake camp. Meantime, we'll give the meat locker a few days to accumulate some carcasses, then pay them a visit."

—

At the police detachment, McNabb left the list of serial numbers with Constable Brown, then they dropped Eric Snyder at his place and drove home. To their relief the phantom hadn't made any changes to the yard ornaments at the McNabb-Williams home while they were at work.

—

1645 – Kirkpatrick Lake, AKA Blue Lake

Reggie Ritchie was picking up another harvested moose. This one at his unofficial camp at the far west end of the lake. Just a tent camp setup. It was his last stop of the day. Once he got this one back to base, there wouldn't be enough daylight for another trip.

"Aw, shit, guys. What'd ya do with the sex parts on this bull?"

"Probly back on the gut pile, Reggie. What's it matter anyhow. Nobody'll check for that."

"Yeah, someone damned well might check it. New game warden just checked the last carcass I hauled in not much more than an hour ago. If you left it on the gut pile, the ravens will've have got it by now. No time to go looking anyway. I really don't feel like having my plane seized for transporting an illegal moose. And you probably don't want your moose seized. And then there's the fines…."

"Aw, fuck. What should we do then?"

"Tell you what," Ritchie scratched his head and sighed. "For an extra five hundred, I'll drop the moose and one of you guys on the beach at Quirk Lake. The other three will come the rest of the way to the base with me. If the warden checks us there, you tell'm you didn't get anything this year. Lookin' forward to next year. Then you shut your gobs, get in your trucks and drive back to Quirk to pick up your moose and your buddy. Got it?"

"Well … I guess. But an extra five hundred bucks? C'mon, man that's pretty steep."

"Call it a warden avoidance surcharge. Take it or leave it. I'm not going to risk it for nothing."

Chapter 10

Monday, October 17, 0805 – Blind River Natural Resources office

The MNR office was located in a rambling two story building built for the Department of Lands and Forests back in the 1950s. The institutional white asbestos tile siding under a red shingled roof was the first thing people noticed when driving up the street. Several additions had been constructed in the 1970s to accommodate growing numbers of staff back then. Rob McNabb and Samantha Williams were given a couple of tiny cubicles in what had once been a small single office. The subdivided room barely fit two desks and was in the back of the original building. McNabb had asked the area supervisor if someone could remove the partition, and this morning he got his answer.

On his desk he found a hammer and a wrecking bar. An industrial-duty vacuum cleaner sat on his chair. He was scratching his head, wondering what that was about when Leo Lyons walked in. Leo was the area supervisor. He was in charge of ministry technicians and the facility, but he wasn't part of the chain of command for either Rob or Samantha.

Leo was a likeable fellow who bore a strong resemblance to the cowardly lion in the original movie, *The Wizard of Oz*. Having grown up carrying that burden, he played on the persona. A sign over his office door read: "The Lyons Den."

"Hi Rob, I meant to leave you a note when I dropped off the tools but got sidetracked. So, you can remove this partition to expand your space. But it is strictly a DIY job. There's no money for contracting it out. The partition was just a temporary addition, built for previous occupants. Maybe they didn't get along … it was before my time. Anyhow, down in the old bomb shelter in the basement, there's probably some paint for touching up the scabs you leave by taking this down. Everything in this place is painted the same boring shade of government beige, so you shouldn't have to sort through too many cans to find a match."

"Okay, thanks, Leo. By the way, who handles the land use permits?" McNabb asked. Wendy, the receptionist, and Leo were the glue that held the place together. If you needed something, one or the other could get it for you, or knew who to get it from.

"Go and see George Almond. He's the big fellow … shaved head … in the Lands office. Guess you haven't met him yet. He's been on vacation."

"Got it, thanks." McNabb wandered through the labyrinthine halls of the old and new buildings. After backtracking, having followed a wrong turn, he found himself in a section more recently constructed, and there he found the correct office. He knocked on the open door. "Good morning, George. I'm Rob McNabb."

"Ah, good to meet you, Rob. My daughter says the kids at the high school are calling you the new sheriff. Sounds like you are making a positive impact in the district."

"First week has been a steep learning curve and if it stays this busy, I might implode."

"Settling in all right?"

"Yeah, it's starting to feel more like home. We could have used a larger phone booth for our desks, but we've got the essentials, and now, Leo's permission to do a minor reno job."

"What can I do for you?"

"I'm looking for the lessee for …," he walked to the wall map across from George's desk, "… this LUP." He pointed to River Lake.

"Oh, sad case that one. Pierre Lachappelle. He had a stroke two years ago. Been bedridden ever since. He's in long-term care. But his wife keeps paying the lease in hopes that maybe one day he'll recover … at least enough so that family can take him up there for a few days at a time."

"Do you know if anyone uses it?"

"Nope … As in yes, I know that no one does. More accurately, I guess, nobody is *supposed* to be using it. Their four kids are scattered across the world on three different continents. They don't get back here except on rare occasions to visit. Why?"

"Someone has stashed a whole lot of food and fuel supplies and a bunch of outboard motors there. There are more than a dozen coolers stacked on the porch with different owners' names on them. Gas jugs and propane bottles enough to supply eight or ten camps for the full hunt."

"The weasels. Caching stuff they've stolen at a camp they don't own. I suppose they figure it gives them plausible deniability … not my camp … not my stuff. I'll keep my ears open in case that ties in with any camp theft complaints we get."

"The police are already investigating a bunch of hunt camp break-ins."

"Do you want Mrs. Lachappelle's contact info?"

"Please."

McNabb took down the phone number and wandered back through the halls to his own cubicle where he made a call to the lady herself. And no, she hadn't given anyone permission to use her husband's hunt camp. And yes, she could provide him with a list of major equipment he kept there, complete with serial numbers. Mr. Lachappelle was meticulous in his record-keeping.

McNabb grabbed the keys for a pool car and drove across town to pick up a copy of Lachappelle's camp inventory, then returned to the office. He called his staff sergeant in the Soo to check in and mention the disabled patrol truck, then placed a call to the police detachment.

"*Constable Brown is not in this morning. I'll put you through to his sergeant.*"

There was hardly a pause before he heard: "*Mitchell here.*"

"Good morning, Sergeant. It's Rob McNabb calling. Just wondering if anyone ran the list of serial numbers I left with Constable Brown last night?"

"*Good morning, Rob. And you can call me Harry. So, your list … I saw it here on my desk … buried now. Just a sec …. There it is. The night shift sergeant ran the numbers for the ATV, the outboards, generators and boat. The four-wheeler and five of the outboards have been reported stolen in the last eighteen months. All different owners. And one of the two generators got a hit, too. You guys are pretty good at this. How would you like to transfer over to police work? We've got vacancies.*"

"No thanks, Harry. If I joined your organization, my income tax would shoot through the roof. Your constables get paid thirty grand more than I do."

"*Well, keep us in mind if you have a change of heart. So, what's the word on the ownership of that camp?*"

"It's leased to Pierre Lachappelle. Do you know him?"

"*Oh, yeah. Sad story.*"

"So I heard. Anyhow, his wife says she hasn't given anyone permission to use the camp. A couple of those serial numbers are for units that should be at that camp according to his inventory. But there's a Grumman square stern canoe that's missing."

"*Could be anywhere by now, Rob. It would be easy enough to fly it out strapped to a Beaver. Anyhow, keep your eyes open. If it turns up at someone else's camp, we'll put the squeeze on them.*"

"What do we do about the stolen goods?"

"You guys have the transportation needed to move that stuff, but you are going to be tied up during the hunt for sure. Keep an eye out for any of it showing up at active camps, then we'll have a better handle on who to lean on, and we'll plan to do a scoop after the hunt. I'll clear it with your air service managers. That work for you?

"Sure, we can do that. We did a lot of cross-agency work like that up north. We'll keep you in the loop, thanks."

Sam came into the office as McNabb was ending the call. "Ready to fly, Robbie?"

"Yup, all set. I've got the pool car signed out. Let's go."

—

0830 – North Shore Air Service

"So, he's all moved in then, Tyler? And you've already played some of the jokes on him, like I asked?"

Tyler Hatch was in his early twenties. He lived at home with his parents. He wasn't the brightest bulb in the room, but whatever task Reggie gave him, it was always completed without any grumbling. He was normally kept busy doing menial chores around the air base and at Ritchie's outpost camps. Running errands, sweeping the floors, cutting the grass, cleaning the shitters, gassing up the planes — just the usual cleaning and maintenance stuff. But once in a while Reggie had given the kid special assignments, and Tyler had proven his loyalty. Now it was time to turn up the heat on McNabb and family.

"Yeah, Reggie. They moved in a week ago, and I done what you asked. But I don't know how funny they found it, findin' stuff moved around their yard like that."

"They're called practical jokes, Tyler. Something you do to folks that they can laugh about later on." When the kid had told him the new game warden was moving in near Tyler's parents' place, it opened all kinds of possibilities in Ritchie's mind. Ways to get under the new game warden's skin. At first that was all he was looking for. But now it appeared that this new CO and his cute little pilot wife could cause him some real problems. Word going around was that McNabb had already charged some guys that everyone thought could never be caught. Now he needed ways to make the newcomer's life miserable — so he'd want to quit, or transfer to another district.

"So this is what I want you to do, Tyler," and he outlined the next set of pranks he wanted the kid to pull.

"You sure he won't get mad, Reggie?"

"Nope, he'll get a real chuckle out of it. That little house needs a lot of upgrades and this first one will give them a head start."

"Okay, then. I could have lots of fun doin' that. And he'll never know who done it."

"You're a good man, Tyler."

Chapter 11

1125 – Over Wenebegon Lake

Sam and Rob were flying from lake to lake, checking hunting parties near the north end of the district. They were over a hundred and thirty kilometres north of Blind River and closer to the town of Chapleau than they were to home. Some of the hunters they checked said they hadn't seen an officer in the area for years. McNabb charged two hunters for having loaded firearms in their power boat and one of the two had chucked a beer can into the lake just before Sam taxied the Beaver alongside. That offence didn't go unpunished either. Most hunters, however, were behaving.

As they flew over the south end of Wenebegon Lake, Sam banked the plane hard left and spoke over the intercom. "Someone down in that cutover waving his orange coat, Rob. Trying to get our attention." They were only six or seven hundred feet above the ground and the guy was easy to spot.

"Yeah, I see him … or her." The person was standing in a logged area only a couple hundred metres from the lake. "Could be a medical emergency, Sam."

"Or lost … if it's a man," Sam took a jab at McNabb.

"Yeah, yeah… wouldn't stop and ask directions, right? Put us down in that bay, and we'll find out what's going on."

She radioed their intentions to the communications centre and circled the intended landing area. When she landed, Sam found a narrow sand beach to back the Beaver up to. As she and McNabb finished tying the plane to a couple of trees, a man came through the bush to meet them.

"Hey guys, a couple of bulls got their horns locked together up there in the clearcut. One's dead and getting pretty ripe. The other one looks pretty beat. We don't have a bull tag, but can we shoot that one? Put it out of its misery?"

"How far is it from here, sir?" McNabb asked.

"Felt like a mile, busting my way through all the blow-down in this stretch of bush, but it's right past the buffer zone." The forest management plan required a two hundred metre buffer of uncut forest back from the water's edge. "With the stress that big fella is under, the meat's probably not even suitable to eat."

"Well, let's take a look," McNabb said, and slid a 30.06 rifle out of a locking case behind the seats. "Coming, Sam?"

"With you all the way."

Ten minutes later they emerged from the bush and approached the two moose. The live bull was exhausted and had been dragging the dead one around for days, probably. Unable to get down to the lake to drink, the poor beast would be badly dehydrated.

When bull moose engage in battle, they occasionally lock their antlers together. McNabb had seen it on YouTube and had heard other officers talk about it, but it wasn't a common event.

"Do you guys have a chainsaw handy?" McNabb asked. "Should be able to cut the rack off the dead guy to set this one free. Given some rest and water, he'll likely recover okay."

"Did have, but one of the other guys backed his pickup over it."

"Bet he's popular around camp now."

"Sure is. Earning his keep cutting our firewood with a bow saw."

"Okay, plan B. Sam, you want to give it a try?" He offered her the rifle.

"Sure."

"She's the deadeye shooter of the two of us," McNabb said. He was every bit as good a shot, but he thought it would be good for the word to get around that the lady bush pilot was no shrinking violet and as good in the bush as any man.

After walking over to take a close look at how the antlers were interlocked, she paced off roughly twenty-five yards from the two moose. She didn't want to be standing right beside the surviving moose when he was suddenly freed. She could get trampled in his rush to get away — even as tired as he was.

The rifle was sighted in to be exactly dead centre at one hundred yards, which meant that the bullet would also be dead centre at twenty-five yards. It had to do with ballistics — the bullet rising through the sightline when it first leaves the muzzle and gravity taking over after that.

She snapped the magazine into the receiver and chambered a round. Paused a moment, then knelt and rested the rifle on a high stump. One shot rang out. The far side antler of the dead moose spun away and landed three or four metres beyond.

The surviving bull, either surprised or terrified by the rifle shot, shook his head and disconnected from his adversary. He trotted a short distance away then stopped to orient himself. The humans stayed motionless and silent. After a brief pause, the moose turned and headed between them, down toward the lake at a slow trot.

"Nice shot, lady. You the department sniper?"

"McNabb would have done just as well." Sam answered his question with a non-answer, and as she spoke, they could hear the rumble of an aircraft engine.

"Piston Beaver," she said. A minute later a white and blue Beaver passed to the east of them, too far away to see its registration. But it had the same colour scheme as Reggie Ritchie's. It was heading roughly north.

The hunter: "Shit, that plane has been all over this area today. Spent some time circling the north end of the lake earlier. You guys have got to do something about that guy. I hear some guys have taken shots at him."

"Would you be one of the guys trying that?" McNabb asked as he watched the Beaver disappear beyond the tree line.

"Nope. I'm a bonded transport driver. A criminal charge would end my career … but I can't say I'd blame a fellow for trying."

"We'll keep our eyes on him," McNabb said. "And if he's using the plane to hunt, we'll be seizing it. Gotta catch him first though, or come up with reliable witnesses who see it happening."

As they talked, McNabb walked to the dead moose and held his breath while he tied a piece of police crime scene tape to its remaining antler. "Reduce the chances of getting an abandoned moose kill complaint. Hopefully anyone who sees it will figure out that it has already been investigated."

"Thanks for your help, officer."

"Thank you for flagging us down."

—

Sam got the yellow bird airborne again and was climbing away from the lake in time to see the same Beaver approaching them on its way south. She looked at her husband — the unspoken question being, where to now?

"Make sure he sees us, then let's mosey up to the top end of the lake. He must have a hunting party that we can annoy somewhere in the area. He doesn't have an LUP camp on this lake, but Eric's map shows he had a tent camp setup here before."

Sam set a course to pass the other plane several hundred feet away. It was the North Shore Air Service Beaver. As they flashed past, McNabb signed, "eyes on you."

Chapter 12

1240 – North end of Wenebegon Lake

Minutes after passing Ritchie's plane, Sam was circling over a hunt camp and preparing to land. They saw a group of hunters gathered on the beach a short distance west of the camp.

"Looks like a party going on down there Rob, but I don't see any moose hanging."

"Maybe that's what Mr. Ritchie was doing up here … carting off another moose. Let's go down and have a chat with them."

Five minutes later, the Turbo Beaver was tied to the dock in front of the hunt camp and the gathered hunters walked along the shore to meet them.

"How's it going, guys?" McNabb gave them his usual friendly opening line.

"Not worth a shit, officer," one man answered. "That asshole Ritchie, dropped these guys off to set up camp right over there … what, maybe fifty yards away? We paid good money to our outfitter for a remote hunt out of this camp. No one around for miles he said. It isn't the fault of these guys, either. Ritchie just dumped them off with their gear and said, 'go to it.' Didn't even leave them a boat."

"Yeah, and we don't want to interfere with their hunt either," one of Ritchie's guests said. "But we've got no idea where else to camp on the lake and no way to get there if we did."

"Okay," McNabb said and unfolded his area map. "We saw a point about halfway down the lake … probably about here. Looked from the air to be a red pine stand with a sand beach out front. Still on this lake, but there's a big marshy bay between here and that spot. A natural boundary of sorts." He looked at the spokesman for the original camp. "Would you guys have any problem with them hunting down below there?"

"No, we don't usually go that far down anyhow."

McNabb to the newcomers: "Call Ritchie on your radio. Get him to come back and move you."

"We tried calling him as soon as we discovered what he'd done, and he wasn't answering. Last time we'll book a hunt through that asshole."

"Okay," McNabb, paused in thought; looked at the Ritchie group spokesman. "How many in your party?"

"Just the four of us."

"Sam, alright if we taxi these guys down to that spot?" Before she could answer, the spokesman for the established camp took charge.

"Hey, we're not paying you guys to ferry hunters around in a government aircraft. You've got poachers to catch. We've just got a light fourteen-footer here, but we'll boat them down. It'll take a few trips, but if we can't help our neighbours, we shouldn't be allowed out in the bush."

"Okay, after we check licences, we'll leave you guys to it. It's good to have it settled on an amicable basis."

Ten minutes later Sam Williams powered the Beaver off the lake and turned east. Rob still had a list of lakes he wanted to check before the end of the day.

"Remember my gut instinct about Ritchie after meeting him yesterday, Sam?"

"There's a lot of territorial rivalry between fly-in operators, Rob. It happens everywhere. The shoestring outfits I flew for before I started flying with the province were always doing shit like that."

"Yeah, our man Ritchie just got moved up on my list of operators to watch. Now we just have to catch him dirty. Too bad there isn't a charge for the unethical camp placements."

"How about 'Interfere with lawful hunt,' Rob?"

McNabb thought about it for a moment. "Actually, depending on the attitude of the crown attorney, maybe that would work. Good idea, Sam. That section of the act was originally intended to go after anti-hunters messing up the hunt for law-abiding hunters, but sure ...why not? I'll ask the crown."

—

Hunters at the next three lakes were behaving themselves, and at two of the camps they grumbled about a Beaver doing a lot of flying nearby. But no one had witnessed any specific action that they could testify to, and the plane they were complaining about had orange trim — not blue — maybe the outfitter from Chapleau. And once again, that plane was too far away to see the registration.

"Let's head home, Sam. After we hangar the bird, I'd like to drive to North Shore Air Service and pay him another visit, if he's there."

"You should probably tell him those guys aren't going to be where he left them."

"I'll try to be polite when I do, Sweetie."

—

1640 – North Shore Air Service dock

Rob and Sam walked down the dock. The Beaver was gone and there was no sign of the dock hand Ritchie had spoken of, but the Piper Super Cub was still tied right ahead of where the Beaver had been docked yesterday.

Since it wasn't locked and the window that made up the top half of the door was already open, a quick look inside wouldn't hurt anything. Sam stepped down onto the float and looked in. The aircraft interior looked a little tired and was devoid of any luxuries. Standard fare for a two-seat working plane.

She noted that there was no built-in aviation radio, but there was a commercial sized Motorola walkie-talkie lying on the pilot's seat. When they first walked onto the dock, they had noticed a plastic packer that had some walkie talkies in it too. McNabb returned to the packer. There were three of the portable radios in it, all identical to the one in the Super Cub. He reached down and picked one up.

"Marine radios, Sam. Smart guy. Good range for a portable. A unit like that would be great for communicating with his hunters without having to land to check each group. And far enough from Lake Huron to avoid getting hassled by the Coast Guard."

"Until now there was little chance of anyone listening in on their conversations," Sam said, and a wicked smile spread across her face. "What channel are they on, Rob?" Marine band radios used different frequencies than aviation and most enforcement equipment. But the government Turbo Beaver was equipped to receive and transmit on marine band frequencies. It was standard gear for an aircraft occasionally tasked with search and rescue duties.

"Well, let's see." McNabb turned on the unit and it came up on channel 10. Just to make sure, he reached for the other units, and turned them on, one after the other. They were all tuned to channel 10. "Looks like ten is the magic number."

"That's where we will be listening in, then," Sam said. Rob put the radios back in the packer. Sam wrote a note about the hunters on Wenebegon Lake relocating and stuck it in the office door jamb as they walked up to the pool car.

As McNabb drove toward town, he began to formulate a plan for the next couple of days.

"We've been seen, at least fleetingly, across most of the district by now, Sam. Word will be spreading that there *is* a new sheriff in town … just like George Almond's daughter said. So, now that we've discovered Ritchie's walkie talkies, what say we spend a day or two going high and following him around? Watching and listening."

The smile was still on Sam's face from when they discovered that Ritchie's radios used the marine frequencies. Now she was beaming from ear to ear. "It's an opportunity we'd be foolish to pass up, Flyboy. Let's do it."

"There's a good camera and a long lens in the equipment locker at the office. I'll take it home and check it out after supper."

The ride back to Blind River went by quickly as they laid out their plans.

Chapter 13

Tuesday, October 18, 0810 – Elliot Lake

It was a bright, chilly autumn morning and the wind was calm. The grass was covered in a light frost, but the temperature would soon creep above freezing, and the Weather Network said it was supposed to get up to 10° Celsius. Eric Snyder sat watching the North Shore Air Service dock across the bay. His chosen observation post was in the parking lot at the municipal boat launch. It was busy enough that he didn't stick out as an obvious spy. A handful of mostly retirees — kayakers and fishermen — were arriving to get in a last day on the water before the cold weather set in for good.

The activity at the air service dock was close enough to see with the naked eye. With binoculars Snyder could pick out the goings on in fine detail. He was sitting in a generic white government compact sedan, except today the car wasn't displaying the Ontario government logo on the doors. He had dipped into his bag of tricks from years past and dusted off a pair of magnetic University of Toronto signs he'd once found abandoned in the bush. They were great for hiding in plain sight. They had never attracted unwanted attention.

He was caught up by McNabb's enthusiasm and was determined to help the new CO snag some serious poachers. He concentrated on the action over at Ritchie's dock, to the exclusion of all else. The pilot and several guests were packing a huge pile of supplies into the Beaver. A knock on the driver's side window startled the old CO. He gathered his wits and ran down the window.

"You university guys doing a research project up here?" a man asked as he set down the kayak he was carrying. So much for not drawing attention to myself, Snyder mused.

"I brought a prof up to attend a meeting in town," he improvised. "I'm just a driver … filling time until he calls me to come and get him."

"What kind of meeting? What field is the professor in?"

"Something to do with quantum physics and new mine startups." More improv. "And don't ask me anything about it. Like I said, I'm just a driver." His interrogator stood silent a moment and showed no sign of moving on. So, Snyder, not wanting to be entirely rude, tried to add an incentive.

"Headed out for a paddle? I hear the wind is supposed to pick up in the next hour or two."

"Guess I'd better get going, then. Thanks." The guy picked up his kayak and headed toward the boat launch. Snyder considered adding *Quantum Physics Faculty* to the wording on his magnetic signs. Surely that would keep folks away.

The pilot and passengers were climbing into the Beaver now. The dock hand stood by the lines while the radial engine cranked over and started up. Eric poked the contact button on his phone to call Rob McNabb.

"*Yeah, Eric?*"

"They're taxiing away from the dock now, Rob. He sure doesn't give it much time to warm up. He's started his takeoff run in the time it took our call to connect. I'll call you as soon as I get a feel for the direction he's heading in."

"*Thanks Eric. We're taking off now.*"

Sam had kept the turbine at idle speed from the moment Snyder called ten minutes earlier to say the Beaver was being loaded. Before McNabb and Snyder finished the second call, she had the powerful bush plane airborne. Today they were going to fly high and watch. Unless Ritchie or his guests committed offences that couldn't be deferred, they would not make contact. From seven thousand feet above, they would log his route and record any radio activity, but otherwise they would try to remain unnoticed. That could be tricky. It was the first time they'd done this.

Sam banked the Turbo Beaver and set her heading to pass over the east end of Elliot Lake. It didn't take long to spot Ritchie's white and blue Beaver ahead, now several thousand feet below them and headed northeast. Sam kept climbing. Reggie flew straight and kept six or eight hundred feet above the rising land below him. This was the boring part of tailing someone. But then, the object of tailing is to keep it boring. Observe but not be seen.

McNabb sat at the convex viewing window in the back seat on Sam's side of the plane. He cradled an expensive digital camera in his lap. It was mounted on a large telephoto lens and was programmed with image stabilizing software. Without that feature, getting steady video of distant objects from the moving platform of the Beaver would be difficult even though the air was smooth that morning.

Nothing happened for the first fifteen minutes of flight until the marine band radio picked up a transmission. On channel 10.

"*Camp seven, camp seven, this is base camp. Got your ears on?*" Close to twenty seconds of dead air followed. But what they were hearing was being recorded. Dead air and all.

"*Base camp. Seven is here.*"

"*How is it goin' fellas?*"

"*Nothing down yet, Reggie. We followed a bull until dark last night. We didn't push him, hoping he'd hunker down somewhere, but he wouldn't settle. Lots of tracks, though.*"

"*Roger that. We'll check on you tomorrow.*"

"He calls himself base camp, Rob. But you can hear the Beaver's engine thundering in the background."

"Yeah. Too bad he assigns numbers to his hunt camps. Kind of hard to know where they are. I had hoped for lake names."

"He's not going to make it easy for you Robbie."

Then without warning, the white and blue Beaver landed on a small sliver of a lake, north of the Mississagi River. The lake was unnamed on McNabb's map. "Slow to stall speed, Sam … plus a knot or two … so we don't fall out of the sky." Through his binoculars, the CO watched Ritchie's plane come to a stop at a small T-shaped dock near the south end of the lake. His passengers and their gear were disembarked in record time. Within a few minutes, Reggie had his Beaver airborne again.

But as slow as Sam had been flying the yellow bird, they had overflown Reggie's plane and lost sight of it behind them. This flight was a learning experience for them both. They had already agreed that circling above the action would draw attention to themselves, even though they were flying more than seven thousand feet up. While Ritchie *might* not notice — his eyes would be on the action around and below him — his hunters on the ground might see the yellow speck circling high above them. But if it wasn't circling, the Turbo Beaver would just appear to be passing air traffic. They hoped.

So, only after passing the lake where Ritchie had left his hunters, did Williams begin a slow turn. By the time the Turbo Beaver was back to where they'd left their prey behind, Reggie's plane was nowhere to be seen.

"Crap, this isn't going to be as easy as I thought, Sam."

"Welcome to the vagaries of aerial warfare, Flyboy."

"Can only…." He was about to say 'hope,' when the radio traffic started again.

"*Camp twelve, camp twelve, this is base camp, come in.*"

"*Gotcha five-by-five, Reggie.*"

"*How's it goin' down there, Larry?*"

"*We're spread out like you told us, but we seen nothin' yet. No tracks even. I thought you said this was a premium area. Where's our moose?*"

"*Cow and two calves not half a mile east of you. I'll circle 'em once, but you never saw me do it. Catch my drift?*" By the sound of Ritchie's comment, he didn't want word to get out — didn't want to get caught. But it sure caught McNabb's attention.

"*Won't say a word, Reggie,*" came the hunter's reply.

"Sam … over to the left. I just caught a flash of white … far side of that bald rock knob."

"Got it." She boosted the power and climbed another thousand feet in hopes of giving McNabb a chance of seeing the action. With the big camera lens suspended from the overhead by a sling, McNabb lined up on the white and blue Beaver when he found it again, far below. He zoomed in until he could see the three moose standing in a clearing below it. But Reggie had already made his circle. All the video picked up was the plane flying past the moose and continuing its northbound flight.

"*I see them now, Reggie. Picked them up with my scope. Good eye, buddy.*"

"*Not hard from up here. But you owe me a roast off that cow.*"

"*No problem. Cut and wrapped by the end of the day. See ya.*"

"Damn. Missed the action. Sorry Rob."

"Not your fault Sam. This *isn't* going to be easy, is it. But we know for sure he's got no qualms about using his plane to spot moose for his hunters. And this is just our first shot at it. He may be a slippery guy, but we'll get him yet."

"We did get him on audio. Do we stick around and wait for them to shoot, Rob?

"No, mark the location on your GPS, then pick up your pace. We'll stick with our main man, practice our craft and see how many more times he incriminates himself. Even if we didn't see it happen, we know he was using his aircraft to hunt. Got that much on audio. We're doing the right thing … just have to be patient," McNabb said.

"After the hunt, we can get a subpoena for his records to track down those guys … maybe persuade them to roll over on Reggie. That's another thing we can discuss with the crown attorney."

As the morning passed, Reggie Ritchie contacted four more groups. The fifth group on his route asked him to land and pick up a cow they'd shot the day before. It was skinned and quartered and ready to go. The night chill had gone, and with the temperature already climbing above what was forecast, the hunters were afraid the meat might begin to spoil.

"Follow him in, Rob?"

"No, I think arriving right behind him, so soon after doing it on Sunday, might make him realize he's being watched. I'll call Eric and ask him to meet him at the dock. Let's check some camps while we're this far north."

Chapter 14

Wednesday, October 19, 0745 – Elliot Lake

With the lessons learned during their first observation flight still fresh in their minds, Williams and McNabb took to the air for another high-altitude flight. They hadn't been able to see the rest of Ritchie's route yesterday because of his early return to take the moose back to town. Eric Snyder had checked it when the Beaver landed at the dock, and like Sunday's moose, it was legal. The only issue was Ritchie's attitude to being checked by a volunteer deputy CO. Said he didn't think Eric had any authority, but he was too busy to make an issue of it.

This morning Eric volunteered to stand by again to check any incoming moose, but McNabb was having second thoughts. He didn't want his unarmed deputy to be dealing with Ritchie without backup. However, Snyder had already used his initiative to talk Sergeant Mitchell, his next-door neighbour, into providing backup. If it was needed, the Elliot Lake detachment day shift would provide someone. At least one unit could be on the scene within ten or fifteen minutes from anywhere in town.

"Okay, but don't approach the guy until your backup arrives," McNabb had insisted. He was pleased that his deputy — more of a partner — was determined to help.

McNabb and Williams were at the airport ready to take off in the Turbo Beaver when Snyder called to tell them that Reggie was going to be using the Super Cub today. The little Cub could only make about one hundred knots air speed compared to the Beaver's hundred and twenty-four, so Sam was going to have to keep her plane reined in tight to avoid getting ahead. But with a fifty-knot stall speed, the Turbo Beaver had a good cushion to work with at the slow end of its performance characteristics.

Ten minutes after Snyder's final call, Sam brought the yellow bird above and behind Ritchie's blue Super Cub, and as soon as she had climbed over seven thousand feet, she powered the Pratt and Whitney turbine way back to match his speed. Ritchie flew over the same route he'd followed the day before. Nothing exciting happened for the first while. There were conversations transmitted between Reggie's "base camp" Super Cub and his numbered camps on the marine portable radios, but there were no moose to pick up and no moose spotted by air for hunters on the ground. The target made one stop at Bark Lake to deliver a forgetful hunter's medications, and back in the air, it turned westbound.

And then it started. High above Rocky Island Lake, they heard Ritchie calling the next group. "*Camp eight, camp eight, base camp calling. Do you read?*"

"*Great timing there Reggie. We need a hand here … big time.*"

"*Whada ya need?*"

"*Outboard won't start. Dummy here, carried it all the way in but forgot the gas line. But that's not the big problem right now. We need you to chase a big bull off the island near the middle of Nigick Lake. Need him to come ashore on the big point to the east of the island.*"

"*Not supposed to use the plane to hunt your moose, ya' know, but seein' as how you've already found it, I guess it won't hurt to give it a little nudge. Be there in a couple.*"

Sam was chuckling. "This should be fun to watch, Robbie."

"Yeah. So, bring us in slow as you can Sam. It's time to get this action on video." McNabb started recording even before he had the camera lined up on the Super Cub. Sam crabbed the

Beaver a little more to the north so the action on Nigick would all take place on the one side of the Beaver — out the one window without Rob having to switch sides.

They watched the Super Cub drop low over the water to the west of the island where the moose was reported to be. It took a minute, but soon McNabb picked out the moose standing in a clearing. The approaching float plane slid into view on the camera's screen. The moose was a big fellow, and he stood his ground as the Cub made its first pass. Reggie made a tight turn, and his second pass was made at speed. He skimmed over the island just yards above the big beast.

Only then did the moose move downhill and into the water. It must have felt the breeze from the propeller wash as the plane passed low over it. But when it began swimming, it headed north, toward a larger island. Not the way the hunters wanted it to go. Reggie flew the Super Cub out ahead of it, turned the little bush plane in tight circles, wingtips dangerously close to the water, but never touching. The moose changed direction, turning south, not east like the hunters wanted. The Super Cub repositioned once more and began the same manoeuvre. The big beast finally began to comply.

"If this goes on for more than three or four minutes, I might have to begin to circle, Rob."

"With the good show he's putting on for us, Sam, our stealth doesn't matter any longer. It will soon be time to take him down."

They watched for close to another minute; Sam banked left in a gentle turn so that Rob could continue recording the action. And then the spell was broken. One of the hunters on the ground had his eyes on the sky.

"*Better break off, Reggie. There's a yellow plane circling way above you.*"

"Aw shit. Well, if he comes bitchin' at me, we'll just say one of you guys lost your gun case. Slid down a rock into the lake and floated away. I was just trying to find it for you. That's our story, guys."

"Ten-four, my man. We're stickin' to it. The word of five of us against one game warden, it'll never get to court."

McNabb was laughing so hard it took a moment before he could ask his pilot: "Can you plug me in to transmit on their frequency, Sam?"

She flicked a couple of radio switches. "You're on, Robbie."

"We're still recording, right?" She nodded yes. McNabb pushed the transmit button on his headset and began to speak, his voice going out on marine radio channel 10.

"Piper aircraft, C-GCUB, that's Charlie Gulf Charlie Uniform Bravo, this is Natural Resources Turbo Beaver OEY, Oscar Echo Yankee on channel 10 and circling above you.

"There are two reasons that alibi won't work, Mr. Ritchie. One: the wind appears to be onshore. The gun case would not float toward that island. And reason number two is: the four and a half solid minutes of video I've captured have nothing to do with floating rifle cases and everything to do with you harassing that moose. Oh, and then there's a number three: the continuous audio recording of you and your clients cooking up your bogus alibi. Won't look good in court.

"Now, we're going to land to let someone off here, then we'll be escorting you back to your Elliot Lake base. In the meantime, break off chasing that moose. And to all hunters ashore, *do not* shoot that moose. Hunters, please acknowledge."

"*Yeah, I hear you.*" The guy sounded a little deflated.

"Reggie, acknowledge."

"*Fuck you, warden.*"

"Well, have it your way then. But we've got at least two more hours of fuel on board than you do. We can just follow you around until you fall out of the sky if that's the way you want to play this. But I'd suggest you get a head start for home. We'll catch up. You can choose wisely, or not. It's your call … I'm not going to tell you again." McNabb cut the transmission. "Sam, get me down there quick as you can, then take off and follow him. I don't know if he's armed or not, so keep your eyes on him. While you are following him, phone Eric and let him know he's going to need his backup at the dock, and they are to seize the plane and its contents the moment it arrives. Ritchie may try to screw around for a while, but his options are limited. I think he'll eventually head for home."

"Got it," said Sam.

"If he does choose to fall out of the sky though, just mark the position on your GPS and come right back to pick me up." He added, "Come back for me either way … I'm not walking home from here."

Chapter 15

There was no beach where the four hunters had gathered on the shore of Nigick Lake, just a sloped, stony lake bottom with trees growing down to the water's edge. Williams applied gentle reverse thrust to back the Turbo Beaver slowly toward the shore until McNabb waved her to stop. Then he jumped off the back of the float, landed in thigh deep water and waded ashore. The Beaver powered up and took off without hesitating.

McNabb grabbed a small cedar tree and hauled himself out of the water. "I'll take that radio now, guys."

"We need that to get in touch with Reggie."

"You'll get it back before I leave." The self-appointed camp captain reluctantly handed over the Motorola. "And you are the one who asked Reggie to round up the bull," said as a statement — not as a question. Less room for the guy to deny it.

"Well, yeah, I guess."

"You guess, or you did?"

"I did. We just wanted him to herd the moose over this way, 'cause we couldn't use the boat. I kinda forgot.... "

"...the gas line. Yeah, we heard all that. You all have licences?" Heads nodded and lips mumbled the affirmative. "In the hunter safety training you all took, can I assume you recall that the definition of hunting includes chasing, pursuing and harassing?" More nodding heads. "And you also heard Reggie saying that using the plane to hunt is a violation of the law?" Still another round of nodding heads.

"Okay," he turned to the hunter who had carried the walkie talkie. "Which of these fellows suggested you ask Reggie to round up the moose?" He kept his voice calm. The hunters, though they were obviously upset, remained subdued and non-threatening.

"The other guys weren't anywhere near me. It was my idea."

"Okay. Good to be upfront about it. Just the same, I am charging you with the offence of 'use aircraft to hunt.'"

"But it was Reggie who flew the plane, officer."

"Yes, his is the greater offence by far, and he is flying into the long arms of the law as we stand here. But you are a party to the offence … aiding and abetting … accessory before the fact. Bet you know all those terms from TV cop shows, right?" Heads nodded yet again.

"You going to seize our rifles?"

"Did any of you fire a shot at the bull?"

"No, it was swimming … can't shoot that … and nowhere near close enough to any of us." At McNabb's request, they each handed him their rifles. He checked each gun. None had been fired since they were last cleaned.

"We only seize items considered to be evidence. The rifles weren't used, so they are not part of the case … aside from the fact that you had them here for the hunt. The court will accept pictures and my word in a case like this." McNabb kept the situation calm by his own quiet demeanor.

The hunters each produced valid moose licences, and their personal identification as requested. McNabb used his phone to take pictures of the hunter who was being charged and a closeup of each hunter's rifle. To finish up, the hunter who called in the air assistance received a summons.

Chapter 16

1025 – In the air over Rocky Island Lake

Sam Williams caught up with the Super Cub within ten minutes of leaving McNabb with the hunters. Ritchie was flying the plane about eight hundred feet above ground level. If he was pushing it for speed, it still wasn't doing much more than its usual ninety-nine knots. But the little plane was heading west, not southeast toward its home base. Sam figured it was time to give the guy a little directional assistance.

She swung the Turbo Beaver wide of the Super Cub and a little farther north. Then she powered up to the plane's rated VNE — the "velocity never exceed." At one-hundred and forty-three knots, she turned and swept across Ritchie's nose, more than a hundred yards ahead of him, pointing in the direction of Elliot Lake. Then, making a tight climbing turn, she reversed direction, came back toward, but above him. One more tight turn placed the Turbo Beaver to the right of the Super Cub, slightly above and behind it, matching it for speed.

Looking to her left, Sam could see into the small cockpit and see Ritchie at the controls. If he went for a gun, he would have to open his window to fire, and she would see that with more than enough time to pull up and away. The poacher had only to look over his right shoulder to see the government plane. And he saw it alright. At first, he continued west, but each time he looked, Sam had edged the Turbo Beaver closer. Her wingtip was only yards from his tail.

"*Okay, okay, you win, asshole,*" came over channel 10. The Super Cub dropped down several yards and peeled off, turning south, then it settled on southeast, with the Turbo Beaver still flying in formation on his starboard side.

Sam got on the phone to Eric Snyder. "Call your backup, Eric. I've got the Super Cub coming in. ETA about twenty-five minutes if he's finished trying to be evasive. The charge is: use aircraft to hunt. Rob says to make the seizure … the plane and everything in it, including phones and or cameras. Take statements if he'll talk, but we've got great audio and video even if he won't."

"*Got it, Sam. Brownie's already here. Brought me coffee, so I'll hang on to him until we make the bust. You going back for your man? Or is he walking out?*"

"He nearly had to swim ashore to deal with the hunters. Be cold and wet by now, so I think he'd prefer the ride. But I'm sticking to Teflon Reggie until I see you guys grab his wing strut. I don't quite trust him to find his way home without an escort."

"*Brownie is listening in, Sam, and says he'll fetch you a coffee if you touch down long enough to swing by the end of the dock.*"

"Thanks Brownie, but I've got full Thermoses here and we've still got our lunch."

—

1050 – North Shore Aviation Dock

From where Eric Snyder and Darren Brown were standing, Reggie Ritchie's face registered somewhere between furious and livid as he taxied the Super Cub up to the dock. The sudden jarring stop he made when the nearside float hit the dock, bore that out. He normally came alongside barely touching.

"You two here just to piss me off while I wait for McNabb to come and harass me again?" he demanded of the officers. He nearly fell between the plane and its float in his angry rush to get out onto the dock.

"Reginald Ritchie," Snyder began as he held up his badge. "Deputy Conservation Officer. You are charged with the offence of using an aircraft to hunt. Do you wish to say anything in answer to the charge? You are not…."

"You fuckin' asshole! You got no right to charge me. You're nothin' but a washed-up old game warden. Got no authority here. Get the fuck off my dock!"

"…. Not required to say anything unless you wish to do so," Snyder easily ducked under Ritchie's first swing, "but whatever you do say, may be given in evidence."

Reggie didn't complete his second swing. Constable Brown had grabbed the man's arm mid-swing and leveraged it behind his back. One cuff went on while Snyder finished giving the police caution, and he could hear the other cuff ratcheting shut as he put his badge back in his vest pocket.

"And after that," Brown said, "we'll be adding the charge of assault peace officer to your tab, Reggie. The same caution applies."

The two officers conducted a thorough search of the prisoner. Each item was placed in a plastic packer they'd brought out onto the dock for the purpose. Keys, wallet, pocketknife and cell phone cleaned him out. Nothing extravagant in the way of potential weapons.

Snyder: "Officer McNabb has also instructed us to seize this aircraft."

"Where is that fucker? Too chicken to come and do this himself, huh?"

"His pilot left him off at Nigick Lake to deal with your hunters. They'll be back later."

"What … that bitch was the only one in the plane? I coulda flown circles around her sweet fuckin' ass up there if I'd known she was alone."

"You haven't heard her flying history yet, then, have you?"

"Can't be that good. Women drivers, you know?"

But Snyder wasn't listening. He stepped down onto the Super Cub's float and leaned into the plane to begin his search. "Bingo!" He pulled out his phone and took several pictures of a Go-Pro camera mounted on a headset that was hung above the opposite side window. The retired game warden figured that with Reggie's big ego, there was a good chance he had activated it during the moose chase. He sure hoped so. He added it to the evidence bin.

The Motorola walkie talkie was still turned on — still set on channel 10. He turned it off and added it to the other seized items. Map pockets in the side walls of the cockpit produced miscellaneous accumulated junk and a map. A quick look at the map showed Reggie's camps and the camp numbering system. Good evidence there too. The aircraft log and several other documents rounded out the evidence collection.

Brown put their prisoner into his cruiser's cage and headed for the lockup while Deputy CO Snyder secured the plane to the dock with a cable lock and posted a seizure tag on it. It would be left there with orders that it not be touched under any circumstances.

—

Sam Williams returned to Nigick Lake. McNabb had finished with the moose hunters. They paddled him out to the Turbo Beaver in their small boat so he wouldn't have to swim out to it. Sam poured him a cup of hot coffee before restarting the turbine and he wolfed down a ham sandwich while she flew.

He phoned Snyder, who assured him that the Super Cub was locked to the dock and Ritchie locked in a cell for the night, but there would be a bail hearing in the morning and the man would probably be kicked loose — although McNabb hoped, after hearing about the assault on Eric, that a judge might hold him over for trial.

"Okay, Eric, when we get in, I'm going home to grab a hot shower and some dry clothes. Can you meet me at the office around two this afternoon? We gotta get everything documented and the other seizures into secure storage."

"Yeah, I'll meet you then. We'll want to download whatever he has on this Go-Pro camera before we put it to bed too, Rob. I'm hoping it was running while he was harassing that moose."

"Wouldn't be the first time a defendant's ego helped to get him convicted."

After Rob and Sam got the plane locked in the hangar in Elliot Lake, they drove straight home. They were pleased to see that nobody had messed around with anything in the yard again today. It had been a couple of days since the planters got moved. Maybe the hazing ritual was over and done with.

—

1355 – Blind River MNR office

Eric Snyder pulled into the parking lot right behind McNabb. The deputy carried the plastic packer containing the loose items seized from Ritchie's plane and Rob brought his laptop computer. They connected it to the Go-Pro first thing.

"Let's see if Teflon Reggie got some video worth looking at … down at moose level." McNabb started the video. Smiles broke out over both their faces. "Gotcha Reggie!" Multiple high fives exchanged before they got down to the serious work.

Chapter 17

Thursday, October 20, 1155 – MNR office

"You've got a bunch of nuisance bear calls to deal with in Elliot Lake, Rob." Wendy caught McNabb as he came into the office to begin an afternoon shift.

"Kind of busy with the moose hunt, Wendy."

"Rick Webb said you would say that. And he told me to tell you that it would provide a boost to our public image if you spent a day getting to know the non-hunting constituents in your district. Some of those folks pay our wages."

"I've been meaning to talk to 'some of those' folks about that." He paused. Looked at his watch. "But, okay, they say variety is supposed to be the spice. And then there's the other saying… carries more weight … the boss is always right. Guess I'll do bear calls.

"But you know, Wendy, some districts actually have a PR person to go on these nuisance animal complaints."

"Used to, Rob. Used to. Remember … budget cuts. We're now a shadow of our former selves in this district, just like everywhere else."

"Okay. How many have you got?"

"Five."

"Crap." McNabb's shoulders slumped. He heaved a frustrated sigh.

"Rick says after you mollify your constituents, you are free to hunt moose hunters for the rest of your shift. Oh, and where's Sam? I've got messages for her too."

"She's stuck in the Soo. Went to get the Beaver serviced this morning and got fogged in there. Says it might lift before dark … or not. I can put them on her desk."

"Okay, and Brownie called. Wants you to call him back. Something about your prisoner."

McNabb sifted through the bear call sheets as he headed for his office, shook his head as he went. He speed-dialed the police detachment on the land line. "Constable Brown, please." Put on hold before he heard the familiar voice.

"*Hey, Rob, sleep-in day, is it?*" Brown gave McNabb no chance to reply. "*Reggie's lawyer bailed him out this morning. He's headed off flying, according to one of the Elliot Lake guys.*"

"Aw, shit. How'd he swing that, Darren? Guess I'm not totally surprised, but he was arrested for assaulting a peace officer and he's out in less than a day? I thought Judge Chenoweth was supposed to be tough on crime."

"*Wasn't her. Some travelling judge did the hearing in Elliot Lake. That's where we put him up for the night. It's our revolving door bail system, Rob … not entirely the fault of the folks behind the bench either. Stinks, I know. Some of these criminals are rearrested on similar charges on the same day they are released, but the bleeding-heart politicians don't think it's fair to keep them locked up until their trial. Anyhow, I just thought you should know.*"

"Well, I guess it's better to hear it from you than from Teflon Reggie himself."

—

1340 – Elliot Lake

McNabb arrived at the first bear complaint and could see a problem as soon as he wheeled his elderly patrol truck into the driveway. A banged-up galvanized garbage can lay tipped over, close to the side door of the residence. The otherwise pristine yard was strewn with whatever garbage the bear had not seen fit to take away. Before he got up to the house, the complainant — a Mrs. Swan, according to the complaint slip — burst out of the door. A slender woman, she appeared to be in her late thirties or early forties and was wearing designer jeans, an expensive jacket and walking shoes of a brand McNabb figured he would never be able to afford. She could have been a nice-looking woman if she wasn't shooting daggers with her eyes.

"Where have you been?" she demanded. "I've been confined to my house all morning because that dangerous bear is lurking somewhere nearby! Didn't you bring a bear trap? You people have to move all those filthy, dangerous animals out of town. It just isn't safe around here with bears roaming loose on every street."

McNabb put on his most disarming smile — or at least he tried to. He had to change the tone of the interaction, or he was likely to lose it himself. "Good afternoon, Ma'am, I'm Conservation Officer Rob McNabb. When did you last see the bear?"

"Shortly after nine this morning."

"Just the one?"

"*Just* one? Isn't that enough? How *dare* you! Implying that we terrorized citizens are over-reacting because there was only *one* hungry monster wandering around our neighbourhood waiting to attack someone. I'll report you to your superiors for that. That bear had to weigh at least four hundred pounds!"

Before McNabb had a chance to answer, a man from two doors down the street, called from his front lawn. "That bear's over here now, Justine. It's up in the maple tree in Joan's yard." He paused while he spoke, then casually resumed raking fallen leaves.

"If you'll wait here, I'd better take a look."

"Take your tranquilizer gun with you. You don't want to go near that thing without it."

"If it has been scared up a tree, it won't be attacking anyone." McNabb said and he walked down the street to where the neighbour was working. The man set aside his leaf rake and led him between the houses and into his neighbour's back yard. Justine Swan followed close behind. The neighbour lady, a chubby, older woman who was introduced simply as Joan, was busy taking pictures of the black bear with her phone. The poor animal was about twenty-five feet up a mature maple tree, huffing and chuffing and gnashing its teeth between pitiful moans. It looked to McNabb to be about two years old and not very big. Seventy-five to one hundred pounds at the most, but not likely that big. Some folks tend to overestimate the weight of bears. In the case of Mrs. Swan, by a factor of four.

"Is this the bear you saw Mrs. Swan?"

"That's the one alright. And the horrible thing is growling at us."

"Actually, it is terrified of us, and is crying 'I want my mommy!'"

"Don't you make light of this, Officer McDuff."

"McNabb, Ma'am." He resisted the temptation to tell her to get his name right when she complained to his supervisor.

"The reason the bear is in the neighbourhood is because it has found one or more easy sources of food." One or more — he was trying to be diplomatic. "At this time of year, bears need to bulk up … put on lots of fat before they go into hibernation. If they don't put on enough, they might not make it through the winter. And that skinny little character really needs to spend the next month at an 'all you can eat' buffet before it heads for bed.

"Now, your garbage can, kept outside like that, is an automatic bear attractant." He looked to the small group in general and asked, "Are there any fruit trees in the neighbourhood? With fruit still on them?"

"Joe and Sandra, across the street, have apple trees," Joan said, "but they picked them all, and what they didn't use, they took to the bush to feed the bears and animals out there. Everyone else we know, keeps their garbage in their sheds or garages." She stared at Justine Swan as she said the last bit.

"Anyone with bird feeders?"

"I think pretty well everyone who feeds, waits until the first major snowfall before they start."

"So, there you have it, Mrs. Swan," McNabb returned his attention to her alone. "If you keep your garbage can where the bear can't get at it, in a few days, it will move on and look for a food source elsewhere. Just think of that poor little creature as an oversized raccoon. It's up there, clinging to that tree, terrified of the bunch of us, not looking for confrontations with humans. If it's left alone, it will come down after dark, if not sooner."

"But aren't you going to move it?"

"No. It has four legs of its own. Like I said, it will leave when it realizes there's no more food here." He left the woman standing with her mouth open. Joan resumed taking pictures and the man who had led them to the bear went back to raking leaves. McNabb got into his truck and started up the street, shaking his head as he headed for the next bear call.

Chapter 18

McNabb got no more than a dozen houses along the street when another man flagged him down. "Crap. At this rate, I'll be in this neighbourhood for the whole shift," he said to himself. He stopped next to the fellow and ran down his window. The guy had to be in his eighties but was so tall that he had to bend down to make eye contact with McNabb sitting in the four-wheel drive pickup.

"How are you today, sir?"

"You the game warden?"

"Conservation officer, yes. Is this about the bear?"

"No. Got a question … Is it against the law to hunt moose with a sniper rifle?"

"What calibre are you talking? A lot of police forces use regular hunting rifles for that purpose … as sniper rifles, I mean."

"Military grade. The guy said it was a fifty calibre."

"Hmm," McNabb thought about it for a moment. "There are more than ten thousand joules of energy in a fifty-calibre bullet, so that would be against the current federal firearms regulations. Why, are you in the market?"

"No, I don't hunt any more. Used to. But my neighbour had some buddies over for a back yard fire and a few drinks last week. Being a nice warm evening, they stayed outside the whole time. The conversation got a little loud, right under my bedroom window, just about. Turns out, the guy who was talking is going to fly some money bags American in at the end of the month to hunt a trophy moose with this monster rifle."

"Any idea who it was, telling the story?"

"Pretty sure it was the fly-in outfitter from down on the lake. North Shore Air Service. You know him? His truck was parked with the others out front in the street all evening."

"Did you hear any specific dates mentioned?"

"The end of the last week of the month, I think he said. Didn't give a specific day."

"Well, thanks for that, Mr…?"

"Smith. Yeah, that's for real. Ron Smith." He shook hands with McNabb — a firm grip. "You won't tell anyone it came from me, will you?"

"My lips are sealed, Ron. Thanks again."

The remaining bear complaint calls went along similar lines as the first one. He received no further poaching tips, though. But that one tip from Mr. Smith was golden. That would be worth putting all his attention and resources on — well, him and Sam. Maybe Eric, too. The prohibited sniper rifle would be a police matter. Maybe they would spring for ride-along constable for a few days. Anyone planning to bag a trophy moose — if there was one to be found in the area — would probably need air support to find it. Use aircraft to hunt — again. Go Reggie! Still got one plane left in your fleet.

It was already dark when McNabb stopped for a coffee, a couple of bagels and a honey crueller at Tim Hortons. No time to eat in, so he took it to go and headed up the highway to visit several road access hunt camps he had been asked to check. It started to rain.

Two kilometres north of town his truck died. The lights and electronics stayed up and running, but the engine quit just as suddenly as if he had turned off the key. He coasted onto the shoulder and shut everything down. He phoned for a tow and called the comm centre to see if there was a police unit nearby to give him a lift. Got the truck towed — again — and a ride back to Blind River in time to end his shift.

If it hadn't been for the moose sniper information, it would have been a wasted day. Reggie's release, though somewhat expected, had been a disappointment and the bear calls pretty much a waste of time — maybe time well spent for the welfare of the bears, but folks in northern communities had to learn to co-exist with the wildlife.

Chapter 19

Friday morning, October 21 – Blind River Natural Resources office

"That's serious stuff, Rob," Sergeant Harry Mitchell said. "A .50 calibre rifle might be a good choice for hunting a T-Rex or an armoured personnel carrier, but a bit of overkill on a moose.

"What I don't understand is how the guy plans to get it into the country. Not that it couldn't be smuggled in, but with the chance of getting caught … that's a fifteen-thousand-dollar toy he's risking there." Mitchell sat on one of four chairs in McNabb's and Williams's tiny office.

Rick Webb, McNabb's staff sergeant, was in the other straight-backed chair. Webb was a fit man in his mid-forties, five feet ten inches tall with greying brown hair worn in a brush cut.

McNabb and Deputy CO Snyder were in the swivel oak desk chairs.

"So, how do you want to deal with this, Harry?" McNabb asked.

"You're sure of your informant? That he heard it right?"

"I can't personally vouch for the guy, but I'm certain he told me what he overheard. And as old as he appeared to be, he didn't display any sign of cognitive or hearing impairment."

"Well, I've…." Mitchell was interrupted by the warbling of McNabb's desk phone. Inside extension calling, despite his request not to be disturbed.

"Sorry guys," he shook his head and picked up the call. "Yeah, Wendy? … Well, we're in a meeting right now … Oh … Okay, if it involves him, then send the guy in." He hung up the phone. “Reggie Ritchie’s lawyer would like a word with me. I have no problem if you guy’s stay … please.”

Three smiles looked back at him. Heavy footsteps drummed on the wooden hallway floor. A man the size of a football defensive lineman appeared, filling the doorway. He looked to be somewhere between forty and fifty. His head was bald, but his face sported a permanent five o’clock shadow. He wore an expensive business suit and shiny, black leather shoes.

“Thornton J. Greene, Attorney at Law,” he introduced himself. His baritone voice demanded attention. “I represent Reginald Ritchie. Which one of you is McNair and which one is Snyder?”

“How do you do, sir? I’m Conservation Officer Rob *McNabb*. Across from me is….”

“You Snyder?” Greene interrupted, pointing at the Deputy CO. He didn’t seem to take notice of the other two uniforms in the room.

“What right do you have to seize my client’s aircraft? You’re just a retired game warden. You can’t take away a person’s means of livelihood unwarranted and unannounced.”

“Mr. Greene,” McNabb cut in. “Deputy Conservation Officer Snyder seized the aircraft on my instructions, based on my personal observations of an offence being committed by your client using that very aircraft.”

“But he’s retired.”

“Deputized, Mr. Greene.” The voice came from beside Snyder. “Deputy CO Snyder is a duly appointed officer under the Fish and Wildlife Conservation Act.”

“Who the hell are you?” Greene looked at the speaker.

“In the rushed introductions, a couple of us appear to have been glossed over.” McNabb’s supervisor stood and held out his hand. “Staff Sergeant Richard Webb. I’m Officer McNabb’s boss, and by extension, Deputy Snyder’s as well. And this gentleman is Sergeant Mitchell, with the provincial police. There's not much room in here, but can we offer you a chair?"

Greene didn't take the offered handshake. "Him, I already know," meaning Mitchell. "And no, I'm not staying any longer than it takes to sort out this vexatious injustice. Nobody can just seize an aircraft from a hard-working taxpayer like my client. And then there's these unauthorized audio recordings you made of the conversation between Mr. Ritchie and his guests."

"Oh, get down off your high horse, Thorny," came from Sergeant Mitchell. "You can be such a pain in the ass at times. Ritchie and his clients were transmitting on public airwaves where there can be no expectation of privacy. Courts have already ruled on that. Years ago.

"These officers were working entirely within their authority under the Act. And I understand Officer McNabb has had previous experience with aircraft seizures. He knows what he's doing."

"I highly doubt he ever seized any from a legitimate business enterprise."

"Rob, perhaps you could enlighten the man," Webb suggested.

"Mr. Greene, it's true that in my brief five-year career, the three aircraft I previously seized were private, not commercial planes like this one. But all four, including Mr. Ritchie's Super Cub, were involved in unlawful activities. Whether or not, upon conviction, the court moves for permanent forfeiture is not for me, or any of us here, to determine. In the meantime, your client still has his workhorse Beaver, legally unencumbered, so far, to continue conducting his business, so long as he obeys the law.

"And the evidence seized from the Cub added a whole lot more weight to our case. You will learn all about the evidence when we submit our disclosure to you after the court documents are sworn and filed."

"I'm putting you on notice, McNabb. I'll be filing a motion with the court to have that aircraft released immediately."

"Well, that's obviously what Reggie is paying you for. So, go for it." The last was directed at the lawyer's back. He was already thundering down the hall toward the exit.

"Guess I shouldn't have said 'go for it.'"

"Water off that fellow's back, Rob," said Mitchell. "Don't worry about it." He scratched his head and paused. "So, before we were interrupted, you wanted to know how we plan to deal with the sniper rifle. I'll make a call to Canada Border Services in the Soo and ask if they would keep an extra watch on hunters entering during that time.

"Beyond that, we are going to have to put eyes on Reggie's facility full-time until whatever is supposed to happen, happens. Doesn't necessarily mean boots on the ground. I'm thinking we can get our tech guys to install a couple of discreet cameras that can be remotely monitored."

Eric Snyder spoke up. "He might have plans to pick up his client elsewhere and fly him directly to wherever he is taking him. There have been rumours over the years that he flies down at night and picks up guys from one of the islands in Michigan, near the border."

"At night? With a float plane?" Webb asked.

"Clear nights, around the full moon."

"Tricky landing on water in the dark," McNabb threw in, "but it can be done.

"Okay," Webb said, then pulled out his phone and flicked through his list of contacts. "I've got a friend at Michigan DNR. We did a couple of cross border operations together while I was on the lake unit."

He punched in a quick text message: **Available to talk?**

"Our reciprocal officer powers might come in handy in this case." Ontario and Michigan COs had authority in each other's jurisdiction as long as the case was being jointly worked. In fact, Ontario conservation officers shared reciprocal powers with COs in all nine jurisdictions bordering the province.

His phone beeped. Text reply: **At self-defence qualifications all day. Call you tomorrow.**

"I'll see if he knows anything about night flights into the Upper Peninsula when he calls me back."

Chapter 20

1340 same day – McNabb's office

The printer was spitting out the last of the documents needed to move Reggie Ritchie's case into the court system when McNabb's desk phone warbled. Call display showed Blind River Court Office. He hadn't been to the court yet nor did he know anyone there, so it puzzled him what they'd be calling about. He answered the call.

"Enforcement, Conservation Officer McNabb speaking."

"Officer McNabb, I am Linda Ward, the court administrator. Welcome to Blind River. I have Mr. Thornton Greene out at the front counter raising a stink because he wants to file a motion for the release of an aircraft that he says you've seized with malicious intent. His words, not mine. But there have been no charges filed with us yet to which I can append his motion. When do you expect to file charges for this case? And no, there is no hurry as far as this office is concerned. He's just being a little impatient."

"I'm sorry Ms. Ward…."

"It's Linda. And no, I'm not trying to interfere with any procedures you MNR folks have to follow. If it still has to be approved higher up in your chain of command, do whatever needs to be done. I just thought I'd ask."

As she spoke, McNabb thought, I shouldn't have told the irritable SOB lawyer to go for it.

"Okay, and I'm Rob. We COs don't have to ask for permission to lay charges in most cases. So that's not an issue. But I'm a one-man operation, and my first week and a half here has been very productive in terms of the number of charges laid. I'm in the field almost every day and I wasn't planning to get most of these cases filed with the court until after the hunts are over.

"*But*, because of the seriousness of this particular case," McNabb continued, "I happen to have completed Mr. Ritchie's information and summons just minutes ago." An information was the document used to initiate the charges against an accused person.

"If there's someone there, that I can swear said documents in front of, then I can be there in ten … no, make it, fifteen minutes. I'd better read this over one more time. Mr. Greene I've already met, and he strikes me as the sort of guy who'd make an issue of the tiniest typing error."

"Rob, I'm a signing JP, so you can swear it here as soon as you arrive. And I've been doing this long enough to be able to spot troublesome flaws. Don't worry, minor errors can be easily amended."

—

McNabb drove to the courthouse in his personal pickup — the disabled patrol truck was still in the shop. He arrived at the courthouse and was met at the front counter by a fuming Thornton J. Greene, who began to tear a verbal strip off him for his tardy submission of court documents and his mean-spirited treatment of poor Mr. Ritchie.

McNabb was about to launch into a rebuttal, but a short, wide, silver-haired woman emerged from an office at the back of the room and got in the first and last licks.

"*Thorny*, don't be such an ass. From what I read in your motion, this poacher client of yours…."

"Alleged poacher, Ms. Ward."

"Don't you *dare* interrupt me *Mister* Greene. This *poacher* of yours was caught just two days ago, but he is charged under an act that has a two-year statute of limitations … three years if there's a complex investigation involved. Did you know that? Did you?" She stared at him but didn't give Greene time to respond.

"This officer could have dragged his feet for weeks, or even months, and you'd have no recourse. So, I expect you to show him some respect for being ready to file so soon after the arrest. Officer McNabb, come this way. We'll swear this information in my office."

Ms. Ward could find no issues with McNabb's documents and the swearing and signing took only minutes. She made a quick phone call, then kept him there, chatting, for an additional fifteen minutes, mainly to get under Greene's skin. But when she and McNabb emerged from her office, she was all business.

"Monday morning, Mr. Greene. Ten o'clock sharp. Her Honour, Judge Chenoweth will hear your motion to release."

McNabb returned to the office and called Rick Webb to arrange for a prosecutor for Monday's hearing, then stopped at the Snyders' place to pick up Lottie. Sam was already there — she had walked from the office after work — and the three climbed into the truck for the short jaunt home.

Chapter 21

1730 – Algoma Mills

As McNabb drove up Center Street toward the house, his attention was on an electric mobility scooter being piloted along the narrow street in an erratic manner by a plus-sized man. Rob figured it was safer to dawdle behind him for the last hundred metres than it would be to pass. Sam's attention was not on the man on the scooter.

"Aw shit! Look at that, Rob. Jerks!"

Someone had splashed blue paint over the outside of their house and used orange spray paint to write "Go away warden" across it. And it had happened in broad daylight because it sure wasn't there when they had left for work.

"Mommy, you said…."

"Don't say it, Lottie," McNabb warned. "Not until you are a grownup. Those words are still a no-no for you sweetheart." The electric transportation device finally progressed far enough ahead that he was able to pull into the driveway.

Sam hurried inside with Lottie. She was concerned that Mae Ling had faced the sight of the vandalism alone when she got off the school bus two hours earlier.

Meanwhile, fuming over the sudden escalation from disturbance to vandalism, Rob did a circuit around the house to make sure that nothing else was damaged. Nothing was, but the paint job was more than enough.

He found an empty paint can lying open in the front ditch — blue latex paint and still wet. The can appeared to have partial fingerprints on it, so he took a picture of it, then carefully picked it up and locked it in the garage. He'd take it to the police in the morning.

He took pictures of the mess to add to the evidence. Who could be doing this? Reggie Ritchie's name would be top of the list if McNabb hadn't known how busy the guy was, running his shady outfitting business. A friend, or someone related to him, maybe? Or maybe someone entirely different. Ritchie wouldn't be the only poacher who didn't like game wardens.

When he got inside, Mae Ling and Sam were sitting side by side on the couch talking. "Don't worry about me, Mom. I'm okay. I know it's all about what Dad does, but stuff like that happening, it's just not fair to you guys."

She paused, close to tears, but she took a deep breath and continued. "Some kids at school say mean things about him, but they couldn't have done that … they live in town, not here. And the ones I'm thinking of were at school all day. Some people said bad things about him in Moosonee, too. That's just the way it is. But most of the kids at school think it's cool that he has caught so many poachers already. A couple guys in my class started saying he's the new sheriff in town."

Rob's heart swelled with pride. Sweet girl, thinking more of her family than of herself. He was about to join the conversation when they all heard a heavy vehicle stop in front of the house. Rob walked into the living room and parted the curtain enough to see outside. "Did you leave something on the bus, Mae Ling? It just stopped out front."

"No. All I had was my backpack … it's right here."

Rob reached the kitchen door just as someone knocked.

"Hi, Mr. McNabb. I'm Roy Hatch, Mae Ling's bus driver. We saw what happened to your house today. I've got a few folks with me, and we'd like to see if we can help get some of that paint off before it sets too hard."

Rob was touched by the sudden sense of community spirit after feeling that the village was a social vacuum during their first couple of weeks there. "Well thanks Roy. I'm Rob, by the way. We came home to the mess just a few minutes ago. The place needs a paint job … or vinyl siding, but we weren't planning on doing anything until spring. And we sure don't want to leave it like it is now." He stepped outside to meet the other volunteers.

"The blue paint is water base … I found the can in the ditch."

"Garry," Roy called toward the bus. "Bring out that power washer, will ya?" He turned back to Rob. "You've got an outside tap? The power washer should make the job a lot easier." And he introduced four others as they came toward the house. "This is Marcel and his wife Lise, and that's Chris and Garry hauling the washer over."

Sam and the girls stood inside the screen door watching events unfold. McNabb made the introductions and Sam went into delegation mode. "I'll put on some coffee and Mae Ling, go get those stuffed chicken breasts out of the freezer, please … and the big bag of frozen veggies."

"No, no, Sam," Roy cut in. "Coffee would be great for now, but the other women are bringing supper from town. Hope you don't mind Chinese." And with that, the village crew set up the power sprayer while Rob ran the garden hose around from the back and found part of a litre of acetone in the garage to deal with the orange spray paint. They removed that before hitting the place with water.

It took no more than half an hour to rid the house of its unwanted art. The power washer stripped some major patches of old white paint too, but McNabb told them not to worry about that. The more he thought about it, the more he was convinced new siding was the best way to go — next year when they could afford it.

Job done, tools put away, everyone was invited into the house. Twelve people ate Chinese dinners on paper plates, sitting on the couch, dining room chairs, cushions, and the bare floor. The unexpected housewarming party almost made up for the thoughtless act of the unknown vandals.

Chapter 22

Saturday, October 22, 0925 – Rawhide Lake

Constable Darren Brown and Rob McNabb helped Sam Williams tie the Turbo Beaver to the dock before the three of them walked up a steep path to the hunt camp at the east end of the lake. It was not uncommon for police and conservation officers to work together. Rob had maintained a great working relationship with the police back in Moosonee District, and Brown had taken a liking to McNabb when they first met on the side of the highway that day in the rain.

This camp was not on leased crown land — was not an LUP. The land and the camp belonged to a private group. The main cabin was a well-maintained building with plywood siding, stained brown. The stain smelled fresh. A generator hummed quietly in a nearby outbuilding.

There was a calf moose hanging on the camp game pole. McNabb could hear a chair scrape across the floor inside as he mounted the steps to the front porch. He knocked on the door at the same time as someone called, "Come on in guys … and lady."

They entered a camp kept as tidy as any they had seen. There were even floral curtains hanging in the windows. Three men sat around the table drinking coffee and a fourth was drying the last two plates in the dish rack.

"Good morning, guys. Nice camp," McNabb began.

"Rob, can we get them to move in with us?" Sam asked. "Look at this place."

"Aw, shucks, ma'am, you should see how we live at home. You wouldn't want us."

When the laughter died, McNabb picked up where he'd left off. "You're having a good hunt so far, I see."

"It's a great hunt, officers. Got our moose yesterday, so today's for R&R. Got one more calf tag, but we probably won't bust our backsides trying to find one. Gotta leave a few for seed. How are the other camps doing?"

"You guys want a coffee?" came from the dish dryer.

"No, thanks. There are no washrooms in this lady's airplane," Brown answered, smiling.

McNabb told the men their impressions of the hunt success across the district and at the same time, he checked their licences. Someone commented that McNabb's was a new face in the area, and Rob gave them a quick biography before asking his next question.

"You guys have been here a few years, have you?"

"Yeah, and our fathers before us, too. And get this … we've got a policeman, a professor, a proctologist and a priest."

"I feel a joke coming on," McNabb said, waiting.

The hunters all broke out laughing. One said, "So far, the joke's on us. We've tried for years to come up with an official camp joke, but every year it changes. If you think of one, stop by any time and enter it in the camp log book. Maybe one day we'll get it right."

"Any problems with other hunters?" McNabb asked.

"If you could arrange for Reggie Ritchie to fly into a hillside one dark and stormy day, we'd have no complaints at all … and I'm the priest. Your secret will be safe with me." Laughs all around.

"Specific problems?" Brownie asked, still smiling.

"No, just the usual shit," another of the men replied. "Mainly missing gas and propane. The guy's a constant pain in the ass … and I'm the proctologist … I know what I'm talking about." More laughter.

The policeman among them added: "After I retire next summer, I plan to spend the whole fall season here. Figure I'll leave some watered gas jugs down by the dock as bait. The guy won't be able to resist that. Then we'll have peace in the land."

McNabb handed out business cards. "Don't forget to invite us to the party. But he might be a reformed soul from now on."

"How's that," the priest asked.

Brown pointed at McNabb and said, "The new sheriff, here, seized one of his planes the other day."

Cheers broke out around the table, but when they quieted down, the camp professor shook his head. "Don't hold your breath, McNabb. Some criminals suffer from severe learning disabilities. That's my field."

Williams, McNabb and Brown made their way back down to the Beaver and were airborne within minutes.

—

1015 – Staff Sergeant Rick Webb's office in Sault Ste. Marie, Ontario

"Hey, Rick, how's tricks?" Michigan DNR Detective Bud Larson entered the office without knocking. He wore a big grin on his face and was carrying two Tim Hortons coffees and a pack of Timbits. He'd called Webb half an hour earlier, said he had to do some shopping in the big Soo and might as well combine it with a business meeting. They sipped on coffee, quaffed down sugar glazed treats and caught up on family and career news for the first ten minutes.

"So, what high crime have you got going on that needs the expertise of a Yooper bush dick?" Larson asked. He had spent his entire CO career working Michigan's Upper Peninsula — the U.P. — folks from the region viewed the Yooper nickname as a badge of honour — or in their case, honor.

"Bud, we've got a rogue fly-in outfitter who, it is rumoured, occasionally flies guests to and from somewhere in your bailiwick. Night flights with a Beaver on floats, around the full moon. And now we've received word that he's got a guest from your great nation who's looking to bag a trophy moose with a military grade sniper rifle … a fifty-calibre model that would never pass a customs inspection at the bridge.

"So, we're wondering if there's someone on your side of the border who facilitates for this guy's occasional red-eye passengers. We're guessing someone on Drummond Island or near Detour Village. But it could be anywhere from here in the Soo on downstream."

"Well, it's interesting you mention that. We've got a fellow we're just about ready to take down for illegal deer hunts and venison sales on the island. Lives in Drummond … the village. He's got a jacked-up Chevy pickup, a couple of 6-seater side-by-sides and a fast boat, and he's all over the place on the island. Constantly on the move. A real poaching entrepreneur.

"We've got enough regular shit on him to take him down now, but it sure would feel good if he went out with a bang. Moving stuff across the border, hunters and their trophies, we could nail him on state and federal violations too. The undeclared entries in and out of the country … in reality, human trafficking … that would be a big score for our Border Patrol guys too. We've gotta stay in their good books.

"The guy used to work alone, but his client list grew to the point he had to take on help the last couple of years. We've got one of our guys embedded with him now. He just got started last week after the state police took down his regular sidekick for a bunch of outstanding warrants. We'd all been saving those up for just such an occasion. Now, *our* guy's having a blast, consorting with the enemy, night hunting, running the bush on a big side-by-side and generally doing the guy's bidding."

Larson finished with the key item Webb had been hoping to hear. "And yeah, our guy hasn't seen it yet, but he says a recent float plane night visit has been mentioned." He popped the last Timbit in his mouth and gave Webb a double thumbs up.

"Okay, Bud, we don't have a specific date yet, but from our information, the guest in question is arriving near the end of this month around the time of the full moon and isn't staying more than four or five days."

"Do you want us to bag him before he crosses? Or let him fulfill his fantasy hunt first?"

"Be easy for us if you guys took down our rogue outfitter when he made the drop at the end of their hunt, but we are hoping to make an example of him at home … keeping you guys in reserve as plan B. If he even goes that route."

"Okay Rick, we'll give you till the end of the month. But if nothing happens by then, we'll have to drop the net on our target guy. If we're not picking up any new dirt on him, our judge will accuse us of joyriding and toss the case. New judge from south of the bridge. He's got no appreciation for our work … never hunted or fished in his life.

"Anyhow, if we hear anything, we'll get the word to you right away. And likewise, you call me any time, day or night."

"Thanks Bud. Will do."

Chapter 23

1110 – Bark Lake

At their third stop of the morning, McNabb and Brown stepped carefully as they made their way up a wobbly dock to one of the outpost camps run by Reggie Ritchie. The camp hadn't seen paint or stain for so many years that the plywood siding was in varying stages of delaminating.

The hunters staying there were legally there, not squatting in some unsuspecting permit holder's camp, but there was nobody in the camp when they looked in the front door. The hunters would be out hunting. A quick check inside revealed no firearms left open to view. Unsecured guns would have been an unsafe storage violation.

Back outside, McNabb went to the left as he circled the camp and Brown headed to the right where he found a generator shelter off in the bush, about fifteen metres from the cabin. It was a shaky plywood structure that wouldn't qualify as a shed.

The generator was shut down and cold to the touch. Someone had painted over a random patch of the generator cowling. The constable took a rag and a small can of acetone from his backpack. A light rub over the painted patch with the acetone-soaked cloth revealed previously painted letters: "Lucky Ducks."

An unlucky camp was probably missing its generator. Brown recorded the make, model and serial number of the generator in his notebook, and then discovered from an earlier entry that it was one of the pieces of equipment McNabb and the others had discovered at the Lachappelle camp.

"There's a forty-pound propane cylinder here on the other side of the cabin with a fresh paint job too, Brownie," McNabb said as he came around the back of the camp. "And a fresh pile of garbage. If we don't get to interview the tenants before they leave, I'll have to add it to Reggie's growing list of charges." As the crown land lessee, Ritchie was the one ultimately responsible.

"Recognize the generator, Rob? Thanks to you and Sam and her wonderful yellow bird, Reggie's starting to run up a real big tab this year."

"Looks familiar, yeah. Same serial?" Brown nodded as McNabb continued. "I'm waiting to see what Judge Chenoweth does with him. Eric Snyder says she's one tough cookie."

"She sure is. Assuming we get convictions on him, Rob, she won't be one bit kind."

While they were talking, four men walked out of the bush, each carrying a quarter of moose. Despite the hundred plus pounds they each carried on their shoulders, three of them looked as if they'd just been carrying a bag of bird seed from the hardware store out to their vehicle in the parking lot.

The fourth man was dragging his ass and barely made it as far as the game pole at the back of the camp clearing. The hunters didn't notice the officers at first and hadn't seen the Turbo Beaver at the dock. The camp blocked the view.

One of the men, likely the camp captain, began directing the others to get the quarters hung. McNabb and Brown stood no more than twenty metres away, hiding in plain sight, listening. No one noticed them until Sam Williams came around the corner of the camp to see how Rob and Darren were doing.

"Oh, shit!" The ass-dragging hunter met up with the uniformed pilot on his way to get a beer and was the first to see the officers. The others looked displeased to see the three unexpected visitors.

"Look at this. The fuckin' game warden needs a cop to back him up," said the presumed camp captain. Wrong attitude for openers.

"Actually fellas, I brought him along to back me up," Constable Brown said. "We work as a tag-team, as you'll see very shortly. Starting with the first question: Who owns that generator?" Brown pointed behind him with a thumb.

"That's Reggie's."

"And this propane cylinder?"

"Reggie."

"There's a big heap of garbage over there, boys," McNabb posed his first question. "You guys create that?"

"That was here when we got here," said a guy who was lighting a cigarette. Sucking hard on it, he was surrounded by blue tobacco smoke.

"Yeah, and you arrived when?"

"Last Saturday."

"A week ago, eh? It rained here all night, two days ago. So how come the cardboard items on top aren't all soggy?" No one answered, but while McNabb was asking the questions, Sam brought him a couple of beer cans.

"The empty is from the trash heap, Rob. This one is right out of the cooler."

"Hey, you can't have our beer," Smokey challenged McNabb. The CO ignored the challenge.

"Where did you buy this beer?"

"Hamilton," Smokey answered.

"Same brand, and the batch numbers on the bottom of the cans match, guys. There's not a chance in hell the same batch number, processed on the same date would be sold in Hamilton and again, somewhere else. We'll deal with this later. Looks like the constable has a few more questions to ask." McNabb saw

Brown checking the rifles that the men had carried into yard with them.

"Whose rifle is this?" he asked. He was holding up an older model, scoped semi-automatic hunting rifle with a particularly long magazine.

"Mine," Camp Captain came forward.

Brown detached the magazine from the rifle, and without counting could see more than five bullets in it. Canadian regulations limited semi-automatic firearms to a maximum five-shot magazine. When the constable finished popping bullets out onto a crude picnic table, there were ten live rounds lying there.

"That mag came with the rifle," Captain said. "I brought a legal five round mag with me, but it wasn't in my daypack when it got light enough this morning to start hunting. Think I left it with my gear in the camp, so I popped that in instead."

"If you'd only kept five rounds in this magazine, your story might have sounded a shade more credible. So, show me your legal mag, and depending on how the rest of our visit goes, *maybe* I'll cut you a little slack." Captain made no move toward the camp. Not a good sign.

McNabb moved on to ask about the quartered moose. "Okay fellas, who shot the moose?"

Captain claimed to be the victorious one.

"Let's have a look at your licence." His tag was valid for a cow. "Is this a bull or a cow?"

"Nice big cow, officer."

The tag had been notched and dated as required, so the tag could not be used on another moose. So far, so good — but: "How come her genitalia are not attached?"

"Oh, numb-nuts over there cut it off when we were quartering it."

"But you didn't think to bring it along … on the off chance that an officer might have a soft spot in his heart … match up some ragged knife cuts and accept your excuse?"

The guy gave a shrug but said nothing.

"Well, I'm sorry, but with no sex parts to verify the gender, we are going to have to seize your moose."

"Both of them?" Numb-nuts blurted out, then just as quickly realized his mistake. "Oh, shit…."

"So, there's more than one moose." A statement, not a question. McNabb was pretty good with that technique. "What's the other one?"

"A calf," came a hurried response from the camp captain. Just a bit too hurried.

"Okay guys, take me to the kill sites. Let's get this cleared up right now," McNabb said.

With their situation rapidly turning against them, the camp captain turned belligerent. "No fuckin' way. You want to see 'em, you go find 'em."

"Alright, you've just blown your one chance at getting an offence notice with the minimum preset fine. Now you have two remaining options."

McNabb paused and cast a serious look at the camp captain first, then each of the other hunters in turn.

"Option one: You can cooperate, starting right now, and lead us to the kill sites. You will receive summonses to court for the offenses you've committed. Unlike the set fine on an offence notice, those charged will receive a somewhat larger fine, but not likely anywhere near the maximum.

"The second option … if you so choose … is to remain totally non-cooperative. Then we get to seize *all* the firearms, cell phones and cameras … anything we determine is evidence in the case; and we call in the canine team to find the moose without your help; and we do full forensics on everything."

Constable Brown chimed in: "Officer McNabb is *really* good at that. He worked up north with the inspector who is probably the top crime scene investigator in Ontario. He learned from the best. And then you *all* go to court. And when she's finished with you, our local judge will slap each of you with a fine that will leave your heads spinning. So, who's going to lead us to the kill sites?"

Chapter 24

There was some grumbling, and a minor mutiny took place, in which the other three hunters demoted the captain. Surprisingly, Ass Dragger took the lead. Without a moose quarter over his shoulder, he was quite agile in the bush.

Nearly a kilometre north of the camp they came to the kill site. Two moose had died within a hundred metres of each other on the edge of a beaver meadow — a dried-up beaver pond now covered in knee high grass.

When they got to the edge of the meadow, Ass Dragger turned and faced the officers. The other two mutineers joined up on either side of him. "You're not going to like this," he said. "But someone got carried away. It'd be called 'buck fever' if this was a deer hunt."

Captain was dragging *his* ass up the last rise, still fifty metres behind the gathered group — still out of hearing range.

"Captain shot them both," McNabb suggested.

"Yeah." Numb-nuts and Smokey nodded their heads in agreement. Hunting in a party that was in possession of the right validation tags would not have been a problem. One hunter could shoot all the moose that a group had tags for. But that was not the situation here.

Captain's "cow" had once been an animal with antlers and male genitals. But no one in the party had a bull tag. Captain's "calf" was a yearling bull with much smaller antlers — a pair of single prongs, several inches longer than his ears, but a bull just the same. Not a calf.

"Okay guys," McNabb said. "We *are* seizing both of the moose. I've got to interview Captain, then we'll get this one quartered and carry it out."

"We'll quarter it for you officer," Smokey offered as he shrugged his daypack off his shoulders and lit another smoke. "You go ahead and deal with my brother. I don't think he'll give you any more trouble. Constable Brown can supervise us … make sure we don't stick any roasts in our pockets." He almost smiled.

Smokey, Ass Dragger and Numb-nuts dove into the job with some help from Brown. The three penitent hunters were surprisingly cheerful despite the trouble they were in. By cooperating, McNabb thought he might let the three of them go with nothing worse than a summons for the litter back at the camp.

Everyone stopped what they were doing when they heard a Beaver approach and fly overhead. Reggie's Beaver.

The marine radio was in Captain's daypack, and McNabb allowed the man to take it out and turn it on. They were expecting a call from Ritchie. None came, and when Captain tried calling the Beaver, there was no response.

—

As he flew past the hunt camp, Reggie saw the yellow MNR plane tied to his dock before he picked out the guys gathered around the moose, a kilometre farther north. He had a pretty good idea that things had gone wrong for the hunters, so when the radio call came in, Reggie ignored it.

"Fuckin' McNabb. Asshole's goin' to ruin my business." Many of his regular customers had been playing loose with the law after the last CO had left the district two years earlier. They wouldn't want to change their ways for the new officer, and might even be inclined to move to other parts of the province.

—

An hour and a half later, the hunters, accompanied by McNabb and Brown, arrived back at camp, The three penitent hunters each carried a quarter of the seized moose. The fourth quarter was carried by McNabb — whose ass was dragging by the time they got it all loaded into the government Beaver. Captain, still in a foul mood, sat on the front step of the camp and watched. McNabb wondered what the group dynamics would be like during the remainder of their hunt.

When the Turbo Beaver took off, it was heavier by two seized moose and one rifle with an oversized magazine. Captain was served a summons to His Majesty's court in Blind River. The others shared one for littering and were given orders to bag up the garbage, ready for Reggie to fly out.

Chapter 25

Sunday, October 23, 0920 – one thousand feet over Mystery Lake

Williams and McNabb were checking hunt camps on remote lakes in the Ranger Lake area, north of Thessalon. The officer who normally covered the area was sidelined following hernia repair surgery, so Rick Webb had asked Rob to work the area for a day. They'd made an early start and had checked two camps before the hunters had set out to start their hunt.

Sam was about to land on Mystery Lake when McNabb's phone rang.

"McNabb, enforcement."

"Yeah, this is Dean Lambert in Iron Bridge. I called the police, and they gave me your number.

'I own Lambert construction, and last year I turned down some shoreline work on Basswood Lake 'cause I knew you guys would never issue a permit for the work that the guy wanted done. My sister-in-law has a place just down the shore, a few lots east from there, and she says while she was away for the last few days, the guy has got himself a machine and done the work himself. Made a real mess in the lake."

Rob made a circular motion with his finger, indicating for Sam to circle, rather than land. She added some power, and raised the flaps, sensing there'd be a change of destination.

"He's digging himself a boat slip for his big pontoon boat. Digging it right into his front yard. She says the water is all stirred up from him working in the lake with a backhoe. Can you take a look? It's off the cottage road on the north shore, near the west end."

"Mr. Lambert, we are in the air right now and can be there in half an hour. Do you know if anyone is there now?"

"*Linda... that's my sister-in-law... she says one of the neighbours is there, giving the guy a hard time but the guy has put the run on him for trespassing. He might give you trouble that way too.*"

"We can deal with that. Thanks for calling Mr. Lambert."

"*No problem, Officer McNutt, was it?*"

"McNabb."

"*McNabb, sorry. After the shoreland work presentation you guys gave us contractors a few years ago, I like to do my part to keep our lakes natural. You won't mention it was Linda, will you? This city guy seems like the sort who'd give her a real hard time over that.*"

"Don't worry Mr. Lambert, it sounds like we'll be able to see it when we fly over it. There will be no need for any names to be mentioned. Thanks, again." He ended the call.

Sam said, "Well, Officer 'McNutt,' new destination, I assume?"

"Aye aye Capt'n Williams. Hard left rudder. Take us generally south." McNabb pulled a paper map from the pocket in the door beside him and easily found Basswood Lake. Then he found it on the Beaver's GPS, created a waypoint for the west end of the lake and entered a GoTo command to get them there. Sam adjusted her course a few degrees to line up with the GPS track.

"Twenty-two minutes to the west end of the lake, Rob. This sure is different from our flights back north, eh? We can fly to any part of this district in less than an hour. We'd be able to see the lake from here if I took us a few thousand feet higher."

"Yeah, but I still miss the James Bay frontier, Sam."

"Me too, Robbie. And up there we never had any ghosts moving around our boat or garden furniture or flower planters."

"Or painting the house."

When they arrived over Basswood Lake, the distinct plume of muddied water led them right to the source. Sam made several passes over the scene while Rob took a series of pictures.

"That looks like a good sturdy dock next door to the west of it, Sam. There aren't any posts above the deck to catch a strut on. Put us down and we'll go and have a word with the guy … maybe hold his head underwater 'til he sees the light."

As Sam taxied the Beaver toward the dock, they saw up close the ugly hack job done to the neighbouring waterfront. The owner was using a big CASE 850 backhoe, which was parked in knee deep water in front of a summer home. A trench perhaps fifteen feet wide had been cut into the yard. It extended a good thirty feet from the natural shoreline. Almost a quarter of the gently sloping front yard had been excavated and the silty clay material was piled high on either side of the trench.

Rivulets of sediment-laden water oozed from the piles and ran back into the already turbid lake water. The remaining lawn that wasn't buried under piles of excavated material had been chewed up by the backhoe's manoeuvres. Any amount of rainfall would be washing a whole lot more silty material into the lake.

As Sam eased the plane up to the chosen dock, they could see two men standing almost toe to toe near what McNabb assumed was the property line between the two cottage lots. It looked as though a heated discussion was in progress. Rob stepped down onto the plane's float and got up on the dock to take hold of the wing strut while Sam feathered the prop and shut down the turbine.

The nearest man who'd been involved in the discussion broke off, crossed the lawn and walked out onto the dock.

McNabb greeted him. "Good morning, sir. Alright if we park our plane here for a bit?"

"Sure," the man said. "Someone call you to come and deal with that idiot?" he nodded his head in the direction of the other man. The backhoe was idling in the trench, its mud-filled bucket resting in the water.

"It was pretty hard to miss seeing it from the air," McNabb replied. "I need to talk to the guy first, but I'd like to hear from you afterward, if you are willing."

"Oh, yeah. You might need to stay the night if you want the whole story. I'm Bob Jordan, by the way." They shook hands. Jordan was over six feet tall, slim and fit and was probably in his sixties.

"Okay thanks. We'll be back in a bit, Bob."

Chapter 26

McNabb and Williams followed a worn path across the lawn toward the neighbouring property — the scene of a significant environmental crime. McNabb began with his usual polite greeting, although seeing the extent of shoreline destruction, he didn't feel one bit like being polite.

"You can't come any farther," the boat slip builder said. He was several inches shorter than McNabb, a stocky build with the beginnings of a beer gut starting over his belt buckle. He looked to be in his forties.

"This is my property. Line's right there. No trespassing. I know the law. Once you've been told, it's as good as a no trespassing sign."

"We are the law, sir. I'm Conservation Officer Robert McNabb and this is Deputy Samantha Williams." Rob stepped over the man's invisible property line, a deliberate move to emphasize his authority. Sam followed and moved to stand beside him. The landowner stood his ground at the line, so they positioned themselves uphill from him. McNabb and Williams had the advantage of the higher ground.

"Do you have a permit for working in the shoreland?" He knew there'd be no such permit issued for this destruction.

"This is my property. I don't need a permit to dig on my property. And you have to *get off* my property."

"Where you are working, sir, is shoreland to the high-water mark, regardless of ownership. Your project here has, in fact, moved the high-water mark considerably closer to your cottage than it was before you started. Therefore, your project is now all shoreland. Unless you have been issued a permit, the Public Lands Act prohibits *any* work in the water or on shoreland, regardless of ownership. And I assure you, my agency wouldn't have issued a permit for work of this nature."

The man started to speak, only to be overridden by McNabb.

"Furthermore, under the federal Fisheries Act, the big plume of silt we see spreading over this entire end of the lake, constitutes a hazard to fish populations. That sediment will settle on the stony shoals that the lake trout will soon be spawning over, and that constitutes several offences … deposit a deleterious substance, and harmful alteration, disruption or destruction of fish habitat."

"What, I'm under arrest?"

"I have no need to arrest you at this point, but you are being charged, sir."

"Did that guy phone you?" He pointed in the direction of his angry neighbour.

"Sir, we couldn't miss it from the air, and no, we received no phone calls from any of your neighbours. Can I have your name please?"

"You can go fuck yourself asshole. Just 'cause you're wearing a uniform doesn't give you the right to come on my property. I already called the cops for that nosey jerk coming on my land. They'll charge you too."

"I look forward to their arrival, sir. Sam, run that machine out of the lake and park it up and away from the water."

"Sure."

She started toward the backhoe, but the man reached out and grabbed her arm, spun her back to face him.

"That's my equipment. You can't touch it." He took a swing at her head with his free hand, but she ducked, and the only damage she sustained was to her hat, which dropped into the mud.

"Now you *are* under arrest, sir," McNabb said, grabbing the man's arm as he drew back to swing again. "Assault peace officer. And if you don't give me your name, we'll add obstruction to your growing list of offences."

"You got no right to be on my private property." His persistence was impressive, but McNabb had dealt with arrogant individuals before and wasn't deterred. He moved quickly to subdue the man, and with the handcuffs secured, he began to recite to the official police caution.

"Do you wish to say anything in answer to the charges…." While he talked, he bent the man forward to keep him off balance and began to search his person, both for identification and for weapons or items that could aid in an escape attempt. The wallet pulled from a pocket of his jeans identified him as Henry Lamb of Barrie, Ontario.

The roar of the backhoe driving out of the trench drowned out the sound of the police SUV crunching the gravel in Lamb's driveway as it pulled in on the other side of his cottage. Quiet descended on the neighbourhood when Sam shut down the backhoe, and McNabb was startled when he heard a familiar voice behind him.

"*Mister* Lamb. What kind of mischief are you up to this week? Hey, Rob. That your pilot doing some work in the water?"

"Hey, Brownie, what are you doing west of Blind River? And no, she's just putting Henry's toys away for him. It's difficult operating all those levers with your hands secured behind your back."

"What's he going in for … this time?"

"Assault peace officer … he took a swing at Sam. Plus obstruction, deposit deleterious substance, alteration or damage to fish habitat and working in shorelands without a permit."

"Well, I'm filling in for the Thessalon team because someone's off sick. But he's going to be real pissed that he missed the chance to scoop Henry … again. They've got history. We've got history."

"Okay, but before you cart him off, I'm not quite finished with him."

"Fuck you, fish cop. This is my property. You got no rights here."

"He wants you to charge us for trespass."

"Forgive them their trespasses, Henry, for the law allows them to do so."

"And that's my lake, Henry, in which you have no right to be messing around without approval. You are hereby ordered not to do any more work on the shoreland or in the water until the court orders you to return it to its original state.

"As standard procedure, the court will be appointing me as your probation officer for the duration of the restoration work. Failure to comply with such order will result in significant financial punishment. Any ordered restoration *will* be performed to my specifications and my satisfaction, and according to a prescribed plan approved by the court. I would, however, strongly suggest you hire a licenced contractor to perform such restoration."

"You know he'll be out on bail by tomorrow, Rob. How are you going to keep his hands off that machine?"

"Glad you mentioned that, Darren. By the powers invested in me under the Fisheries Act of Canada, Henry Lamb the backhoe is hereby seized."

Bob Jordan from next door cheered. He was standing with his toes right up against Lamb's property line. "There is a God!" he said.

"Fuck you, Jordan."

"How far is it from here to the Thessalon detachment, Darren?"

"About fifteen klicks."

"Can you give me a ride back here after I ferry the machine down to the compound there?"

Jordan called over, "I can tail him down and drive him back, Brownie."

Apparently, the neighbour was on a nickname basis with the police — the sole advantage of living with an arrogant troublemaker next door.

"You okay with that, Rob?"

"Works for me. DCO Williams is going to be a while taking pictures and measurements of the crime scene. Depending on how fast this thing goes Sam, I should be back in an hour or so."

"Less time than that, Robbie. It should be able to do thirty-five or forty klicks. And it's got half a tank of fuel. You could go all the way home on that if you want. There's that stump in the front lawn I want pulled…." She finished, laughing.

"You son of a bitch, you better not…."

"She's kidding, Henry," Constable Brown shook his head. "Where's your sense of humour?" He led the prisoner up to his cruiser. McNabb got the backhoe running and followed the police vehicle out the gravelled cottage road. Bob Jordan followed close behind in his Prius.

Brown was waiting at the Thessalon detachment when McNabb arrived with the backhoe. He unlocked the gate to the secure storage compound, and they hung an MNR seizure tag on the machine before locking the gate again. McNabb stopped by the cruiser before getting into Jordan's car. "Mr. Lamb, I'll leave a seizure receipt for the backhoe on your door back at the cottage."

"When do I get it back?"

"When and if the court says you can have it back."

"I'd damned well better get it back or you'll be out of a job."

McNabb didn't bother with a reply.

—

"How do you put up with that guy, Bob?" McNabb asked Jordan as they headed back to the lake.

"Well, he won a big lottery jackpot a couple years ago. Eight or nine million, I think. Bought this place and another place in Florida and a big motorhome and still kept his place in Barrie, so he's only seasonal, and only here intermittently, at worst. When he's here, I spend as much time as I can with my lady friend a few doors farther up the shore. We just got back early this morning after a few days in Las Vegas to see this mess.

"The fact that you got here, I presume she called you this morning?"

"Like I said to Lamb, no one from *this* neighbourhood phoned us," McNabb finished with a smile.

"Ahh, I understand. Well, it worked, anyhow.

"So, change of subject," Jordan continued, "I hunt moose with some buddies north of here, up by Peshu Lake. Every year, there's a guy flies around there, constantly circling … low over the forest. We're sure he's looking for moose. Probably driving them away from us toward his clients. It's a real piss-off. Almost as bad as having Henry as a neighbour."

"White Beaver with blue trim?" McNabb asked.

"Yeah, that's the guy. North Channel Outfitter or something like that."

"North Shore Air Service."

"That's the one. Is there any way you can get him to stop?"

"Well, I told him he wasn't allowed to do that, but he did it anyhow." McNabb said. Then he grinned. "And so we seized his Super Cub on Wednesday."

"Good show. So, we won't see him up there this year?"

"No guarantees, Bob, he still has his Beaver. Let's just say he's a work in progress."

"Glad to hear it. We need more bush enforcement in the area. Did you know there used to be four officers for this district?"

"Oh, I sure do. As busy as things got in my last district … and there were just two of us for a district as big as the state of Minnesota … I was never so run off my feet in my five years there as I've been in the two weeks since I moved here."

When he returned to Henry Lamb's waterfront disaster, McNabb helped Williams take the last few measurements of the unauthorized work. Sam had already gathered water samples and taken pictures of the mess while he was gone, so they decided to head north and check at least a few more camps in the Ranger Lake area.

Chapter 27

1250 – North Shore Air Service office.

Reggie Ritchie was mulling over the flights he had planned for the rest of the day. He was pissed that he hadn't been in the air hours ago, but he'd spent the morning replacing a fuel line on the Beaver — a job that couldn't be put off.

He'd also received word from his friend, Peter Wolf, that the new game warden had flown off in the direction of Reggie's first planned stop. Pete was an unemployed guy who sometimes did things for Ritchie. The outfitter had asked him if he could give him a heads up each time the yellow Turbo Beaver left the airport. He was getting frustrated by McNabb's habit of showing up when and where he wasn't wanted.

Peter had driven his old camper van out to the airport parking lot prepared to spend the next few days there. He pretended to be broken down. Anyone seeing the aged vehicle sitting there with alternators, water pumps and other miscellaneous parts dropped carelessly around it would have no problem believing it was disabled. And it wasn't a busy airport, so nobody bothered to send the guy packing.

Now Reggie's Beaver was buttoned down, refuelled and ready to fly. Daylight hours in October were short, and now the day was more than half wasted. He couldn't wait any longer. He had to pick up the group that had called in by satellite phone last night. Hell, as long as the guys weren't dirty, then there'd be no harm in being checked by asshole McNabb yet again — other than causing another delay.

Reggie cast off, started the engine, and taxied CF-OMG away from the dock, turned into the light wind and prepared for takeoff. Twenty-five minutes later, he was circling over Upper Green Lake, almost due north of Elliot Lake. There was no yellow government plane in sight.

When he landed, he was met at the beach by his three guests. They were all excited about their great hunt. Reggie loved satisfied customers. He immediately began to feel his stress level ease. He had been stewing over nothing.

"Well, what've you got, fellas? You're the guys with calf tags only, right?" When he had flown them in for the hunt, they told him that it was their first ever moose hunt, and none of them had been drawn for a cow or bull tag. They lived for the annual fall hunt, but ducks and deer were their normal quarry, and their entire hunting experience before now was in southwestern Ontario — flat farm country and woodlots near the shores of Lake Erie.

"Yup, couple of big ones, Reg. Just standing together out there in an open marsh. Perfect shots, and down they went. Musta been orphaned … there was no sign of the cow."

The more the guy talked, the more something sounded off to the outfitter. "Let's have a look at them, guys," and he followed them up to where the moose were hanging from the game pole. He could see a problem right away. The fact that the carcasses hadn't been quartered to fit inside the aircraft, wasn't the main problem. That these two moose were not calves, *was* a problem.

"Got yourselves a couple nice yearlings, boys." One had a pair of antlers the same length as his ears and the other was probably his twin sister. Yearlings were not calves. Small adults. Definitely not calves.

"If I get caught transporting illegal game in my plane, I'll be in as deep shit as you guys will for shootin' them. Deeper even. New game warden here's got a real hate on for me."

"Aw, c'mon, we can't just leave them here."

"You're right about that. Even bigger fines for shooting the wrong moose and then abandoning them. And after what I've heard, I'm comin' to believe that the mean son of a bitch can find a dead squirrel buried out in the bush five miles away." A slight exaggeration never hurt when opening financial negotiations.

"So, what do we do then?"

Ritchie was almost beginning to enjoy this. Or at least he would if it weren't so risky. But it had worked before, so it would again. He sighed and ran his fingers through his hair. Had to draw out the suspense — make the guys realize his solution was the only way to resolve their problem.

"Tell you what. For an extra two grand, I'll fly the meat to an alternate destination."

"Two thousand dollars? You've got to be kidding. That's freakin' highway robbery, man."

"Maximum fine for this kind of shit is twenty-five grand … per person. If either him or his deputy check us landing at my base with those yearlings on board, we'd all be roasted like pigs on a spit."

"So … what … you're going to fly us out and drop us on the coast of Hudson Bay or Baffin Island?"

"That'd be pretty stupid, wouldn't it. Besides, the Beaver doesn't have the range. No, it won't be more than a couple kilometres out of the way for you on your way home … but about fifty klicks extra, each way for the Beaver." Exaggerated again, for effect. "And like I said, I'm risking my plane and my business just carryin' illegal game. So, we'll drop one guy with the meat at a dock with good road access and fly the other two of you back to my base for your vehicles."

The three hunters looked at each other, shrugged their sagging shoulders and grudgingly agreed to pay the extra airfreight.

"Now let's get these fuckin' beasts quartered. Told ya that's how I wanted them prepared for the flight. I should charge another five hundred on top, just for doin' what you were supposed to do before I showed up."

—

An hour later, Ritchie scanned the sky, looking for the dreaded Turbo Beaver before loading the two quartered moose into his plane. Couldn't see it, nor could he hear it. No yellow bird nearby. They loaded the plane with meat and all their gear as fast as they could. The quarters of moose were placed close to the back doors, on Reggie's instructions.

As he began to taxi down the bay, he warned them, "If that game warden's plane shows up while we're still on the water, all that meat goes out the door toot sweet, got it?"

"What!"

"Don't worry. They'll sink immediately. Then, no moose, no extra freight charge. It's what you'd call a lose-win situation. Not as good as win-win, but a shitload better than twenty-five grand in fines … each."

There was still no government plane in sight, so he shoved the throttle forward and his old Beaver roared across the lake, slowly lifted off and turned south.

"Just keep your eyes peeled for a bright yellow plane, boys," he hollered over the roar of the radial engine. He nodded to the two guests sitting in the right-hand seats. "Pay real close attention to the sky nearest the sun." Beware of the Hun in the sun, was a World War I saying used by allied pilots. That was where the Kaiser's aircraft had the best chance of getting close enough to attack before being seen.

—

Half an hour later, Reggie banked the plane in a sweeping left-hand turn and scanned the water below for obstacles. In the early 1900s, Serpent Harbour, on the North Channel at Spragge, would have been covered by rafts of logs waiting to be sawn into lumber at Cook's Mill. The mill and the log rafts were long gone, but individual logs — deadheads — still wandered the bay, lying low in the water, just waiting to damage speeding boats and aircraft floats alike.

The pilot checked carefully, but didn't see any deadheads, so he turned into the wind and settled the Beaver on the choppy water. He taxied to the municipal dock, just east of the North Channel Yacht Club. The boating season was over and only a few bodies were visible over at the club. Those who were there were too busy preparing their boats for winter storage to pay much attention to the arrival of the float plane — but it would be noticed. There were no vehicles in the municipal dock parking area. That was good.

"Okay, guys. Time to unload. Find a dry spot up there in the tall grass to lay your quarters. And whoever is waiting here, don't go and mingle with the folks at the yacht club. Too much risk of getting into a conversation and letting something slip. Some might even be antihunters or tree huggers … might take exception to guys taking moose out of their sacred forest. Got it?"

The hunter who volunteered to stay with the meat, agreed to stay put.

"It'll probably be close to an hour before your buddies get back here. I'll show them the turn-off when we get airborne."

Chapter 28

Monday October 24, 0120 – McNabb-Williams residence

McNabb woke to the throaty growl of the family cat. Tigger had learned to open interior doors with latch handles, rather than doorknobs. Just jump, hang weight on the handle, forward momentum pushes the door inward, drop and enter at will. Easy peasy.

Right now, the big tabby was perched with his hind paws on top of the headboard and his front paws on the windowsill. He was the only cat McNabb had ever heard with such a deep growl. Something was out in the yard.

"What's he going on about, Robbie?" Sam asked.

"Probably raccoons, or maybe a fox," he answered as he reached for the laser flashlight under his bedside table. He knelt on the bed beside the growling cat and peered through the window. By the light of the moon, he could see it was neither fox nor 'coon out there but a human. The person had just put a lawn chair up against the house right under Lottie's bedroom window.

"Son of a bitch." Rob was just about to dash to her room to check on the child when the intruder took the chair that was nested on top of the first one and moved along to place it under the master bedroom window, right in front of him.

McNabb pressed the high-powered flashlight tight against the glass and turned it on. "Gotcha now, asshole." The dazzling light beam blinded the guy who stood stunned, with a look of terror on his face before he turned and stumbled away from the house, half blinded, heading for the bushes. The flashlight lit the way for the intruder as he picked up speed and raced for the treeline. Rob killed the light when the guy reached the edge of the bush.

Plunged into sudden darkness the guy tripped over a fallen sapling and hit the ground hard. There was a moment of silence, then cursing loudly, the intruder struggled to his feet and began staggering on into the bush and out of sight.

Sam was up by then and watching too. Rob said, "Good thing I cut those stumps flat and low to the ground." Landing on a sharp, small stump, cut at an angle with an axe, could be deadly, so Rob had sawn them flat in case he or a family member wandered into the bush and tripped.

"That still had to hurt," Sam said. "I don't think he'll be back."

"Not tonight, anyhow. Thanks Tigger. Good kitty, now scoot." He chased the cat out of the bedroom, checked on the girls in their rooms, made sure their windows were locked, then gave the cat a handful of treats on his way back to bed.

—

Same morning, 0710

Breakfast time. Rob was chopping onions and adding them to the spaghetti sauce he was building in the slow cooker. Sam was in the shower and Lottie was sitting at the kitchen table dropping Cheerios from her cereal bowl to the cat — one toasty "O" at a time. Mae Ling had already breakfasted and was dressed for school. She walked slowly into the kitchen, staring at the screen on her cell phone.

"Dad?" The disconcerted tone of her voice and the look of alarm on her face caught McNabb's attention.

"What's wrong, sweetheart?"

"I got this on Instagram," she handed the phone to her father. He looked at the screen and did a double take.

"Crap. When did you get this?"

"Just now."

He looked back at the screen again. A picture of Mae Ling getting off the school bus in front of the house was followed by the caption: "Hot body, China doll. I know where you live. Tell your old man to back off — or else."

"Damn. This bullshit is getting out of hand." The toddler's open ears were forgotten. "Drop in the onions and give this a stir Mae Ling, then put the lid on it. As soon as I'm dressed, we're going to the police detachment."

Sam walked in just then. "What's wrong?" Mae Ling handed her the phone as Rob hurried off to get changed. "Oh, shit!"

"Oh, shit what, Mom?" came from the breakfast table. "Is that like bullshit?"

"Lottie, *no*! Daddy and I sometimes use words you are too young to say, Baby… you can't say them until you are forty years old. Mae Ling, do you know who sent you this?"

"It isn't from any of my contacts and the username is just a jumble of letters. Dad thinks it's that Ritchie guy you are all trying to catch. The word at school is he's in a rage about you guys seizing his plane."

"Okay, then if Dad's taking you to the police station, you'll miss the bus. Get everything together so he can drive you to school from there. He's got court this morning too." Sam shook her head. "Guess I'll have to drive Lottie to Nancy's before I head up to Elliot Lake. How to screw up a morning."

Rob called out from the bedroom. "No, sweetie, we'll get her delivered. You've got your Sudbury flight to do. We'll deal with the rest."

Chapter 29

0735 – Police detachment, Blind River

Sergeant Mitchell listened to McNabb's report of the night visitor, then looked at Mae Ling's phone. "Yeah, I'd say that's a definite threat, Rob. Only, in legal terms, probably classed as an implied threat. And proving who sent it is technologically beyond me, even though I agree with you that it has to be Reggie. You haven't pissed off anyone else this badly yet, have you?"

"The salmon shooter."

"He's in district jail in the Soo."

"Maybe some of the hunters we've charged … but not local folks," Rob said. "The clients I've upset the most are all from down south and still in the bush. Not likely they got out of the bush just to stalk my family … or repaint our house."

"Well, I think we've got a solid lead on that, at least. Results from the fingerprints on the paint can … just a sec … Rhonda," Mitchell looked over at the clerk where she was typing up summonses. "Call Constable Mary Miller. She's just gone off duty but get her back here ASAP. We need her digital-savvy mind for this." Then he turned back to McNabb. "The constable used to be in cyber protection for one of the big banks.

"Anyhow, the prints on the paint can belong to Tyler Hatch. He lives in your fair village, about a ten-minute walk from your house."

"Related to the school bus driver?"

"Yeah, that's his father. Tyler's basically a good kid, but he's … uh … Rhonda, what's this year's politically correct word for mentally slow?"

"Don't know, they change every six months or so. But I can give you a list of all the out-dated ones."

"Ah … no … thanks. Anyhow, the kid, he's twenty-four now, doesn't have the imagination to initiate any of the things you've experienced … not without direction from someone else. And seeing as how he works part time for Teflon Reggie, I think that's the direction in which we should be looking."

"Well, crap. We figured Reggie'd be involved somehow. Tyler's folks will sure be upset."

"Yeah, good people. Anyhow, as for this latest development, Mae Ling, I'm going to have an unmarked unit follow your bus home this afternoon. As soon as you get off the bus, the constable will accompany you into your house and make sure no one is lurking there. Then you lock yourself in when she leaves and don't let anyone in but your folks or one of us, okay?"

"Yes, sir."

"Good. I *would* have her pick you up at the school, but we don't want everyone in town starting a bunch of rumours and going into a panic." He turned his head, as someone whisked into the room.

"What's up, Sarge? Oh, hi Rob."

"Jeez, Mary … did you teleport yourself back? That took you less than a minute."

"Haven't been home yet, boss. I just finished washing my car in the garage."

"Oh, okay. So, this is Mae Ling, Rob's daughter. Take a look at this message she got. Can you trace who it came from? And if so, can you save it as evidence without hanging on to her phone? She needs to be able to stay in touch with her folks … and with us if need be."

"Give me a couple of minutes. C'mon Mae Ling. I'll show you how we do this. And how insecure our social media accounts really are." McNabb's daughter followed the constable into the squad room, where they sat down at a computer.

The sergeant offered Rob a coffee in the lunchroom while they waited, and it was barely half gone when the girls tracked them down.

"Looks like Reginald Ritchie is the primary user on this account. I'm guessing the scrambled letter username was his amateurish attempt at hiding his identity."

"Amateur for sure," Rob said. "Not much point trying to hide it, considering he's trying to get us to back off his case. Stupidest anonymous letter I've ever seen. How did he expect us not to guess it was him?"

"Yeah, not too smart."

"The more important question is, what do we do about this, Harry? I don't want to put my family in danger, but I'm sure not backing away from the guy."

"We'll handle it, Rob. I've got a senior constable, who I guess you haven't met yet … Archie's *really* good at explaining things like this to the misguided among us. That'll be his assignment this morning. But at least for today, let's go with our security plan, okay?"

McNabb dropped Mae Ling at school then went to the office to catch up on some deskwork before heading for court.

Chapter 30

0959 – Blind River court room

Mark Wilson, a substitute provincial prosecutor, hurried into the courtroom, located Rob McNabb and took him aside. At the same moment, the judge's door opened behind the bench. As she stepped up to her seat, Her Honour, Diane Chenoweth, saw the hurried conference being carried out at the back of the room and was not pleased. Someone had arrived late for the hearing.

Wilson said to McNabb, "Sorry to drop this on you on short notice, McNally, but the defendant's lawyer is making a big deal about the seizure of his airplane. I got called in at the last minute. I do traffic cases. Never handled wildlife stuff, so I need you sitting with me."

"Okay, and it's McNabb, sir. Rob McNabb." His heart sank into his gut. If this guy has never done any natural resources cases, we could lose our seizures. And now the scowl was growing fierce on the judge's face. Looking over her half-glasses, the tall, silver haired, sixty-five-year-old made it abundantly clear that she was a no-nonsense adjudicator.

It made for an inauspicious first appearance in her court. McNabb followed Wilson as they brushed through the swinging gate at the front of the courtroom and took their places at the prosecutor's table. The clerk began to call the court to order even before they had their chairs pulled out to sit.

"Cutting it a little fine aren't we, Mr. Prosecutor?"

"Truly sorry, Your Honour."

"And you are….?"

"Mark Wilson, Your Honour. I've been assigned this case at the very last minute … just arrived from the Soo as you entered the court. Furthermore, wildlife cases being alien to me, I'll be leaning heavily on Officer McNally … with your permission, of course."

The judge looked briefly at the information in front of her, then turned to glare once again on Wilson. "I believe you'll get along much better with Officer *McNabb* if you learn to get his name right."

"Yes, Your Honour. My apologies to the court and the officer."

"Mr. Greene, this is your show. Why don't you lead off?"

"Good morning, Your Honour. I'll keep this brief and simple. We contend that Officer McNabb grossly overstepped his authority when he instructed an unpaid volunteer, through an intermediary no less, to seize the aircraft belonging to my client, Mr. Ritchie, owner and operator of North Shore Air Service. The aircraft is a Piper Super Cub, Canadian registration C-GCUB. This abusive overreach of his authority, and that of the volunteering individual, occurred in the midst of my client's busiest season, seriously depriving him of one of the most important tools of his trade.

"Said seizure being a breach of Mr. Ritchie's constitutional right to carry on his business, we are asking that the court order Officer McNabb to immediately release the aircraft and return it to my client." The big man sat down and gave McNabb and Wilson a look that said, just try to beat that.

"Unusually brief for you, Mr. Greene, thank you. Mr. Wilson, what does the Crown have to say?"

McNabb had already opened his copy of the Fish and Wildlife Conservation Act and used a highlighter to hurriedly mark the definitions of an officer, and the powers of search and seizure. He handed it to Wilson who stood for a moment, flipped through the pages and looked entirely lost.

"I'm waiting, Mr. Wilson."

"Court's indulgence, Your Honour? I need to familiarize myself with the statute."

"It's an extensive piece of legislation, Mr. Wilson, and I wasn't planning for a full day session. Your time's up."

McNabb's heart just about stopped. That's it. The guy just lost us our seizure without saying a word.

"Officer McNabb, would you be comfortable responding to the defence motion?"

McNabb half stood. "Uh …." Oh boy, he thought, this is not going well at all, but he stood the rest of the way and responded, hopeful for the chance of a reprieve. "I … yes, I think so Your Honour." He sat back down, mainly to buy himself a little time. He needed to get this right.

"Mr. Greene? Any objections?"

"None whatsoever, Your Honour." He looked at McNabb and gave him a Grinch-like grin. Greene versus the greenhorn prosecutor, an alligator versus a frog. This ought to be easy.

"Don't worry Officer McNabb," the judge reassured him. "This is not a trial. The sole purpose of this hearing is to listen the defence motion, the crown rebuttal and then rule on it."

McNabb nodded toward the judge and looked at Wilson, who had sufficiently recovered from the judge's scolding to scribble a brief message on his legal pad: *Keep it simple. Respond directly to A – your authority under the Act and that of your deputies; and B – aircraft not the only one in his fleet.*

McNabb took a deep breath, then stood again. "Yes, Your Honour. In answer to Mr. Greene's first point. I am a conservation officer, appointed under the Fish and Wildlife Conservation Act, Revised Statutes of Ontario.

"The person I instructed to search and seize the aircraft in question is Deputy Conservation Officer Eric Snyder, a retired conservation officer in good standing. I was acting as his supervisor and made the lawful request to him by relay through duly appointed Deputy Conservation Officer Samantha Williams. She is the ministry pilot in charge of the aircraft from which we both observed the defendant's aircraft chasing a moose.

"Unlawful use of an aircraft to hunt is an offence under the act. The definition of hunt includes, among other things, the acts of pursuing and harassing.

"It is true that Deputy Snyder was acting in a volunteer capacity. But as an officer under the Act, being an unpaid volunteer in no way undermines his authority to make the seizure.

"Section 92 of the Act gives an officer the authority to seize anything, *without* a warrant, that he or she believes on reasonable grounds was used in the commission of an offence or may provide evidence of an offence. My instruction to seize the aircraft and its contents, provided him the reasonable grounds needed to make that seizure." McNabb paused for a moment in awe of the fact he was about to deliver a constitutional argument — something definitely above his pay grade.

"In answer to the defence question on the matter of depriving Mr. Ritchie of his means of conducting business, we would point out to the court that only one of the two aircraft in his fleet was seized. He still has a fully operational De Havilland Beaver at his disposal." When he sat down, McNabb realized that his knees had been shaking throughout his presentation, but he felt his confidence return when Judge Chenoweth flashed him a brief smile.

"Thank you, Officer McNabb. Mr. Greene, do you have anything further?"

"Your Honour, my client is concerned that certain personal items were removed from the aircraft at the time of the seizure. He would very much like to get them back."

"Seized as evidence perhaps, Officer McNabb?" Judge Chenoweth looked at Rob as she spoke.

"Yes, Your Honour. All catalogued and receipted by Deputy Snyder, a copy of which was given to Mr. Ritchie at the time of his arrest."

"All right then. Final disposition of all seized items and equipment will be ruled on following a trial or other resolution of this case. We are adjourned." She immediately stood. Her long robe flowed behind her as she swept out through the door to her chambers.

"Good job, McNabb," Wilson muttered. "Sorry I wasn't much help." He stood and prepared to walk out of the courtroom.

Greene stuffed some papers into his briefcase and fixed a piercing glare at McNabb. "I'm not done with you yet, McNabb." Then he stood to follow Wilson out.

"Nor am I done with you, Mr. Greene," McNabb stood as he spoke. "Simply put, you ought to instruct your client on the legal consequences of threatening a peace officer, his family, or inciting vandalism of his home." He handed Greene a paper printout of the picture and the message that had been posted on Mae Ling's phone, and another printout of the paint splattered on his house. "Now I *am* finished with you."

Greene stood there, silent, as he looked at the images. He wasn't accustomed to having lowly law enforcement personnel talk back to him like that. But the message on the photo of Mae Ling and the threats spray painted across the front of the house told him he needed to keep Ritchie on a short leash.

"I'll pass that along," he said, then turned and left.

McNabb sat down, heaved a relieved sigh. He picked up his copy of the act and turned to follow the others out.

"Officer McNabb," the judge called from the doorway to her chambers. He looked back at her. "Do you have a few minutes?" she asked. And when he moved toward the judge's bench, she continued.

"Nice work. I usually like to meet with new law enforcement arrivals in my district before they do business in my court … give them a pep talk about dress and decorum, but after witnessing you pull the fat out of the fire this morning, I see there's no need. Please, come with me."

McNabb skirted around the bench to follow her into her office. He'd been in courtrooms often enough during his brief career, but never in chambers.

"Welcome to my world. Is it Robert, Rob or Bob?"

"I generally go by Rob, Your Honour, but in court…."

"In court, you are Officer McNabb, and I am Your Honour. Anywhere else, I'm Diane. Coffee?"

"Sure, thanks."

"Tell me a bit about yourself, Rob."

"Yes, Your Hon … excuse me … Diane. I'm southern Ontario born and raised." He took the offered mug of coffee.

"I've been a CO for five years, and until now I was in Moosonee District. Samantha Williams, the pilot and Deputy CO I spoke of in the hearing, is my wife. She flies government Turbo Beavers, and as a deputy CO she has occasionally been called as a witness. She's very good at both.

"We have two girls. Lottie, age four, and Mae Ling, who will turn seventeen just before Christmas."

"I take it from her name, Mae Ling is adopted?"

"Yes. We pulled her out of a life-threatening situation while working a poaching case that crossed paths with human trafficking. Rather than being sent back to her country of origin, which could well have been a death warrant for her, the province put her into foster care.

Because we were considered by some to be too young to adopt a teen, Sam and I had to jump through an awful lot of extra hoops, wrapped in a tangle of red tape, to be able to have her join our family. But she quickly fit right in. She's a smart young woman. Wants to save the world."

"Word gets around, Rob, and I recall hearing about a couple of your cases up north. A polar bear poacher, wasn't there?"

"That's when I met Sam."

"And poachers who were into sex with underage teens? That's where you found Mae Ling?"

"Yes, and one of those guys murdered my partner at the time." McNabb paled at the memory of it and Chenoweth allowed him to take a moment before he continued. "Anyhow, our successes up north marked us for special treatment, and we were chosen to move here to tame the human flying creatures of the forest."

"Well, it's been a pleasure meeting you, Rob."

"Likewise. And thanks for helping me get through this morning's hearing. I've never had to do that before."

"You handled your part admirably. And a word of caution, Rob. Be careful out there. Watch your back. Some folks really don't like conservation officers."

"I'm aware of that, thanks." He stood and she extended her hand. The handshake was firm, despite her slender, piano player's fingers.

Chapter 31

1115 – North Shore Air Service base, Elliot Lake

"Kinda late, aren't you, Tyler?" Reggie Ritchie heard the old pickup's door squawk shut and the lad approach behind him as he hung the fuel nozzle back on the avgas pump. He turned toward his helper.

"Jesus, boy. What the fuck happened to you?" The kid had a big round bruise over one eye. Four Band-Aids did a mediocre job of patching a group of lacerations on his left cheek and a cut on his neck — and he was walking with a decided limp.

"I don't think I want to play any more jokes on the game warden, Reggie. He might know who I am now, and my folks will be real pissed when they find out what I was doing. They weren't real happy about the blue paint on his house.

"Them and some other neighbours in the village went to help the warden's family clean it off that night. And they said the warden and his family are real nice folks and now everyone's real mad about someone doing all that stuff to them. I thought jokes were supposed to make people laugh, Reggie."

"What do you mean he might know who you are?"

"I was putting the lawn chairs under the windows just like you told me, and he blinded me through the window with a real bright spotlight. When I ran into the bush behind his house I tripped and fell and hit my head and got cut up real bad.

"My dad says the jokes ain't makin' them want to leave. He says it's like waving a red cape at a bull in a bull fight. Makin' him real mad."

"Don't you worry, kid. He'll be wavin' a white flag when I'm done with him."

"Aye, do ye think so, Reggie?" A booming voice came from an officer who had just emerged from a black and white police cruiser. Senior Constable Archie McEwen was a tall, sturdy Scot who bore the appearance of a traditional rough British Isles copper, a man who could break up a bar room brawl single-handed. He'd never had to, but that was because he looked as if he could — and would. He had left the Scottish police in mid-career to join the provincial police in Ontario. He wanted to be closer to his only brother, who was a miner in Sudbury.

"Wee bit of a rough night, was it, Tyler me lad? I hear ye got tangled up racing through the McNabb Forest."

"Yes sir."

"Aye, the woods can be a dangerous place in the dark. And what can ye tell me aboot this photo of his bonnie young lassie gettin' oot o' the school bus?" McEwen held up a tablet with a copy of the image Mae Ling had found on her phone just a few of hours earlier.

"I didn't send it to her sir. Honest. I took the picture for Reggie and sent it to him a couple days ago."

"Keep quiet, Tyler. Don't say nothin,'"

"Aye, Reggie. Ye'd be talkin' aboot the right to remain silent, would ye? Advice ye might well consider fer yairself." The big constable moved into Ritchie's personal space for emphasis. It was the move that had almost always settled bar room brawls singlehanded.

Reggie chose to remain silent.

"Aye, well it makes no never-mind. I've been sent tae tell ye tae lay off the silly-bugger shite ye've been puttin'

McNabb and his family through. There'll be additional charges … threatenin' a peace officer and the likes o' that, added tae yair docket. But I'll no be arrestin' ye today. That'd just make for another bunch of aggravatin' paperwork when we've already got plenty enough on our hands.

"And Tyler me lad, if ye plan tae hang aboot wi this wicked man, ye have chosen the wrong fork in the road. But if ye choose tae retire from yair position here, Officer McNabb and his kind wee wife have asked that we no lay charges against ye, seein as ye were only doin' this evil man's bidding.

"And right noo, I need ye tae accompany me back tae the station house and make a sworn statement aboot yair recent related activities. Will ye do that for me lad?"

"Yes, sir, Constable. Sure thing … Um, Reggie. I think my folks'll want me to quit now too, okay?"

The senior constable got back in the police car and Tyler got into his own beater pickup, prepared to follow the cruiser down to the Blind River detachment.

"Fuckin' asshole Scotchman. *Shit!*" Ritchie broke his silence and stormed down the dock toward his Beaver.

Chapter 32

After court, McNabb picked up a burger at the A&W, then went hunting hunters on the bush roads south of Elliot Lake. He wanted to check the scattering of moose hunters he and Sam had seen on flights over the area. He hadn't been through this part of his district by road yet and wanted folks there to know he was on the job. Today he was working solo because Sam was flying Sudbury COs to remote locations in their district, and Eric Snyder had a dental appointment.

Two hunters, riding ATVs near the west end of the Christie Lake Road carried loaded rifles on their machines. McNabb issued tickets for that offence but since they were polite and didn't grumble about it, he let them off with a warning for not wearing their helmets. Two other hunters got tickets for littering, but the dozen others he checked were behaving themselves. Having made his presence known on the west side of highway 108, he headed back out with a plan to drive in the McCarthy Lake Road on the east side. The entrance was only four kilometres farther up the highway, but the truck was low on gas, so he ran up to Elliot Lake to fill up.

Driving south again, he hadn't made it down to the McCarthy Lake turn-off before an oncoming pickup flashed its lights and pulled onto the far shoulder. Rob pulled off the road on his side of the highway and ran down his window as the other driver jogged across the road to talk to him.

"You the game warden?"

"I'm the conservation officer, yes. How can I help you?"

"I was going to go fishing down at Lake Two, just up from the highway 17 junction, but somebody parked across the entrance trail, blocking the way."

"It isn't much of a walk from the highway to the lake. Couple hundred yards at the most."

"I know, and I walked in, but there's a guy camped right at the lake. Said I wasn't welcome there. That's crown land, isn't it?"

"Well, I'm new here, but that would be my guess." McNabb opened an area map — a well-used paper map of the district. Private land was shown in orange and the Crown land in pale yellow. Lake Two was surrounded entirely by pale yellow. "Yeah, that's all crown there. You want to follow me back down? I'll negotiate a peace settlement. Either that, or an eviction."

"No, I've already wasted over half of the hour I had allowed myself. I just wanted to take a bit of a break from my office. But thanks."

"No problem. I'll check him out anyhow." McNabb watched the fellow return to his pickup, then restarted the HVEV and headed south.

—

1515 – Lake Two, Lewis Township, south of Elliot Lake

Highway 108 ran alongside the small lake called Lake Two. McNabb had heard that the brook trout introduced there in the 1980s were thriving.

He arrived at the short access road, a simple two-track trail, and it was indeed blocked. Someone had parked a 1990-something Oldsmobile Alero right at the entrance. There was no way to drive around it. The patrol truck's licence plate reading app chose that moment to freeze. He rebooted the system but didn't stick around to wait for results. He got out, locked the truck and headed in on foot.

He didn't have far to go, but since he was looking for a guy who didn't want others around, McNabb took his time keeping his eyes open and his senses on alert. Every few yards, it appeared as if something had been dragged along the trail — inbound, judging from the way the drag marks pushed up small ridges of dirt. The marks would disappear for a short distance before showing up again. As he approached the campsite, the marks disappeared altogether.

First thing he saw when he arrived at the landing was a small pup tent pitched in the middle of the track, just yards from the water's edge. The tent was barely large enough for an adult. McNabb stood and listened for several minutes. There was no one around.

Between the tent and the lake, a small campfire sat hissing inside a ring of stones. The fire was mostly smoke. Smoke that smelled of wet wood. Wood piled beside the fire ring was fresh cut birch. It was too green to burn properly. McNabb wondered at the apparent lack of wilderness experience of whoever had laid this fire. At least there was little danger of it taking off and causing a wildfire.

He looked inside the tent. The only thing inside was a thin, cheap sleeping bag. Might keep the occupant warm on a hot August night, but it sure wouldn't be comfortable on a chilly autumn night. And there was a frost warning out for the coming night.

Beside the tent, leaning against a tree, was a bargain rack fishing rod. It was the sort of thing you bought for a kid you didn't want to encourage to take up the sport. It was the cheapest Walmart rod and reel available. Beside it was a plastic tackle box — same quality as the rod — with half a dozen cheap lures, best suited for pike or bass, not for the brook trout in this lake.

Also leaning against the tree was a well-used Garant round nosed shovel — a quality tool someone had paid good money for. It had probably cost more than all the cheesy camping gear on the site. Okay, the shovel is for digging a latrine.

McNabb wondered though, would someone as ill equipped as this camper appeared to be, think to dig a dump pit? Or maybe someone was setting up the cheap stuff to "reserve" the site for the weekend when the real camping equipment would arrive. That happened quite frequently at prime unregulated campsites.

Now he heard someone coming through the bush. There was no more time to ponder the situation. The camper was coming home. McNabb saw the man before the guy noticed him. He was a tall stocky man, late twenties or early thirties, at least four inches taller than McNabb. How would this guy fit in the skimpy sleeping bag in that tiny tent? He could have been a bar room bouncer if he had been better dressed — it looked as if his clothes were rejects from a donation bin. He had on a ratty fall jacket, and the cuffs of his scruffy jeans were tucked into coarse wool socks that showed above a pair of black rubber boots. Okay, so the guy is a bit down on his luck. Act accordingly.

"Good afternoon. I'm a conservation officer," McNabb announced. "How are you today?"

The guy looked a little surprised to see someone in his campsite. He didn't respond to the question. He looked at McNabb with a blank expression, aloof, then looked away.

"Here to do some fishing, are you?"

"Yeah." No eye contact.

"You will need to find some dry wood if you plan to get any heat out of that fire. I passed a standing dead cedar beside the trail, halfway between here and your car. Nobody'll complain if you cut that one down."

No response.

"Do you have a fishing licence?"

"Yeah."

"I know you aren't fishing at this moment, but if I check it now, then I won't need to come back."

The guy pulled a wallet from his jeans pocket, took out a temporary licence printout and handed it to McNabb. Hands were steady. Interesting, he thought — most folks being checked by law enforcement, even when they aren't doing anything wrong, tend to get at least a little nervous.

The temporary licence identified the holder as Anthony Bailey from Mississauga, Ontario and it had been bought just a day earlier. His eye and hair colour matched, and his age looked appropriate, but height and weight indicated someone shorter by a couple of inches, and lighter by as much as thirty pounds, McNabb would have judged.

"What's your current address, Mr. Bailey?" McNabb asked, attempting to verify that the licence really belonged to this fellow. The guy told him the address that was shown on the document. The inconsistent height and weight were still puzzling, but McNabb decided to let it go. He could ask for his driver's licence for comparison, but the guy looked as if he had enough challenges in life without nitpicking over licence details. Especially since the guy was unlikely to catch any fish with the cheesy fishing gear.

"Okay, you're set to go. Just one thing. This is crown land. Anyone is entitled to use it, so if someone comes through here to do some fishing, you may not impede them in any way. I spoke to a fellow a while ago who thought you might not want him around. He maybe just misread the situation?"

"Yeah, I guess he did." Bailey pocketed the licence, picked up the cheesy fishing rod and started to tie a lure onto the line. A lure best suited for catching pike. Tied on with granny knots. The guy was so much out of place that McNabb couldn't bear to watch.

"Okay, good luck fishing. And please move your car so it no longer blocks the access." He turned and walked back toward the truck, scratching his head as he walked. Something weird was going on there. Or it *was* just a case of the guy being down on his luck. Maybe someone else bought the licence for him and just guessed at his height and weight. That could explain it.

Back at the F-150 patrol truck, McNabb made some notes, then noticed that the licence plate app on his laptop had come up with the ownership for the Olds. And it wasn't Anthony Bailey. Ray Rogers, also of Mississauga, was the owner of record.

"Shit." But neither was the Olds listed as stolen. "Hmm. Not listed as stolen *yet*, anyhow." He began to imagine different situations but kept coming back to what he had seen. A strange character who appeared totally out of context with his surroundings, camping with an obvious lack of bush sense, using entirely inadequate equipment — except for the shovel. And driving a car not registered to him. Older model, but in decent shape. Borrowed from a family member, perhaps? Is he really Anthony Bailey? And what about the unexplained drag marks on the trail. All his camping gear together was nowhere near heavy enough for a guy that size to have to drag it down the trail.

"So, do I call in the blue crew?" he pondered aloud, thinking of the police. "Naw, they've got enough going on without me laying my thin suspicions on them. Not yet anyhow." Instead, he locked up the truck again and started back to ask Mr. Bailey a couple of follow-up questions.

Chapter 33

Before he'd gone fifty yards down the access trail, McNabb saw Bailey coming the other way. The guy had already passed the dead cedar tree, and he wasn't carrying a saw. Good, he's coming to move his car.

"One quick question Mr. Bailey," McNabb said. "I just learned that the car isn't registered to you. What's the story there?"

"Father-in-law loaned it to me. And maybe you want to leave now." Bailey's hands were jammed in the pockets of the big coat and staring straight at McNabb. It was a creepy kind of a stare — a predatory stare, not the aloof look he'd first exhibited. He kept approaching.

"You're getting involved in something that's none of your business," Bailey said as he continued his slow approach, almost like a cat stalking a bird or a squirrel — but without the pauses between steps.

If he'd said no more after the bit about his father-in-law lending him the car, McNabb probably would have turned and left, but something strange was going on here. Creepy strange.

"Stop there for a minute, please."

But Bailey kept coming, and said, "Get in your truck and drive away while you still can."

What the hell is going on? McNabb's mind raced through the possibilities. If the hair stands up on the back of your neck, it is happening for a reason — a lesson from his enforcement training. Had the shovel already been used to dispose of a body? Father-in-law's car. Was the old man's body in the trunk? In the ground? Am I overthinking this?

Bailey was less than ten yards away now, and still coming — not fast — but still coming. The time for speculation was over. McNabb had five years on the job and had experienced several life-threatening situations in that short time. His next move was instinctive. Just ahead of him, off to the left side of the track, was an abandoned car — a wreck from the 1950s, lying on its side. He gripped his pistol butt ready to draw, stepped behind the wreck, and once again he told Bailey to stop. A quick, left-handed thumb push on his walkie talkie sent out a silent call for assistance. The HVEV radio would pick up the signal and relay it directly to the police comm centre — if the relay was working.

"Stop and take your hands out of your pockets. Do it now!"

Bailey stopped, but his hands stayed in his big pockets and whatever was in the pockets made the coat bulge. His right hand was moving inside the pocket. McNabb knew that the guy wouldn't have to pull a handgun out of the pocket to shoot. One more hole in the shabby old coat wouldn't be noticed.

"Hands up *right now!*" McNabb ordered as he drew his Glock pistol and aimed it at Bailey. His heart was pounding. He steadied his hands on top of the old car. It wasn't perfect cover, but the steel remaining in the old junker was probably twice the thickness of a twenty-first century auto. He had a slight advantage, and Bailey was standing in the middle of the trail with no cover.

Now the guy took his hands out of his pockets. Nothing in them.

"Take off your coat and set it up here on the car. Then step back. *Do it now.*"

Slowly, Bailey pulled off the coat and dropped it on the ground in front of him — not on the wreck.

McNabb let that slide. On the ground was almost as good. "Step back from the coat. Three giant paces." Bailey shuffled back a little. Not nearly enough.

"Back farther. The longer you take, the longer this goes on." When McNabb was satisfied with the distance, he stepped back onto the trail. "Now, put your hands on top of your head, fingers laced together." Bailey paused before raising his hands.

The slow compliance was frustrating and unnerving, but the guy hadn't done anything yet to warrant an arrest and McNabb was concerned that he was overstepping his authority. If he was, there were lawyers who would have to sort that out later. But right now, every hair was standing up on the back of his neck and his mind whirled through a long list of possibilities.

He stepped forward and picked up the coat, then stepped back behind the wreck and laid it on top. He checked the left-hand pocket: balled up winter glove. Right hand pocket: the other glove — and something hard and heavy under that — brass knuckles. A prohibited weapon in Canada. A feeling of vindication and relief came over him. The guy did represent a potential threat.

There was still something hard inside the coat. He heard it clunk when he flopped the coat over on the sheet metal bodywork. Inner pocket check. Right side: nothing. Left side: an ugly looking spring knife — well worn, at that. Also illegal in Canada.

"Any more weapons on you?"

"Nope."

"You go by Anthony, or Tony?"

"Mr. Bailey, to you."

"Okay, Mr. Bailey, put your hands behind your back and lean forward for a minute. I'm arresting you for possession of prohibited weapons." McNabb holstered his pistol and pulled out his handcuffs. He snapped on the first cuff, but Bailey held his other arm rigid and out of reach.

"*Put your arm down now!*" McNabb yelled and jerked the cuffed wrist high up Bailey's back. The guy had thick muscular arms, but with the cuffed wrist pulled tight between his shoulder blades, he soon complied. The second cuff ratcheted shut.

"You've made a false arrest, asshole," Bailey snarled. "You better turn me loose before this gets any worse. Your life won't be worth living if you don't."

"I'll turn you over to the police as soon as they arrive. If they agree with you, then I'll leave it to them to turn you loose. In the meantime, I'm going to frisk you for other weapons. You make *any* aggressive move, and you will severely regret it." He pulled out his collapsible baton and snapped it open to back up the threat.

His careful search came up empty. The guy had no more weapons. "Okay, move." McNabb pushed him toward the highway. Police sirens were approaching fast. The emergency relay signal must have worked. The first of three cruisers arrived at McNabb's truck at the same time he and Bailey did.

Constable Mary Miller stepped out and took charge of Bailey even though he dwarfed her. He started to resist and get pushy.

"No tiny bitch cop is going to lock me up."

McNabb jerked the handcuff chain hard upward once more, pulling both arms toward Bailey's shoulder blades and enforcing compliance. He helped Miller force the prisoner into the back seat of her caged cruiser. They shoved the door closed just before two backup constables arrived.

All four of them walked back down the trail to pick up the weapons still lying on the wreck while McNabb gave them a brief verbal report. Miller returned to her cruiser to quiz the prisoner on the whereabouts of his father-in-law while the other two constables headed down to Bailey's campsite.

McNabb returned to his truck to make notes. He knew that he would have to fill in a whole set of ministry forms and probably be subjected to an enquiry after drawing his pistol on the guy.

Halfway through his note taking, he stopped to take a phone call from his comm centre. "McNabb, badge 415."

"*Rob, Mary Ellen here. We've got a call from a hunter who says that another hunter is trying to claim the moose he shot this afternoon. They are parked on the side of highway 639 at the top of the Cobre Lake hill, north of Elliot Lake.*"

"I'm inclined to think that's a police matter, Mary Ellen. But since I've now got three of their units tied up here, I guess I'll take it."

"Police matter if one had stolen it from the other, Rob. This is a case of both having shot it. Each one claims to have made the kill shot."

"Okay. I've got another five or ten minutes of notes to write up and I'll need to finish conferring with the police. It might be fifty minutes or more before I get up there."

—

1610

Rob phoned Sam just before he was ready to leave the Lake Two incident. She was returning from her day with the Sudbury officers.

"Hi Sam, it's going to be a long day here. I just got handed another occurrence to attend. Are you able to pick up Lottie?"

"*Hey, Flyboy. Busy, huh? Don't worry, I'm less than ten minutes from Elliot. After I refuel and hangar the bird, I should be able to pick her up at Snyders' by five-thirty.*

"So, are you still liking the fast pace of a southern CO?"

"Rick warned me on the first day that I'd be doing the work of four officers. I guess the phone booth sized office wasn't an accident after all. Anyhow, right now I'm about to head for a moose kill dispute between two hunters. Ever since leaving court this morning I've been going all out. Think I'll turn off the phone and cut the wires to the radio after this call so I can sneak home. How was your day?"

"Good, until one of the COs slipped and broke his ankle climbing onto the float. We got some loaded rifles in power boats before that happened, but then we had to fly him back to Sudbury. Screwed up the rest of the shift for his partner, though.

"Anyhow, I'm about to go on final approach. Gotta do some piloty stuff. We'll see you whenever you get home. Love you, Robbie."

"Love you too, Sam."

Chapter 34

It wasn't five seconds after he disconnected the call that Rob's phone rang. Call display said "Webb."

"Hey boss, what's up?"

"*I hear you drew your pistol on a citizen this afternoon.*"

McNabb's face paled. It had just happened, and the shit had already hit the fan. "Uh … yeah, Rick. It was literally a hair-raising experience. How'd you hear about it? I haven't even left the scene yet."

"*Staff Sergeant Sawyer just called me. He says he hasn't met you yet. Said he wanted to let me know about it before any lawyers or media got hold of it. He said that from what Constable Miller reported to him, it was a justifiable action, so don't get your shirt in a knot. But you know how it goes … I'll need to interview you, and we'll have some paperwork to do.*

"*You're busy there now, so I'll see you at your office later in the week. Supposed to rain on Friday. Maybe we'll do it then. I'll get back to you. Don't sweat it, Rob, it's just procedure. You're not being hauled up on the carpet.*"

"Linoleum tile."

"*Huh?*"

"The floor covering … in my office."

"*See you Friday, Rob.*" McNabb could hear his staff sergeant chuckling as the call ended.

—

1705 – Hwy 639 at the top of Cobre Lake Hill

McNabb pulled into a small gravel pit beside the highway. There were three pickups and a couple of minivans already parked there. Wasn't much space left for the patrol truck, so he left it blocking in several vehicles. When he got out of the truck, he could hear loud voices off in the bush. Had these guys been arguing the whole time since one of them called it in? He followed the noise for seventy metres up a trail into the hardwood bush. About a dozen orange-clad hunters were gathered around a cow moose carcass.

"Good afternoon, folks. I understand that there is some disagreement over possession of this moose." His greeting and the uniform got their attention and a few seconds of silence followed, but before he could say anything more, it seemed that at least half of the crowd wanted to have their say all at once.

"*Hold it everyone!*" McNabb had to raise his voice and hold up his hands to get their attention. Silence settled on the crowd again. "One at a time, please. Now, who shot the moose?"

"I shot the fuckin' thing first," a big man in his late thirties or early forties spoke up. He was at least a couple inches taller than McNabb and he wore a surly look and three- or four-days' stubble growth. "This guy says it's his but he's full of shit. We tracked it to here from where I shot it. We're ready to dress it out and haul it away but these assholes are holding us up. They say we can't take it until you arrive. So now you're here we can take it, right?"

"I'd like to hear both sides of the story before anyone takes it," McNabb said.

The other shooter was short and thin — maybe twenty years older than the big guy. He gave the impression of being a white-collar office type, but it was hard to tell, him being all decked out in his hunter orange coat and coveralls. This fellow was keeping his cool — waiting his turn to speak, which he did at the invitation of McNabb's gesture.

"I heard shots a distance to the east of me and about ten minutes later this moose came through the brush. I was over there about eighty yards … sitting on that ridge. I couldn't see enough of her to take a clear shot for almost a full minute, then she stepped forward a pace. Perfect position for a heart-lung shot. She dropped right here. I didn't know she had already been shot until I came down to check for signs of life. She was stone dead. That's when I saw all this damage." He was referring to a scattering of bullet wounds in the right hind quarter of the moose and one in the abdomen.

"Ooh, gut shot, yeah," McNabb said. "Okay, first things first. Can you two please show me your hunting licences." They both had them ready. Both licences were valid for shooting a cow moose.

"Randi Thompson," McNabb addressed the big guy. "You are hunting with a party?"

"Yeah. These are my buddies," he pointed at four others standing there. "Look, it's getting late. Can we get started gutting this old girl now?"

"Not yet, no. So, Leonard Fountain," he turned to address the other man. "Is the rest of this group with you?"

"No, it's just me and my brother, Harold," he pointed at another slight man standing quietly to one side of the gathered throng. Strong resemblance. Could have been twins. "The others just showed up while we were out by the road discussing the situation with Mr. Thompson. That's when Mr. Thompson called your office. They suggested we should wait for you to come and settle the matter."

"Okay guys. The bottom line in a case like this is that ownership of lawfully hunted wildlife goes to the person who made the kill."

"Well, that's my killing shot *right there*!" Thompson snapped, as he pointed to an entrance wound in the rib cage right behind the front shoulder.

"I don't think so, Mr. Thompson. If you had put a bullet right there, this animal would have dropped like a stone where it was standing when you shot."

"Goddammit! *That's my shot*!"

Leonard Fountain just stood, quietly shaking his head.

"Mr. Thompson," McNabb asked, "what are you hunting with?"

".44-40 Winchester. Easy hundred-and-fifty-yard shot. I emptied my mag at this bitch. Sent ten rounds her way. She's mine, goddammit."

"And you, Mr. Fountain?"

"Model 70 Winchester, 7-millimeter magnum rounds."

McNabb quickly saw the way to wrap up the discussion. "Each of you give me a live round."

"What, you goin' to shoot her again?" Thompson scoffed. "And no, I ain't got no bullets left. Used 'em all on bringin' her down."

"No, we're not shooting her again. I think she's had enough. You both agree that this was the killing shot?" McNabb pointed to the entry wound in the chest cavity.

From Thompson: "Yeah, that's my fuckin' shot."

From Fountain: "Definitely, officer." He handed McNabb a live 7-millimetre bullet.

McNabb took one of his spare magazines from his service belt and popped out a 9-millimetre round. He held the two bullets up, side by side.

"Mr. Thompson, your .44-40 round is even bigger in diameter than this nine-mil. Am I right?" The big man nodded his agreement "And there's a two-millimetre difference in the diameter of these two bullets. Almost an eighth of an inch.

"Uh, yeah." The man began to sound deflated even before the demonstration could begin. He could see that McNabb hadn't been fooled.

"So, do we need to go poking bullets into this seven-millimetre entrance wound to see which one fits?"

"Naw … you win Fountain," Thompson said, totally beaten. "But it was worth a try."

McNabb stood there, shaking his head. Fountain's brother came forward and muttered in Leonard's ear. Leonard nodded and said, "Look, there's only the two of us, Thompson. Harold is widowed and my wife doesn't like wild game. If you'll give us a hand, you can have a couple of quarters."

"Aw shit, man. After the hassle I gave you, you don't have to do that."

"It's the only way I can see to getting rid of that hind quarter with all the lead in it," he chuckled. Thompson's sudden laugh was a bellow that would wake any sleeping moose for five miles around.

"Randi," McNabb said before leaving, "that's a dandy rifle you've got for shots under a hundred yards. But long shots like you say you took … well, there's a lot of damaged meat there."

"Yeah … I know. My buddies keep telling me my old British .303 would be better for reaching out long like that. Guess I should take their suggestion. Thanks, officer. I appreciate you showin' up.

"Oh, before you go, I heard you put Slippery Ritchie out of business."

"Well, as city lawyers say when they are talking to the news media, 'I can't comment while it's before the courts.' But, seeing as it's already public knowledge, yeah, we've seized one of his floatplanes."

"Shoulda grabbed them both," one of the bystanders said.

"We can only seize items involved in the offence for which he's being charged."

Another hunter said, "I heard he's still at it and laughing at the ministry, but real pissed off with you. You wanna be watchin' over your shoulder for that guy. He can be a real mean shit."

"I'll keep my antenna up, thanks. But if any of you see him doing anything out of bounds, please give us a call," McNabb said, and he handed out half a dozen business cards. "There's no limit to the number of times I can charge a fellow. And I still have thirty years to go before I retire." That drew more smiles.

McNabb walked back to his truck. The cheerful banter of the reconciled hunters faded behind him as the daylight began to fade around him. Good to know that guys like those fellows wanted Reggie Ritchie taken down too. But he shook his head thinking, I didn't really need to be here. If Thompson had kept his cool from the beginning, I bet the Fountain brothers would have given them part of the moose anyhow. Especially the damaged quarter. Won't be much meat to salvage from that.

—

1830 – Lake Two, Lewis Township

There were four police cruisers, and a large RV-style crime scene truck parked along the shoulder of the highway when McNabb came by on his way home. A dizzying display of red, blue and white flashing lights lit up the parked fleet.

A staff sergeant, who McNabb hadn't met before, was working traffic management in the southbound lane, and when he saw McNabb's truck inching forward at the tail end of a line of vehicles, he flagged him down.

"You'd be McNabb, I'm guessing?"

"Yes, sir."

"I'm Staff Sergeant Jim Sawyer."

"Pleased to meet you, Staff. Is it normal down here for top brass to be stuck on traffic management?"

"Shift change. A replacement hasn't shown up yet. And I'm trying to stay out of the way of the experts at the crime scene."

"So, Bailey was up to no good, then?"

"You got it wrong, McNabb. He didn't come up here to bury his father-in-law." Sawyer paused to flag down a vehicle approaching from behind. But before McNabb could apologize for raising a false alarm, the staff sergeant continued, "The father-in-law paid Bailey to bury the mother-in-law, after her loving hubby pushed her down the basement stairs at home. The crime scene guys are in the bush exhuming the unfortunate deceased right now. Good call, Detective McNabb. We're going to have to transfer you to our team. And Constable Miller would like you to attend the detachment tomorrow morning. She needs to take your full statement."

"Yes, sir. I'll add it to my to-do list. As for your job offer, thanks but I've already turned down previous recruitment attempts. I sure do enjoy working with you people, but I enjoy my independence even more." He drove away, freeing up the traffic that had accumulated behind him.

Chapter 35

Tuesday October 25, 0745 – Elliot Lake Airport

Sam Williams taxied the Turbo Beaver from the hangar, past the terminal building and headed for the runway. Much to her husband's chagrin, another day's enforcement flight was cancelled by circumstances beyond his control. Someone in the air service had decided it was time for Sam's six-month check-flight, almost a month ahead of time. Something to do with scheduling conflicts. So Rob planned a solo ATV excursion to the north end of the district while she was off demonstrating her ability to drive a floatplane.

Sam wasn't happy about it either. So much for having an aircraft dedicated full-time to McNabb's efforts to tame the district's poachers. This would have been a perfect day for more remote hunt camp checks. The check-flight itself wouldn't have pre-empted a whole day's air patrol, but the senior-pilot wanted her to fly to Sault Ste. Marie to do the obligatory flight from there. Most of the day would be shot by the time she returned to the district.

She returned the wave of an early morning jogger as she taxied past him near the aviation fuel pumps. She thought she recognized him as one of the police constables from the Elliot Lake detachment.

A hundred metres farther along, she stopped the plane at the edge of the runway, checked for incoming air traffic and radioed her intention to take off. With no control tower, it was the responsibility of each pilot to avoid collisions. Nothing coming, she taxied onto the runway, turned into the light wind and began her pre-takeoff checks.

—

When Constable Luke Wilmot wasn't on duty, he was running. It was an obsession. He'd done well at several marathons, but his goal was to run the Boston. This morning, he had been up before dawn to run one of his favourite practice routes which started and finished at the airport. Most of the loop took him along gravel foot paths and ATV trails lying to the north and east of the airport. The hilly terrain, including several long steep climbs were perfect for feeling the burn.

When he'd started his run, he'd noticed the 1980s piece of junk — Dodge camper van — sitting at the corner of the parking lot. He'd thought little of it, other than maybe he'd take a closer look when he finished his run. He was police, after all.

Now, with his run behind him, he was walking in cool down mode, and he waved at the pilot in the yellow MNR aircraft taxiing toward the runway. He continued walking as he approached the parking lot and passed close to the questionable van. The MNR Turbo Beaver had just taken off and the roar of the turboprop began to fade as the plane banked and headed west. In the near silence that followed, Wilmot could hear someone talking on the other side of the beat-up van. Sounded like a one-way conversation — or one side of a phone conversation. At first, it meant nothing to him. Not his business. At least it wasn't until he heard one key word.

"Reggie, I swear he's headed west … No, didn't see who got in the plane. I was takin' a piss in the bush, but it's the game warden's plane for sure … Yeah, I said west."

Constable Wilmot wasn't involved in working Reggie Ritchie's case, but everyone in the detachment had been briefed to keep their eyes and ears open. He didn't stop to talk to the guy — didn't want him to suspect he'd been overheard, but when he climbed into his Mustang, he made a call of his own.

—

0755 – Police detachment, Blind River

Constable Mary Miller poked her head into Staff Sergeant Sawyer's office. "Sir, I just got a call from Luke Wilmot. He says there's a guy at the Elliot Lake airport spying on the MNR Beaver. He just overheard part of a call to Reg Ritchie, telling him the plane had just taken off."

The staff sergeant looked up from what he was reading. "Did he interact with this uh, spy?"

"No sir. Said he didn't want to mess up whatever we have going on with the case."

"Good. Okay, I'll pass the word to Harry and Brownie when they return this afternoon. You're working radar through town today?"

"As soon as I take Rob McNabb's statement, yes sir."

"He made a good bust up there yesterday. He'd make a good cop."

"I know sir. Detective grade. We probably never would have found the woman's body if Rob hadn't gotten suspicious."

"Slim chance for sure. Okay, carry on. Oh, tell McNabb what you learned from Wilmot. We need to keep him and Sam Williams up to speed on anything to do with Ritchie."

"Hello, anyone home?" came from the squad room.

"In here, Rob," Miller answered. Seconds later, McNabb appeared beside her in the staff sergeant's doorway.

"Someone gave you the door code, McNabb?" the staff sergeant asked.

McNabb grimaced. Had he just pulled a faux pas? "Sorry Staff. If they shouldn't have, I can erase the code from my memory and never arrive uninvited again. But I'm not telling you who gave it to me."

"Nope, not a problem, Rob. I could narrow it down to two suspects with one guess, but you are welcome here as long as you don't abuse it. Consider it a step in our stealthy effort to recruit you. Mary, get him going on that statement, and don't forget to tell him about the airport spy."

"Yes sir."

—

0810 – North Shore Aviation base

As long as it wasn't a false lead, Reggie Ritchie was pleased to know McNabb's plane was not flying north. He had a full day ahead of him and didn't want to be watching over his shoulder for the damned game warden. One group that hadn't seen any sign of moose insisted on moving to a different lake, and several other camps needed supplies. He would be in and out of his cache at River Lake at least a couple of times and didn't want the nosey CO to discover his secret storehouse of borrowed supplies.

As soon as he was airborne, he decided that his first flight would be to pick up one batch of supplies at River Lake. He would drop propane and outboard gas at Bark and Upper Bark Lakes. Then he'd move the guys out of Rocky Island down to Mewburn. Short hop, but that was a big gang, and they had a lot of gear. Might take three trips. McNabb would be free to check him then. Those guys were regular clients and had always been squeaky clean.

Chapter 36

1510 – Near River Lake in Thorpe Township

Rob McNabb was on his government ATV headed toward his HVEV. After giving his statement at the police detachment in the morning, he had phoned Sam to tell her about Ritchie's airport spy and Constable Miller's suggestion to mess up the spy's communications. They figured it would give them a leg up on Teflon Reggie when the sniper rifle guy headed out for his hunt — if he was really going to show. McNabb still worried about that. He was beginning to wonder if he had been fed a line, or was it actually going to happen?

He'd spent most of the day exploring old logging roads and bush trails in an area fifty kilometres north of Elliot Lake.

He had toured through some spectacular country and got north as far as the Mississagi River near Bark Lake, where he'd surprised two hunters motoring down the river with loaded rifles in their small boat. He charged them for that offence, but because they passed the attitude test, let them off with a warning for having open beer in the boat. They just had to dump their suds overboard.

While he was finishing up with them, Ritchie's Beaver flew overhead, going north. No circling, but his overflight sparked a comment from one of the hunters.

"That asshole's been flying around here for days, officer. I think he's got every moose in the district spotted by now. Can't you do something to stop him? He flies low enough it would be tempting to put some lead up his ass … but of course we'd never do that, y'know."

"First, I don't even want to hear that," McNabb replied. "If by chance, he did draw fire one day, I'd have your name here in my notes … along with a few others who've also suggested that, and I'd be obliged to pass that along to the investigators. You don't need that kind of trouble."

The hunter raised his hands and said, "Point taken."

"As for what can be done, we seized his small scouting plane last week. Let's just say he's a work in progress."

"Good luck, then. Sooner that plane is locked up the better."

"I don't mind hearing comments like that. Have a good hunt." He handed them each a business card along with their offence notice.

Half an hour later, he came on a cow moose standing with her two calves in the middle of the trail. The cow put herself between the ATV and her youngsters and didn't look as if she was going to let McNabb pass — not, at least, until Ritchie's Beaver flew low overhead. The Beaver banked steeply, either to begin a turn, or just to get a look at the moose. But Reggie would have seen McNabb right there, shaking his head "no" and holding his badge, extended toward the passing bush plane. He could understand why some folks might be tempted to take a shot at the jerk.

—

Up in the Beaver's cockpit, Reggie Ritchie looked down at McNabb. "Don't you flash your shield and shake your head at me, fuckface," he said. "I know where you parked your ride." A wicked grin spread across his weather-beaten face.

—

McNabb rode into a few side trails that gradually petered out. They were abandoned logging roads, long out of use, grown in and choked with birch and poplar saplings and tangles of alder. Nothing going on there.

He followed one trail that, according to his GPS, should join up with another road that ran parallel to the logging road he had started out on. Nope, that one ended up at a precipitous washout overlooking a deep gorge. Impassible. But camped right before the washout was a group of five hunters.

"Conservation officer," he announced. "How are you fellows doing?"

"Just set up camp today."

McNabb checked their hunting licences as they talked, and all were in order.

"You seein' any sign?" one hunter asked, then took the last swallow of beer from his bottle.

"There are a few out and about. Saw three earlier today. Cow and her twins. Remember, no loaded firearms on your ATVs, right? I've been laying a lot of paper for that since the season opened. Beginning to get writer's cramp."

"You won't find nothin' to write up here," the fellow said. He punctuated his declaration by tossing his beer bottle into the bush.

McNabb winced as it flew through the air and waited a second. When he heard it shatter on a rock, he shook his head and gave out an audible sigh. The guy's shoulders suddenly drooped. He knew what was coming.

"Guess I spoke too soon, huh?" the hunter said.

"You know, if it hadn't broken, I might have been willing to cut you some slack and just asked you to go fetch, but you're right. Guess I'll have to smear some more Voltarin on my writing hand before the end of the day." McNabb walked over and peered into the bushes where the bottle had landed. "You know I don't feel so badly about writing this one up after all. You guys get in there and pick up the rest of that garbage."

"That's not all ours!"

"Maybe not, but I see at least three more of the brand you just tossed, and several others that haven't seen any weather yet. You clean it all up and I'll just write the one ticket. If not, I'll see who is drinking what, and then match batch numbers with what I find in the bush."

All five men began combing the bush for garbage, and filled a garbage bag almost full before McNabb had the ticket written up.

When he finished with that group, he had to backtrack along much of his original route to return to his truck. The ten-year-old Honda Four-Trax ATV ran well, but it was down to less than a quarter of a tank of gas. It was enough to get back to the truck, but he was wishing he'd brought the spare ten litre jug along for the ride. Spare gas wasn't much use to him, sitting in the truck box a dozen kilometres away, but he made it back with a few ounces to spare.

As he approached the patrol truck, the bullet holes were not the first thing he noticed. It was the smashed lightbar that drew his immediate attention. And then the curse words, spray painted down both sides of the truck in blaze orange boundary marking paint warning him that game wardens were not welcome in the area. It was a discouraging way to end what had been a productive day. He took it to mean that another of his constituents didn't appreciate his good work.

"Gives an entirely new meaning to the HVEV designation," he said with a sigh. He was used to talking to himself. A healthy discussion with oneself sometimes helped provide solutions to tricky problems.

And then he saw the bullet holes in the front fender. "Shit … this goes way beyond crap." There were only three holes, but the doors were locked, and the electronic key fob proved useless. He used the backup key from inside the fob to get the driver's door open. The windows were all untouched and the electronic enforcement equipment was still intact. But like the door locks, nothing electronic was working.

When he popped the hood, it became obvious why there was no power. One of the three bullets had wrecked the battery. The other two just screwed up the body work and flattened themselves on the engine block. The boss had said that the eight-year-old pickup was scheduled for replacement soon, but McNabb doubted that he'd intended for it to happen quite this soon. Without power, he couldn't use the satellite phone to call the office, and his cell phone was useless this far in the bush. No cell towers anywhere nearby.

It was 3:15. He figured he wouldn't be missed by the folks at the communication centre for another hour. The jug of gas had been stolen out of the back and there wasn't enough left in the ATV to drive to the nearest lodge where the only landline phone was located, so he would have to MacGyver his way out of the situation.

McNabb had spent much of his youth hanging around in his dad's small-engine repair shop. As he got older, he was allowed to help, and eventually he worked there for pay. Now there wasn't much in the line of mechanical equipment he couldn't fix, or at least cobble together a temporary fix to get out of a tight situation. Like this.

There was no drain plug under the pickup's gas tank, and with the anti-syphon barriers in the fill pipe, there was no way to transfer gasoline to the ATV. But maybe the Honda could provide electrical power to the truck. Before going to the trouble to remove the tiny ATV battery and install it in the pickup, he hooked up jumper cables between the ATV and the pickup's battery cables.

That gave him power to the electronics, but not enough for the starter motor to roll over the V-8 engine, not even with the Honda motor running to boost the voltage. But while he had the power hooked up, he could call out on the satellite phone.

He was just about to do that when he heard an aircraft taking off from a nearby lake. According to his GPS, the most likely waterbody was River Lake, a little less than two kilometres to the northeast of him, the same lake where he and the others had found the big cache of stolen hunt camp supplies a week earlier.

McNabb could hear the aircraft getting louder. Radial engine. Sounded like a Beaver. It turned in his direction, and when it came into view, he was looking up at Teflon Reggie's Beaver. The plane wasn't close enough to see the pilot's face, but there was no doubt as to who it was.

"Well, crap. Reggie. I bet *that's* no coincidence."

He got back into the truck and powered down all the electronics except for the satellite phone, then hit the speed-dial for the provincial dispatcher.

"*Comm centre, Mary-Ellen speaking.*"

"It's Rob McNabb, badge 415, checking in."

"*Where've you been, Rob? Are you alright? Your tracking signal went off-line over an hour ago. We've got the police headed your way.*"

"I'm okay thanks, Mary-Ellen. Didn't mean to cause any trouble, but my truck was vandalized while I was out on my ATV."

"*Much damage, Rob?*"

"They put a bullet through the battery. It's toast. And smashed the light bar. Bright orange graffiti down the sides suggests that I'm not welcome here. But I've already got a suspect in mind."

"*Quick work.*"

"Yeah, he's already running a tab with us, but the case file needs some additional evidence before I can take this newest incident to court."

"*Need a tow?*"

"I don't think a tow is required, thanks. I'll get a boost when the police show up."

"*They should be there momentarily. Their track dot is almost on top of yours.*"

"Uh-huh, they're pulling up now. Thanks M.E. We'll talk later."

Chapter 37

A provincial police Ram crew cab arrived as McNabb ended the call. It was towing a trailer carrying two ATVs. The driver pulled up nose to nose with his disabled government truck. He couldn't see who'd come to his rescue, because of the glare off the Ram's windshield.

But Sergeant Mitchell and Constable Brown emerged from the police truck at the same time, both looking at the HVEV and shaking their heads.

"Thanks for coming guys."

"What goes around, comes around, Rob. Thought we'd come looking for you to return a few favours," Constable Brown said, chuckling.

"I didn't know I was missing until I called in just now. They didn't put trackers on my snowmobile or my aluminum boat up north."

"As soon as your truck was disabled, your comm centre lost its tracking signal and called our dispatch. Harry and I were up this way to check out some more hunt camp break-ins, so we got the call."

The police turned serious when they saw the paint job on the CO's truck.

"Oh yeah. Serious artwork."

The sergeant looked skyward. "Has this got anything to do with the Beaver that just flew past?"

"I'm guessing it has everything to do with Teflon Reggie," McNabb said as he led the police around to look at the mechanical damage. "These other ATV tracks seem to lead into the bush over there," he pointed to a small gap in the forest edge. "His plane took off from over that way just before it flew over. I'm assuming it came from River Lake. It could just be a coincidence, but my spidey sense suggests a strong connection."

"Yeah," Mitchell said. "For your ears only … Sam's too, I guess. We've got an undercover operation going on that I can't tell you about. Not Ritchie, but folks who know him. Our guy that is imbedded with them reports that he's heard Reggie has got a real hate on for you. Our UC guy is suggesting extreme caution for you and your family."

"Shit. I've been threatened before, but when the threat extends to my family, that really pisses me off. But you already know that. And we really appreciate the extra police presence around our home." He led them to the patrol truck's front fender.

"So now there's this," McNabb said, pointing at the bullet holes. "I'm guessing he used a handgun. There's no exit wound from the battery. If it had been a rifle shot, I think it would have gone right through, and maybe gone on to wreck even more stuff in there."

"Judging from the limited damage, you're probably right, Rob," Sergeant Mitchell said, then paused, thinking. "Reggie, Reggie, Reggie … Yeah, with Lachappelle's camp just over the hill, full of stolen goods, there's every chance this has to do with him. Good chance too that he's the one who's been hitting the other hunt camps we checked out today. Bunch more stuff missing … usual complaint."

"Harry," Constable Brown said. "Perfect spot for a trail camera."

"What, here?"

"No, at the camp with all the stolen stuff these guys found. We could offload the ATVs and follow these tracks in. You know where the camp is, eh, Rob?"

"From the air, yeah. Never off-roaded there, but these ATV tracks should be easy enough to follow through the bush. Eric said the trail out from the camp probably ends up here, and I'd know the camp if I saw it again."

"Okay," Mitchell said. "Let's shift our butts and get that done first. Then we'll deal with this rolling wreck before the government gets ticketed for littering. Rob, do you need gas for your quad?"

Ten minutes later the three enforcement ATVs were putt-putt-putting through the bush, following the winding trail left by the suspect machine. When they got to the Lachappelle camp, there was a lot less gear than Rob and Eric had inventoried on their first visit, but still plenty to draw Ritchie back for more. They mounted the trail camera in a concealed location, and an hour after that, they were back at the trucks using the second battery from the police Ram to get McNabb's disabled patrol wreck back home.

While they loaded his ATV into the back of the now, extra high visibility vehicle, he let the pickup run for several minutes. There might be damaged hoses or wiring that they missed on their initial inspection. But nothing leaked, squeaked or reeked, so he closed the hood, climbed in and followed the police truck out toward civilization.

The graffiti-covered patrol vehicle lived up to its high visibility name, turning heads as they convoyed through Elliot Lake, and again, forty minutes later, on entering Blind River. McNabb parked the pickup in the police garage and Sergeant Mitchell walked up as he got out.

"I doubt the CSI team will find anything that we haven't already seen, Rob, but you'll need to leave it here. It *is* a crime scene."

"Yup, I kind of figured that. Can you find out if Ritchie owns a handgun?"

"I already assigned that little task to Brownie as we drove. If he's registered one, we should know before you get back to your office."

"Thanks, Harry … for everything today."

They offloaded the ATV from the back of the crippled truck and McNabb drove it back to his office.

Chapter 38

Wednesday, October 26, 0755 – Blind River MNR office

A steady drizzle and a cold wind made for a gloomy day, typical weather for October and November in this part of the country. Rob McNabb arrived at the office with a box of donuts for the lunchroom. He figured that being the new guy, it was probably his turn. There was no one else in the room right then, so it became an anonymous donation. Maybe that made him part of the team. He grabbed a couple of coffees and headed for his office.

Sam had arrived just before him and was shaking rainwater from her jacket before hanging it on a hook to dry. She'd arrived in the pool car she borrowed yesterday.

"This pool car business is the pits, Rob. The techs in the other services are grumbling that we should have a second enforcement vehicle so they would always have the pool vehicle available. And I agree with them, but…."

"Yeah, me too. Kind of hard to do though, when we can't even keep our one truck on the road. I left a message for Rick about the truck at end of shift yesterday. Was hoping he'd have gotten back to me by now. Meanwhile, let's sign out the pool car as much as we can. That might inspire the rest of the folks here to gripe to management to do something about our situation."

He had barely finished speaking when Wendy poked her head into the tiny office. "Hey Rob … morning Sam. Rick called. A replacement truck is being driven over from the Soo this morning, but you'll need to drive the guy back there. And no, you're not getting a new one. He says it's the same year … and higher mileage. I guess they want to see if you can get through more than a week with it undamaged before they trust you with something newer.

"He also said to tell you not to spend any time or money on your wreck. Arrangements are being made to haul it away after the police are finished with it. So just clear out any of your loose gear before it gets towed."

"Thanks Wendy. Let me know when it arrives. And since the replacement is also in its senior years, I'll be signing out the pool car to drive the guy back."

"There'll be a grumpy face when someone hears that, Rob. Better grab the keys now, 'cause I think Leo is going to a meeting later this morning. That was his planned ride, but his name isn't on the sign-out sheet … yet." She gave an evil grin as she retreated up the hallway. And just then, McNabb's desk phone warbled. Darren Brown showed up on the call display.

"Hey Darren, what's up?"

"*Morning Rob. There are no restricted weapons registered to Ritchie. But that doesn't rule out an unregistered one. Considering yesterday's vandalism to your truck, along with the reports and rumours we keep getting regarding his undying love for you, you guys really do need to stay on your toes. Eric Snyder too.*"

"Yeah, I know, Darren. And like I said yesterday, we sure appreciate the extra patrols by our house. The folks at the store have even been commenting on how good it is to have a full-time police presence in the village."

"*Ha, they'll be bitching about the lack of policing when this dies down and we go back to our usual routine.*"

"Well, Sam and Mae Ling and I won't complain when things return to normal … whatever that is.

"By the way, that wreck I drove in yesterday is going to be towed away for scrap when your CSI folks are done with it.

So, there's no need to take up garage space or secure storage when they finish. I just gotta grab some gear from it before it goes. And of course, I just replaced the wiper blades on it the other day. Have to grab them too. Would be a shame to send it to the crusher with sixty bucks worth of new hardware on it."

"I'll pass the word, Rob, thanks. There's been some grumbling about it taking up the bay some staff think of as their private car wash."

—

1115

The rain had let up and McNabb had just completed a circle check on his replacement patrol truck. He was amazed that it passed inspection. It was way past its "best before" date and the body looked to be in even rougher shape than his last ride. But all systems, except the satellite phone, worked, and nothing leaked — not too much, anyhow. The wildlife technician who had delivered the HVEV was in a hurry to get back to Sault Ste. Marie.

Sergeant Mitchell wheeled a police cruiser into the lot and pulled up beside them. McNabb pulled some change from his pocket and handed it to the impatient tech. "If you think it will make it there and back, could you run down to Hortons and pick me up a coffee, please. Medium regular. And get one for yourself if you want. I need to have a chat with the sergeant for a few minutes. Then we'll leave.

"Good morning, Harry."

"Hey, Rob. Nice wheels. Think it will make it out of the parking lot?"

"If it survives the coffee run, I'll arrange for CAA to follow me around. I've got a platinum membership."

"Good luck. Anyhow, I just talked to the CSI guys. The bullet in your battery took too much of a beating to learn anything more than it was from a .32. Not a popular calibre any more so that's one thing in our favour if we ever find a gun."

"Yeah, and Brownie called earlier to tell me there's no restricted weapons registered to Reggie. I'll just have to keep my eyes open and my head down."

"I sent Constable McEwen back to see Ritchie for a follow-up visit regarding the truck vandalism. The lout denied it of course, but when Archie left, he said there was no doubt in his mind that some of Reggie's Teflon is beginning to wear thin. He said he was showing signs of a nervous shake when he finished explaining the facts of life and death to him."

"Thanks Harry. I worry about my family more than I do about myself. I've got the training and have been in enough hair-raising encounters that I have a pretty good idea how to deal with guys like him. And Sam's resourceful in a pinch, too. But I worry most about Mae Ling. Young, real pretty and, well…."

"Don't worry. We'll keep with the extra patrols as long as we need to Rob."

"Thanks."

The delivery driver returned with coffees a few minutes later and McNabb drove him back to the Soo in the white sedan. He wanted to save his replacement patrol truck for when it was really needed. Three hundred and seventy thousand kilometres was a lot to ask of a truck that had spent so much of its life driving on bush roads.

Chapter 39

Friday, October 28, 0755 – Blind River MNR office

It was another dreary autumn morning. Cold rain lashed against the windshield. It had been raining hard ever since midnight. The view through the windshield stayed blurred even though the wipers were going full speed. After leaving Lottie with Nancy Snyder, McNabb drove the family crew cab into the office parking lot with Sam by his side.

Yesterday, McNabb had managed to catch up on almost all his deskwork, and had finished his shift at the courthouse, swearing informations and getting summonses signed. This morning, he figured he'd get the last of his deskwork done while he waited for Rick Webb to show up.

Today was the big fact-finding interview. He had to justify his actions to his boss, when on Monday, he'd drawn his pistol and aimed it at Anthony Bailey, the guy who'd buried his mother-in-law at Lake Two.

"What's with the extra CO trucks, Rob?" Sam asked, as he backed into a staff parking spot. Parked beside his new eight-year-old patrol beater was a brand-new F-150 HVEV, and beside that was a Chevy Suburban, not new but not old either, both done up in enforcement livery.

"I can't believe he's here already. And I guess the regional Staff Superintendent invited himself to the inquisition. Crap."

"Why is it that the guys who don't work in the field have the newest trucks?" Sam wondered aloud.

"Probably because they won't get scratched, dented or shot up like they do out in the real world." Rob sighed. He pulled on his hat and prepared to leave the truck. "I'd better get this over with." Despite Webb's assurances that it was just a procedural formality, not a hauled-up-on-the-carpet deal, McNabb had stewed about this meeting all week, and it didn't help that a senior manager had also shown up.

On entering the building, it got worse. Wendy pointed at McNabb as he and Sam headed toward their office. "Leo's office Rob. They're waiting for you there."

Double crap, he thought to himself. That office *does* have a carpet. When he stepped into the Lion's Den, he saw a man he hadn't previously met. It wasn't the regional Staff Superintendent. Rick Webb was standing with the guy by the Keurig machine where they had just finished making coffees for themselves. Leo the lion was absent.

"Rob," Webb said, "Do you know Bill Steele? Bill wanted to sit in on this."

McNabb was stunned. That's just great … not. The Deputy Chief of Enforcement Branch. Things were going from worse to worser. Now he felt absolutely miserable. Nothing good could come from an inquisition led by head office.

Steele was a stocky man, not quite as tall as McNabb. With silvering hair in a businessman's cut, he had to be in his late forties. He had worked as a field officer across Ontario, all the way from Cornwall to Kenora. He had a good reputation among the ranks, but that didn't ease McNabb's anxiety one bit. Especially when the big boss was there in full dress uniform.

"Hi Rob, it's good to finally meet you." He shook McNabb's hand. Firm grip, not some wussy deskbound, rubber handshake.

"I've been following your career. Seems, right from the get-go you've solved some tough cases and endured more crises than most other COs experience in their entire career." The friendly intro took McNabb by surprise, but still, waiting for either shoe to drop was agonizing.

"I was coming up this way anyhow," Steele continued, "and thought I should be here for this. We're not here to tear you to shreds. Just gotta find some facts and check off some boxes. What flavour coffee do you want? I think I've got the hang of this thing now."

Okay, McNabb thought, maybe they're not planning a lynching. He was briefly lost for words but managed to ask for a dark roast. And Steele picked up the conversation while he stuck in a pod and started the coffee brewing. "That'll take a minute. How are you liking your new district?"

"Beautiful part of the province and really nice folks here in the office, sir…."

"Bill. Go on."

"We're getting lots of help from the police and from Eric Snyder, a retired CO, who's now my deputy. But…." McNabb paused, realizing that maybe he wasn't in the best position to express his concerns. Not today anyhow, not in his present circumstance. But Steele didn't appear to be offended, or maybe he was waiting for McNabb to put both feet in his mouth.

"But I take it you have concerns, Rob. Go on. Speak freely. I need to know what worries the folks on the thin green line."

"Well, if you don't mind my saying so, it's a lot to expect one CO to cover an area traditionally protected by four." He hesitated again, but Steele waved him to continue.

So, he obliged the man. "It's particularly frustrating trying to do the job right with an old enforcement truck that's got a satellite phone that doesn't work and was sent to replace the other old truck that had to be towed three times in the two and a half weeks I've been here, before it got trashed by a disgruntled constituent." He looked over at Webb and added,

"Sorry, Rick, but this one doesn't look any healthier than the other one."

"I understand Rob. We're on it. I promise," Webb said. "Something happening on that front shortly."

"You're right, Rob," Steele added. "You shouldn't have to do the job with clapped out equipment, and as Rick says, we do have something in the works." The coffee was ready, and they took seats around the desk. "So, getting to the business at hand … Rick, this is your meeting. Pretend I'm not here," he held up his hands and rolled his seat into the corner, away from the desk.

"Easy for you to say, boss," Webb said, paused, then looked at McNabb.

"Rob, I know you've been down this road before with the polar bear poacher and the ivory runners," Webb said. "Just tell us what happened at Lake Two on Monday."

McNabb retold the story in detail, and the two managers listened without interruption. Webb made a few notes as he spoke. It didn't take long, and he wrapped it up, saying, "Going back to ask him supplementary questions was simply a continuation of my fisheries investigation … clarifying his identification in light of conflicting information. The other anomalies certainly piqued my curiosity. I planned to report to the police about those things, not act myself. The confrontation took place entirely on Bailey's initiative. And that's pretty well it, Rick."

"Okay, so the only part I can see giving anyone gas pains Rob, is why you drew your pistol at the moment you did. And we aren't trying to second guess your actions. You were there and we weren't."

"I felt I had no choice due to the escalating circumstances. In the first place, the guy was way bigger than me. Size and build of a bar room bouncer. I don't think I'd have stood a chance in a hand-to-hand scuffle. And he had progressed from the aloof look he had when I first met him, to the piercing glare of a predator.

"He kept advancing on me, despite my demand to stop. When he told me to 'drive away while you still can,' I took that as a genuine threat. And finally, even though his hands were in his pockets, and I saw no weapons, I flashed back to our last self-defence training when they showed us a body cam video of a guy shooting at an American state trooper, without taking the gun from his coat pocket.

"If I had waited… I didn't believe the guy was going to stop. Gun or no gun," he finished.

"Do you have any questions for him, Bill?"

"Nope. I think you handled it appropriately, Rob. Far better to get home alive, even if it means having to answer some questions later. It seems like you went with your training."

"Okay," Webb resumed his summation. "We've both read the police report on the guy. Turns out he has a lengthy record of assaults; some being described as spontaneous vicious attacks. We have no problem with your response to the situation, so we're done here. That file's closed."

Chapter 40

The deputy chief stood and carried his empty coffee mug to rinse in the sink. He looked around the office with a degree of admiration. "This Leo fellow has quite a setup. His own coffee maker, kitchenette, corner office. Nice."

"I think the Lion's Den was part of a larger staff lunchroom at one time," McNabb said. "I'm told the whole building has undergone continuous renos ever since it was built in thc 1950s."

"That's the case with a lot of these old government buildings, Rob," Steele said. "By the way, I'd like to meet your pilot."

"Let me take you to the low rent section then," McNabb said, leading the way toward his office. "We're not nearly as pretentious back here."

Sam was entering her activities into her online timesheet when McNabb showed Steele and Webb into their office. "Samantha Williams, this is Deputy Chief Bill Steele, next in line to the enforcement director's throne."

As he shook hands with Williams, Steele looked around at the tiny space they shared. "*This* is where they stuck you two? The sole protectors of the realm, and they hid you in here? Jesus, guys, I bet there's a storage closet bigger than this somewhere in the building. I'll get you a more appropriate space before we leave."

"Actually, it's kind of grown on us," Sam said. "Especially after Rob took out the partition between the desks.

And when it's sunny outside, that dreary streetscape you see out there becomes a classic Norman Rockwell painting."

"And the shabby room," McNabb added, "is more in character with my various patrol trucks."

The deputy chief started laughing. "Rob," he said, "Rick and I have been pushing your buttons this morning. Cruel as it was, I'm impressed that you came out and told it like it is regarding your working conditions. The main reason I came up here was not to sit in on your debriefing, but because your staff sergeant here, has been a real pain in the ass about delays in equipment replacement. There hasn't been a day go by that my inbox or my voicemail didn't have at least one cranky message about your transportation needs."

He laid a pair of key fobs on McNabb's desk. "Special delivery, Officer McNabb. Your brand-new truck awaits you outside. Being stuck behind a desk most days, it's not often I get to do fun jobs like this.

"Just remember though, HVEV stands for high *visibility* enforcement vehicle … not high *velocity* … although I do have to admit, it does scoot right along.

"Anyhow, before we leave, I want all your issued gear stripped out of that rolling wreck out there so Rick and I can try to get it back to the Soo."

"You aren't taking the Suburban back?"

Webb: "An early Christmas present. That's your pilot's *temporary* new ride. In the rush to create and execute this airborne team concept, no one thought to consider that you two wouldn't always be going in the same direction, and therefore not always be able to carpool. And Leo's people have been doing a lot of grumbling about that too. So the air service has something far more mundane on order. Just don't get too used to the luxury, Sam. I want my limo back as soon as your aviation folks deliver on their promise."

"Anything's better than thumbing, Rick," Sam said. "This day is turning out a lot brighter than you thought it would, Robbie."

"Not bad, considering my being hauled up in front of the deputy chief. Thanks Bill and Rick. Oh, is it bullet proof?"

"You're a pain, Rob," Webb said. "Now, change of subject. Any word yet on the sniper guy's arrival?"

"Not yet. Our daughter saw the Beaver fly over the house a few days ago, headed southwest, but she said it flew back the other way twenty minutes later. Not nearly enough time to get to Michigan and back.

"But," he added, "our Mr. Ritchie sent her an Instagram message on Monday morning. Made implied threats against her and us if I didn't back off."

"Did you report all this to the police?"

"Oh yeah. I took her over the same morning, and they verified it was from our rogue outfitter. Dumb, sending an anonymous threat but specifying a demand that pointed right back at him. Sergeant Mitchell sent a persuasive constable from the old school to talk to Reggie about being nice to the game warden, so things have been quiet for the last couple of days."

"Good to have the police in your corner, for sure," the deputy chief said.

"Yeah, especially when the word coming in from various sources is that the guy has me … or us … in his sights. The police are taking that seriously, watching the house when Mae Ling gets off the bus and hovering nearby until one of us gets home.

"Regarding the preparations for the sniper, the police have their camera surveillance up and running on Ritchie's shop and waterfront. They've seen nothing unusual yet. But even if the sniper guy doesn't materialize, we and the police are building a long list of wildlife and criminal charges against Ritchie."

"Weather is supposed to clear tomorrow by midday," Sam said. "It's the end of the month, light winds, nearly full moon … good conditions for airborne smugglers. If it's going to happen according to the timing that was reported, it will have to be sometime this weekend."

"Anything else you might need for this project?" Webb asked.

"Do you have a spare portable satellite phone?" Rob asked. "There's no cell service at ground level past the first line of hills north of Elliot Lake, and even when you are airborne, it peters out not much farther north."

"I'll get one to you if I have to drive back here myself."

"Sam has one in the Beaver, and I'm also planning on carrying the portable marine radio we seized from Ritchie, as a backup. Those of us prowling the bush will have the little Motorola FRS walkie talkies to talk between ourselves. But planning the actual takedown will have to be something we do as the situation unfolds. We have no idea yet where the sniper is going to hunt."

"Give me a call as soon as this thing starts. Anytime, day or night."

Chapter 41

1235 – Blind River high school cafeteria

Mae Ling was working on a math assignment and taking an occasional spoonful of fruit cocktail. Four other studious kids were likewise multitasking at the same table.

Randy Ritchie, the son of Teflon Reggie, saw her there when he entered the room and wandered closer. "Hey, here's the game warden's hot Chink little girl," he announced to everyone in the cafeteria. He looked straight at Mae Ling and continued: "You better get your old man to lay off hassling my pop, little girlie. He keeps it up, he'll end up buried in a swamp somewhere."

The hair raised on Mae Ling's arms. Even without the threats, she couldn't stand the guy. He was the school's number one bully. At eighteen years old he was still in the eleventh grade. He stood six foot two and weighed over two hundred and twenty pounds — had played on the school football team before being scratched for using excessive violence. And he always dressed like a slob. Today it was a dirty white T-shirt and faded black sweatpants splattered with red paint stains.

Mae Ling pretended to ignore the big oaf, but knew she was in for a hazing of some sort. She kept her eyes on the page in front of her but could almost feel him approach, even before she could smell him. The one lunchroom teacher kept his attention glued to his cell phone. No help expected there.

Mae Ling had endured a horrid life before Rob and Sam rescued her from the sex traffickers, and if there had been an actual school of hard knocks, she would undoubtedly qualify for a post graduate degree — summa cum laude.

During her first couple of weeks in this new school, she had stayed under the radar. She'd watched and learned, choosing which kids were safe and which ones to steer clear of. But she did have her own strengths, and Rob and Sam had reinforced those, encouraging assertiveness and self-reliance.

"Wanna dance, sweet pea? I'll show you my Chinese noodle." He came closer.

While it was tempting, she refrained from commenting on the tiny size of Chinese noodles. She knew that Ritchie was expecting a delicate oriental girl who would shrivel up and cry. For this situation she could go either submissive or assertive — passive or aggressive. Whichever she chose, he weighed more than twice as much as she did, so she wasn't going to win if things got physical. But her mind was made up.

She turned in her chair to face the bully. She didn't stand — that would just emphasize her small size. From her chair she gave him a long cold stare before speaking. "Get this through your head, idiot: Threatening my dad, or the police, isn't going to make them stop. It just makes them even more determined to bring that asshole criminal father of yours down, bonehead. And anyone harming a peace officer, or his family, is just going to bring a whole shitload of cops and game wardens down on themselves."

"Fuckin' Asian bitch. Time you learned some manners." Young Ritchie sat down on the chair next to hers and moved it, tight against Mae Ling's chair. He laid one big, tattooed arm across her back, and began to paw at the front of her blouse with his other hand.

"Go away. You stink, you dumb jerk. You need a shower."

"C'mon, then sweet cheeks. You and me can shower together." He stood and dragged Mae Ling to her feet.

"Leave her alone, *asshole*." Mae Ling looked toward the speaker, a potential rescuer. Totally unexpected. But her hope slipped away as quickly as it had risen. Ross Mitchell, the sergeant's son was no taller than she was, and probably weighed eighty pounds less than the bully. A brave but foolhardy move, she thought. But that didn't stop Ross. He moved right into Ritchie's personal space. "I said *let her go*!"

"Fuck off, runt. You're goin' to be late for your sissy music class."

"Let her go … *Now*!" As he yelled the last word, Mitchell kicked the bully in the shin with everything he had. He'd aimed for a kneecap but missed.

Ritchie remained standing, but his temper flared fast as the sudden pain reached his brain. He tossed Mae Ling aside. She cracked her forehead on the lunchroom table going down and ended up underneath in a tangle of chair legs and student legs. Ritchie grabbed Ross Mitchell in a headlock and squeezed. Ross was not a fighter. Hadn't been in a scuffle since the third grade, and he'd lost that one. There was no way he had the strength to break the headlock, so he went with what his dad always told his sister … but grabbed, rather than kicked or punched.

"*Aaayyyyy*!" Ritchie's scream brought any remaining activity in the cafeteria to a standstill. One kid hurried over to alert the lunchroom monitor — still concentrating on his cell phone, and not one bit eager to deal with Randy Ritchie.

"*Let go! Let go*!" Ritchie half screamed. He could be heard all the way down to the office wing.

Mitchell found the strength to squeeze even harder and the bully's screams increased in volume and climbed several octaves toward soprano. Two of Ritchie's buddies moved in to help him, but three more of Mae Ling's classmates blocked the way and started throwing punches at the bully's buddies.

Ritchie was beginning to fold slowly toward the floor but didn't give up the headlock until, on the verge of collapse, he let go and proceeded to head-butt the poor Mitchell kid. But he got it wrong. Badly wrong. Instead of using his forehead to bash Mitchell's nose, he smashed his own nose against the shorter boy's forehead — and went down hard — crying.

Mitchell sure felt the blow to his head — felt his brain get jarred — but he still hung on to the big jerk's junk. He didn't let go until Mr. Niganobe, the vice-principal, gently talked him down. Barely more than two minutes had gone by since it all started. The VP was a big man, an Ojibwe leader, recently retired from the neighbouring first nation police force.

"Boys, and young ladies, my office. Right now," he spoke softly, but with all the authority needed to bring order to the sudden chaotic outbreak. "Go on, get moving Mr. Ritchie."

"But I'b bleeding … by doze is broke."

"It's not fatal, Randy. Man up and get moving." He handed the big kid a large wad of paper napkins from a nearby dispenser. "And don't bleed all over Mr. Cyr's clean floors."

—

1310 – Police detachment, Blind River

Sergeant Harry Mitchell hung up the phone, shaking his head, then picked it up again and dialled an internal line. It was answered on the second ring.

"Brownie, grab a couple more bodies and run down to the high school. There's been a minor donnybrook in the cafeteria, and retired Sergeant Niganobe has three miscreants he would like us to arrest. Two for assault and one for sexual assault and assault causing bodily harm.

"All three are eighteen, so there's no need to give them the young offenders kid-glove treatment. Treat them like the big men they think they are. In fact, take Archie with you. One of them is Teflon Reggie's big oaf kid. You'll need two vehicles, because the oaf needs to stop at the hospital to have his nose pulled back out of his face before we deal with him here."

He thought for a few seconds before adding: "And when the inevitable irate parental phone calls start pouring in, either you guys handle them, or refer them up to the staff sergeant … my son was involved, so I've got a potential conflict of interest."

Chapter 42

Saturday, October 29 – McNabb-Williams residence, Algoma Mills

Rob and Sam were scheduled for two days off, although they were holding their breath — the situation could change at any moment. The moneybags American with the sniper rifle had to arrive soon if he really was coming. Regardless, everyone in the household had slept in.

Slept in, that is, until Lottie came screaming into her parents' bedroom just before eight o'clock — carrying a mouse — who's teeth had a firm grip on her finger and refused to let go.

Rob sat up, jolted from his sleep by the panicked child. "Aw, jeez Lottie. What are you doing picking up a mouse?" he asked. He looked around for something to grab the critter with, settled on yesterday's sweaty T-shirt and wrapped it around the little rodent. Reacting to the new threat, the mouse let go of Lottie's finger, and Rob opened the bedroom window and fired the shirt and its passenger out into the back yard.

Through her tears the four-year-old said she had rescued it from Tigger who was playing with it on the kitchen floor. "He was being mean to the mouse, Dad," she sobbed.

"So, you rescued the mouse, but instead of thanking you, it bit you, right?"

"Uh huh." Murmured through her tears.

"Well, my thoughtful little animal lover, even though these mice live *inside* our house, they are still considered wildlife

… not domestic pets. And what have we told you about touching wild animals?"

"Don't touch wild animals," followed by a shaky, tearful sigh.

"Right." He gave her a comforting hug. "Let's go wash your hands with lots of soap and water. Mice can have some bad germs on them that could make you very sick, so we need to wash away the germs." Rob pulled on his jeans and carried Lottie down the hall to the bathroom while Sam got up to start breakfast. "And from now on, young lady, we'll have to let Tigger catch the mice … even if he is a little bit cruel. And we'll buy some traps when the hardware store's order finally comes in."

"That's not the only one he caught," said Sam, from the kitchen. After turning on the coffee maker, she swept the remains of two more mice from the counter into the dustpan and pitched them out the side door. Then she proceeded to wipe down the counter with bleach for the umpteenth time since they had moved in. "Goddamned rodents."

Rob did up a batch of pancakes and fried some bacon for breakfast. Loved his bacon and pancakes smothered in maple syrup. Just as he and Mae Ling finished doing up the dishes, there was a knock at the door. Sam went to open it. Harry Mitchell was standing there in civilian clothes. She invited him in for a coffee.

He stepped through the door and spoke. "Mae Ling, we came to make sure you are alright after yesterday's dustup at school," he said.

"We?" Sam asked.

"Ross came with me … he's out in the car … a bit shy about coming in."

"Get him in here…." Sam and Rob spoke at the same time. Mae Ling nodded, smiling, and went to the door to beckon to him.

While they waited, Harry spoke: "Young Ritchie is out on bail, as I'm sure you guessed he would be. But he shouldn't be any problem in Blind now. He has been permanently expelled from the school, and his mother, who has suffered through a continuous string of his screwups, has thrown him out too. Last night his old man picked him up and took him to his place. Now he'll be a pain in the ass in Elliot Lake."

Mae Ling opened the storm door for Ross and introduced him to Rob and Sam. Rob stood and shook the boy's hand. "Thanks so much for standing up for Mae Ling. That was a brave thing to do considering the size and reputation of the threat you faced."

"I couldn't just stand there, Mr. McNabb. Not after the way she told him off. I've never heard a girl swear like that in school! And never I heard *anyone* talk back to Randy Ritchie."

The adults all got a chuckle out of that, and Sam began laughing even harder. "Look at them." Standing side by side, Ross and Mae Ling each had nearly matching bumps in the middle of their foreheads. "They look like a pair of budding unicorns."

"Where are the unicorns, Mommy?" Lottie dropped her Barbies and raced from the living room into the kitchen, eager to see her favourite fictional creatures.

Mae Ling cut in, quickly changing the subject, "Ross, I finally figured out the second math challenge question Mrs. McKelvey gave us. C'mon, I'll show you."

They moved to the living room couch, and she opened her laptop. Harry smiled. He knew his son had feelings for the girl. Rob poured coffee and gave Sam a hug from behind. Their girl was growing up.

"So, where is your sniper, Rob?"

"Harry, I've been trying to compose an apology to everyone, in case the guy is a no-show. The information, as it was given to me, has almost reached its expiration date.

I mean, it should have happened this weekend. I'll feel really stupid if the whole thing was a red herring."

"Don't be so hard on yourself, Rob. Sometimes shit doesn't happen."

Part 2

Chapter 43

Late the same evening – East end of Drummond Island, Michigan

The Ontario 32 sailing sloop, *Better Times* ghosted up False Detour Passage in bright moonlight on the last breath of the west wind. There had been a light wind all day, and the sail from historic Mackinac Island had taken almost fifteen hours, but Alex Ferguson was not in a hurry.

Widowed for the past six years, he was savouring the final week of a long dreamt of circumnavigation of the Great Lakes. To his left, on the west side of the passage, was Drummond Island, Michigan and to his right, barely two miles away, Cockburn Island, Ontario.

The retired Toronto police detective had enjoyed every slow mile of the gorgeous autumn day. The autohelm kept a steady course, from which the skipper had deviated only twice, to keep clear of passing lake freighters.

With the wind gone calm in the lee of the island, he started the Yanmar diesel, then furled the sails and motored past a spot shown on his GPS chart plotter as Shale Beach. He pulled into a small bay just north of there and dropped anchor.

Tomorrow he would sail to Thessalon on the north shore, where he would check in with Canada Customs. And for the rest of the week, he planned to dawdle eastward through the myriad of beautiful islands and coves of the North Channel, arriving finally at Little Current, where the boat would be hauled out for the winter.

Satisfied that he was secure for the night, Ferguson lit the rail-mounted barbeque and grilled a small bacon wrapped steak while his vegetables heated on the galley stove. He didn't bother switching on the anchor light because there were no other pleasure boats out this late in the season, and commercial vessels could not get this close to shore.

He ate his meal in the cockpit under the nearly full moon. Beautiful night. Margaret, his late wife, would have loved this. As he sat enjoying the serenity of the location, he became aware of a faint rumbling in the distance. An engine. Boat or aircraft, he couldn't immediately place it.

The sound gradually increased. It came from the east. Yeah, it was an aircraft, flying over Cockburn Island just a couple of miles across the passage on the Canadian side of the border. Now he could see the navigation and landing lights as the plane descended toward the island. There was a small airstrip there according to his navigation charts.

The plane's lights disappeared, but the rumble of the engine continued to get louder. And then, in the moonlight, he could see a light-coloured float plane coming across the passage, low over the water, but still airborne and now showing no lights. If it stayed on its present bearing it would end up in the bay immediately south of him. Or end up in the trees if it didn't soon land or pull up. Just as it seemed the pilot was not planning to stop, the engine died to an idle and the floats touched the water almost immediately. The pilot killed the engine as the plane coasted into the adjacent bay. It looked like a De Havilland Beaver.

The plane turned sideways to the beach and drifted for several minutes. The pilot climbed down onto the float. He was cursing — presumably talking to himself, or maybe on a phone. "Where the fuck are you guys? C'mon I can't sit here all night."

Sound travels clearly across calm water. The retired detective could hear every word.

At first, Ferguson wondered how it was the guy never saw him. But then again, from more than two hundred yards away, his boat's dark blue hull would be nearly invisible on the dark water, and the pale grey cabin top would appear in the moonlight to be about the same shade as the limestone beach behind him. He stayed quiet. Old habits die hard. He had no idea what was about to go down, but at this time of night, there was a ninety-nine percent chance it was something illegal.

The pilot swore again, then jumped into waist deep cold water and began to turn the plane to face out into the passage again. Going to leave without making contact? No, maybe not. The guy began to pull the Beaver backward, toward the beach. The aircraft registration was displayed on the tail. His binoculars quickly picked up the letters: CF-OMG.

Ferguson was mulling over the evidence as it accumulated. Canadian registered plane arrives from Canadian airspace in the dark, no running lights showing and lands in U.S. waters. Up to no good for sure. He was guessing human trafficking, drugs or firearms, the three most likely cross-border night crimes. These days handguns and assault style rifles poured across the border into Canada like water through a sieve. Humans and drugs crossed in either direction.

If his presence was discovered during the intended transaction, things could get ugly for him, so he slipped below and fetched the only weapon he had aboard. The plastic, single shot twelve-gauge flare gun would be useless for any long-range shots, but it would make a dazzling and painful deterrent for anyone attempting to board his boat. He dropped a flare into the breach and quietly closed the action, then laid the five remaining flares on the seat cushion beside him.

Moments later he heard several ATVs approach the beach from somewhere inland. Heavy twin-cylinder jobs by the sound of them. Must be side-by-side quads. He knew that some of those machines could carry five or six people. Sure enough, a pair of the big offroad machines emerged from the trees and backed down the beach, stopping close to the Beaver. A man got off the driver's side of each quad and waded into the water. The two of them helped the pilot pull the plane up to the beach. Ferguson could hear the aluminum floats rubbing on the stony bottom.

He heard the pilot's voice again, but the wake made by the plane landing had reached his bay and was washing over the stony beach, obliterating the speaker's words. The voice sounded annoyed, but for several minutes he couldn't distinguish what was being said. Another minute passed and everything went calm again — the conversation easy to hear now.

"We need to get moving. The drone-free window is already half gone. Gotta load up and get out of here, like right now!"

"Careful with that," from a different voice. "That's a McMillan TAC-50 rifle in that case. Better still, I'll carry it." The apparent owner of the voice, and the big rifle, stepped down from one of the ATVs along with a fourth man. The voice belonged to an overweight man who picked up the oversized rifle case and carried it down to the water's edge. He handed it up to the pilot before hoisting his considerable bulk up onto the aircraft float. Despite his sense of urgency, the pilot handled the case with an unusual degree of awe.

Alex Ferguson's last detective assignment had been on the guns and gangs squad. He knew guns. He'd never handled a TAC-50, but he knew exactly what it was and what it could do. The arrival of a single .50 calibre sniper rifle quashed his human trafficking guess. And gun runners don't show up with just one firearm. Someone was planning a deadly force event of some sort.

Duffle bags and a couple of daypacks were transferred from the ATVs to the Beaver, and at the pilot's urging, the two passengers boarded the plane in a hurry.

Before he climbed into the plane himself, the pilot handed an envelope to one of the ATV drivers. Payment for services, Ferguson guessed, although he had expected the payment to go the other way — here's your cut for getting this guy into your country. Didn't really matter. Someone was being paid for something.

A moment later, the Beaver's engine started, and taking very little time to warm up, it went to full takeoff power. Less than a minute later, the ATVs started up and roared away, back into the trees.

Chapter 44

Alex Ferguson pulled out his cell phone and brought up his contact list, selected a name, touched the screen, and waited for the call to connect. Dan Fry, an old friend, was an inspector with the provincial police. The call to his home phone was answered quickly for such a late hour.

"Hello."

"Hey Dan, it's Alex Ferguson. Sorry to call so late, but this could turn out to be something urgent."

"Fergy, I thought you were off sailing the world. And no, it's not too late. Jane and I were just watching the news.

"So, what's up that 'could be urgent?' Have you gone back to work?"

"No, still retired, Dan. Look, I know this isn't your branch, but I figured you would know someone to take it to, to get things going quickly.

"I'm anchored at the northeastern-most corner of Michigan, no more than a mile from the Canadian border. Just saw a strange transaction involving a Canadian float plane taking on two passengers who claimed to be carrying a McMillan TAC-50 rifle." Then he launched into considerable detail, *every* detail observed by the experienced detective's eyes and ears.

"Oh, and when the Beaver took off, it was holding a course pretty damned close to zero-five-zero degrees. Never deviated during the few minutes I could track it in the moonlight. Still wasn't using his navigation lights. And that course would take him either to, or over, Elliot Lake."

"Okay Ferg, I'll call our Northeast Region comm centre as soon as we hang up."

"Thanks Dan. I'll let you go then."

"I'll keep you advised, Ferg. Bye."

The retired detective decided that called for a shot of rum before turning in.

—

2330 – Flying Low over the North Channel

Once Reggie Ritchie got the Beaver airborne, he trimmed it for level flight when it was just fifty feet above the water. He wouldn't climb any higher until he was comfortably into Canadian airspace. He was pissed that his client hadn't been waiting at the beach when he landed. The window during which US Homeland Security drones were not covering the border near Drummond Island was narrow and if a drone caught a tail wind, it could arrive early. He'd be up the creek if they caught on to him. He didn't talk for almost ten minutes, flying white-knuckled until the Beaver approached the north shore. Only then did he take it up to a safe thousand feet above the water.

"So, what was the holdup, Warren?" he finally asked, shouting over the roar of the engine. "How come you guys weren't waiting when I landed? That was the deal."

"Sorry about that, Reggie. The game wardens were running a check station at this end of the Mac bridge and some idiot pulled out on the highway and caused a wreck. Northbound traffic wouldn't have been affected if some other idiot hadn't been gawking and started a chain reaction pileup on our side. We just had to wait it out." Beyond providing that brief explanation, Warren Fitch seemed unaffected by Ritchie's concerns, and now that the pilot appeared open to conversation, he used his thumb to point at the guy in the back seat and introduce his companion.

"Reggie, that's my right-hand man, Wayne Parker." Parker was a tall cadaverous looking man, but under the death-warmed-over appearance was a wiry, tough-as-nails man who was Fitch's fixer. Any kind of trouble Fitch generated for himself — and there always seemed to be something — Parker took care of it.

"We've hunted just about everything there is to hunt all over North America. Been to Africa too. He didn't make it up here for that last hunt, but that's the only one he has missed." Fitch stopped long enough to take a drink from a water bottle. The yelling was giving him a scratchy throat. Then he switched topics to highlight an upcoming big business deal that meant nothing to Ritchie, and just as suddenly switched to this weekend's hunt. A touch of attention deficit disorder, Ritchie figured. He remembered that from a previous hunt.

"So, what have you got lined up for us this time, Reggie?"

"Got a lake picked out. Good dry cabin. Plenty of room for the four of us," he yelled. "There's a real nice bull on the next lake east. Biggest I've ever seen in this area. He's got a fantastic rack. There's a ridge just north of our camp with a good view of the island the bull is stickin' to. Hasn't moved off in over a week. Lots of feed, good cover, so he's not interested in leaving. He's not shy … comes down to the water, two, three times a day. It's a thousand-yard shot from the ridge. Perfect for that McMillan. Man, I wanna see that happen. But if you don't like that range, you can work your way down to the shore and cut the distance in half." Reggie didn't mention that this bull had cost him the seizure of his Super Cub.

"No way man," Fitch said. "I bought this bad boy for the long shot. You set me up on that ridge and I'll wait the beggar out. You said four of us?"

"Yeah, my young lad's finished school. Time to teach him the trade. He won't be no trouble, and if we've got anything heavy to pack out, he's built like an ox."

"Okay, long as he knows to keep his mouth shut. Don't want the law coming down on us 'cause he had to share a story with his buddies."

"He's cool. So tonight, I've got you booked in at the hotel in town. You can get a few hours shuteye before I pick you up at seven-thirty. We wanna be in the air by eight."

Twenty-five minutes after leaving Drummond Island, the white and blue Beaver gently touched down in the path of the moon on the calm waters of Elliot Lake. Five minutes of taxiing took them to the dock, and Ritchie had his clients delivered to the hotel by half an hour after midnight.

Chapter 45

2355 – Northeast Region Communication Centre

"Sergeant," one of the police dispatchers pushed back from her workstation and flagged down the shift supervisor.

"Yes, Giselle?"

"I just got off the phone with an Inspector Fry, a traffic coordinator at GHQ. He got a call at home from a retired Toronto detective about someone flying a couple of guys with a sniper rifle from Michigan into Ontario. Our region." She handed over a transcript of what she'd recorded during the call and waited until the sergeant had read it through.

"Could be something serious in the wind. That size of rifle isn't legal here, but I wonder if it could be as simple as some big hunter with a teeny weenie wanting to bag a moose? Or maybe … are there any unpopular politicians planning a tour up this way?"

"They're all unpopular up this way, Sarge."

"Too true. Anyway, look up the aircraft registration. See who owns it and get the contact info. And while you are doing that, I'll call Blind River detachment to give them a heads up. If it looks like hunting, we'll read in the MNR folks too. But the rifle is still going to be our problem."

Five minutes later Giselle, entered the sergeant's cubical. "The aircraft belongs to North Shore Air Service in Elliot Lake. Owner is Reginald Ritchie. He's got a website. Specializes in fly-in hunting and fishing packages."

"Okay … You're ahead of me now. I got sidetracked. I'll call Blind River detachment next and let them know. You give the MNR comm centre a dingle. I think they've got a CO over there now with ready access to an aircraft … *We* should be so lucky … a plane available any time we need it…."

"I don't know, Sarge. I heard you get airsick in small planes," she said, grinning as she headed back to her workstation. A moment later she connected with the dispatch centre that served Ontario's entire complement of conservation officers.

"Comm Centre. Mary Ellen speaking."

"Hi M.E., it's Giselle at Northeast Comm. Got something for you."

"Hi Giselle. Okay, let's have it."

"I've just emailed it to you, but here's the dark and dirty gist of it." She gave a short summary. As soon as Giselle finished speaking, the MNR dispatcher had the email and was ready to text it to McNabb.

"Got it, thanks. And yes, I'll get Rob McNabb to work with your folks on it." She didn't have to explain who McNabb was. By now his was almost a household name with the provincial police.

Chapter 46

Sunday, October 30, 0012 – McNabb/Williams residence

Rob McNabb was sitting on the edge of the bed yawning and rubbing sleepers out of his eyes. He had hit the sack just an hour earlier, and now he was half awake as he read the message from Mary Ellen at the MNR comm centre. Before he finished, the phone began to vibrate in his hand. Harry Mitchell.

"I won't ask what's up, Sarge. I'm already reading a message that came from our end." But to be sure, he asked, "This *is* about the sniper rifle guy, right?"

"*You got it, Rob.*"

"I'm betting they'll stay in Elliot Lake tonight and fly out early in the morning … if they didn't fly directly to their chosen hunt location.

"*No, our cameras have them tying up the plane at Reggie's base right now, Rob.*"

"Are you guys going to lie in wait and take down the rifleman before he boards the plane in the morning? I'd like to be there for that."

"*That's what I wanted to talk to you about. We can do that, and it would be the end of the rifle and the rich guy. But you and I would still have Teflon Reggie as our perennial thorn in the flesh.*

"So, I'm thinking … moneybags is likely looking for a specific moose. He is probably going to want eyes in the air. If we take a pass on the morning takedown and follow them to where they go hunting, we have a better chance than ever of snagging Reggie again. With two planes gone and

a double set of charges against him, we'd be rid of him once and for all, and we'd still get the rifleman."

"Sure sounds tempting, Harry. While it goes against the grain, me being a keeper of the flock and all, I think mother nature would forgive us for risking one moose for such a noble cause. That's if we don't bag the poacher before he shoots. But we would need to find where they've gone first, so Sam and I have to be airborne as soon as they are." McNabb paused, thinking, and then continued.

"What about your organization? Surely there's going to be some grumpy old inspector or superintendent, high in your chain of command, who'll be ready to tear you a new body orifice for not going after the bird in the hand. You know, a simple takedown, based on information received. Smuggled firearm taken out of circulation … brownie points all round."

"*You sort of remind me of a staff sergeant I used to work for, Rob. And yes, if we do this, I will be kind of sticking my neck out … but Jim Sawyer is all for it, and if my boss is that pumped, then, it's on. Also, there's a whole lot of my folks who would love to sideline Ritchie. Taxpayers too, especially all those hunt camp owners missing equipment and supplies. I mean, the COs who were here before you have never had an aircraft at their beck and call, so we were never able to consider doing something like this.*"

"Hmm. Take some planning, but my pilot just got out of bed to start the coffee, so there's interest on that front. Are you awake for the night, Harry?"

"*Meet at your office?*"

"Uh, let me think a second … coffee, socks, underwear, childcare and my faithful retired deputy … how about in an hour?"

"*Sure. Brownie is off for a couple of days, but I know he'd be real pissed if we left him out of the action. Besides, we'll need a second pilot if we manage to seize the Beaver somewhere out in the bush. I'll wake him up next.*"

"And I'd better call Rick Webb. He's supposed to be bringing me a sat phone."

"*See you at your shop.*"

"10-4, Harry."

Chapter 47

Same morning, 0710 – Elliot Lake airport

Rob McNabb turned his new HVEV crew cab off the highway and drove in the short airport road. The new truck was a delight to drive. It came equipped with all the latest enforcement electronics and had ample comfortable seating for him and his three companions: Sam Williams, Eric Snyder and Darren Brown.

A plan had been hatched at their wee hours meeting in the MNR conference room. Jobs had been assigned and weaknesses in the plan assessed and acknowledged. With several unpredictable moving parts to their plan, everyone knew that flexibility would be a necessity. But the first part was simple enough. Follow Ritchie's Beaver.

As they approached the terminal building, Constable Brown activated a cell phone signal blocking device — Constable Miller's idea for messing with the spy's communications. Everyone in the truck chuckled when they saw a light come on in the beat-up camper van occupied by the spy.

"The guy won't be able to get through now. Not until it's too late to warn the Teflon man, anyhow," Brownie said. "I'll set this thing on the airport manager's desk with a note to shut it off when he arrives for work." He took a key for the terminal building out of his pocket as he left the truck.

The only available landline phones at the airport were inside the terminal building, which wouldn't open until nine o'clock — too late to warn Ritchie. An ancient telephone handset at the fuel pumps was a designated line that went directly to the airport manager's house in town.

Once inside the hangar, Sam did her pre-flight inspection under the bright lights in the building. Rob and Eric loaded their personal gear and a crate of supplemental oxygen equipment for their high altitude flight, into the plane. The pale morning twilight was just beginning to give shape to the landscape when McNabb rolled open the hangar doors. Then the three of them pushed the Turbo Beaver out onto the parking apron. Darren Brown joined them as Sam began to go through the prestart checklist.

In town, Rick Webb had parked his Chevy pickup at the municipal boat launch. His first call told McNabb that Ritchie and guests had just arrived at his air base.

"Okay, light her up, Sam," McNabb said in the silent cabin of the government yellow bird. The starter motor whined and the turbine fired and came up to idle speed while they waited for Webb's next phone call. The wind was calm and in the increasing dawn everything in view was covered in frost. There was not a cloud in the sky. Perfect flying conditions. No wind meant water landings and takeoffs could be made in any direction.

—

Peter Wolf grabbed his cell phone and punched in the number for Reggie Ritchie. The outfitter would want to know that the MNR truck had arrived carrying four people, and that the Turbo Beaver was warming up. But his call wouldn't connect. His phone showed lots of battery, but no signal.

Reggie would be pissed if he wasn't warned that the game warden was about to fly, so Peter kicked some spare parts in front of the van out of the way and climbed into the driver's seat. He turned the key, but nothing happened. He tried again with the same result.

He got out and raised the hood. He looked around and wiggled the battery cables. One connector was loose. He twisted it onto the battery post to improve contact, then went to his toolbox in the back of the van and picked out a wrench. He returned to the front and tightened the nut on the cable clamp. Back inside the van, he was relieved to hear the starter motor when he turned the key. The old V-8 fired and started, spewing a cloud of smoke from the exhaust.

Peter shifted the transmission into drive and headed for town. He was about to turn onto the highway when the van stalled. He looked at the gauges. Out of gas. He'd burned a bunch of gas idling the engine to keep warm at night. But he had left two spare jugs of gas back where he had parked. Now he had to walk back for his spare gas. Two hundred metres there and two hundred back.

—

Eight kilometres away, Rick Webb sat in his pickup and watched Reggie Ritchie and his clients carry their personal gear down the dock toward the North Shore Air Service Beaver.

Webb got on his phone again. "They're loading the plane, Rob. There are four of them. One in charge is obviously the pilot." Webb had never met Ritchie and was going by McNabb's description. "There's a big, tall lad with a bandaged-up face … a dock hand, I presume…."

"*Ritchie's son, I'm guessing. Interesting. There's a story there for later. Let us know if he goes with them.*"

"And the two other guys I assume are the guests the way Ritchie is catering to them. One's tall and narrow and the other one medium height and overly wide, carrying an oversized gun case."

"Okay, Rick. We're about to take off and go high. Let us know when they cast off."

—

Samantha Williams taxied the Turbo Beaver toward the runway. Constable Darren Brown, sat beside her. Rob McNabb and Eric Snyder sat two rows back, next to the rear doors with convex viewing windows.

Everyone was wearing intercom headsets and they each had an oxygen mask either dangling loose around their neck or in their lap, ready to wear. The air gets a little thin above ten thousand feet in a non-pressurized plane.

McNabb pocketed his phone and toggled his intercom switch. "Okay, Sam. Rick says Reggie and his people are loading their gear. Let's head for the sky." He heard a double click affirmative, and Sam lowered the flaps and applied takeoff power. The 680-hp turboprop pulled the Beaver into the air with plenty of runway left over.

Sam trimmed the bird to climb and turned southeast and away from Elliot Lake. They wanted to gain lots of altitude before turning to follow Ritchie. If they were seen, they would just be a tiny dot, high in the sky. Reggie knew that they had watched him from six or seven thousand feet above, so they planned to double that today. When the ministry plane climbed past six thousand feet, Sam began a gentle left turn and kept climbing.

McNabb's phone went off again. He listened and then acknowledged, ended the call and spoke on the intercom. "Reggie's passengers are boarding, Sam." Double click. The Turbo Beaver continued to climb.

Ten minutes after they were airborne, Sam announced over the intercom, "You guys might want to start on oxygen now. We're above ten thousand feet. We'll climb another three, I think, and hold there."

McNabb's phone rang. It was Webb again. "*They're off the water, Rob. And the kid with the big bandage is travelling with them.*"

"Bogey in sight, nine o'clock low," Eric Snyder announced at almost the same time.

"I always wanted to say that" he said, chuckling. "Probably watched too many World War II movies in my teens." He kept his eye on Ritchie's Beaver as it left the lake far below and turned to head slightly west of north.

Sam confirmed she could see the tiny white dot climbing away from Elliot Lake. She powered the turbine back to allow Ritchie's Beaver to pull ahead.

Chapter 48

At the stalled camper van

Peter Wolfe struggled under the load of two twenty-litre jugs of gasoline. He'd started out carrying just one, but the imbalance made walking difficult, so he had gone back for the second. Now he was no more than ten metres from his van when his phone played a 1950s jazz tune.

He set down the gas jugs and pulled out the phone. A hang-up. Wrong number, maybe? But now that he had a signal he had to call Reggie. Right away. His phone was out of range of the blocking device here. Had been all along.

—

In the white and blue Beaver

Twenty minutes after taking off from Elliot Lake, Ritchie scanned the sky around him. He missed seeing the Turbo Beaver flying high above and hidden from view by his own Beaver's wing. Even if he'd seen it, at that altitude, he would have assumed he was seeing an aircraft in transit between two distant places.

The noise inside his old Beaver drowned out the urgent ringing of his cell phone, and with the phone tucked in an outer pocket of his fall jacket, he never felt it vibrating either. Sneaky Pete's repeated calls went unanswered.

A few minutes later, far from cell phone range, he began a wide left turn and pointed at an island on a lake they were passing. The Beaver was flying no more than six or seven hundred feet above the ground.

"That's Nigick Lake, Warren," he shouted over the roar of the radial engine. "The middle island … the one with the high pine knob surrounded by a hardwood covered ledge … that's where he's hangin' out. We won't go any closer than this for now. Don't want to spook the big fellow. You'll be sitting on top of that ridge over there." He pointed ahead and to the right before continuing his narration. "Our camp is on that next lake, just ahead. Man, I'm sure looking forward to seeing this happen.

"I'm going to keep this wide turn going so we get lined up to land on Loftus. If you glass this end of the island, you might catch a glimpse of him." He handed a pair of binoculars to Fitch. Fitch had to look across the pilot and through his hazy side window, so he handed the binocs back to his right-hand man, Parker.

"Wayne, any sign of a bull on that middle island?" he shouted.

The cadaverous fixer lifted the binoculars, adjusted them and then steadied his gaze on the island. He panned slowly from left to right — saw nothing. He was about to give up when he saw movement in the trees.

"There's something in there," he yelled at his boss. "Can't identify it because of the shadows, but it's big enough to be a moose."

The Beaver's engine quieted as Ritchie throttled back to idle speed and the plane began its descent. "Okay guys, seatbelts on, seats and trays in the upright position." Ritchie's attempt at humour. There were no trays, and the canvas seats had only one position. "Landing Loftus Lake in two," Ritchie said. He didn't have to yell with the engine at idle. Moments later, they passed through a gap in a stand of tall pine trees. Seconds after that, the floats touched the mirror calm surface of the lake in a picture-perfect landing.

"Camp's down in the bay here," Ritchie said, pointing to the right as he turned the plane toward their destination.

Chapter 49

In the MNR Turbo Beaver at thirteen thousand feet

"He's taxiing toward the camp," Eric Snyder said, over the intercom. He had his binoculars trained on Ritchie's plane as it approached a dock at the north end of Loftus Lake.

Sam pulled the power back some more and lowered the flaps a touch. At eighty-five knots they would be able to watch the action below them for several minutes longer. It was unlikely that even after getting out of his Beaver, Ritchie would regard them as anything other than a transient speck in the sky, more than two miles up. He certainly wouldn't be able to detect their reduced speed.

"They're at the dock." Now Snyder was having to look slightly behind, but he figured on another minute of unobstructed view. And just before the white and blue Beaver was obscured by the trees, he saw what he needed. "Not wasting any time down there. Looks like they're unloading their gear. And … I've lost sight of them now."

"Okay, Sam," McNabb spoke up. "Keep this heading for a couple more minutes, then we can start a wide right turn and position ourselves to pass over them on a southwesterly heading. We'll just appear to be an uninterested aircraft in transit from the northeast.

"We've never seen him take more than five minutes to offload, so if his Beaver is still there when we circle back, I'm betting he's staying with the sniper. At least long enough to do some spotting for the guy." That was all they could hope for. Ritchie hadn't given them an itinerary to follow. From here on, it was going to be guesswork, and hopefully a major dose of good luck.

—

Loftus Lake hunt camp

Reggie Ritchie, Warren Fitch and Wayne Parker were hiking up to the ridge behind the camp to set up and watch for the moose. Randy Ritchie got stuck with camp chores and was humping supplies from the dock up to the camp. This was probably Ritchie's best outpost. He'd stained it only eight years ago. The outhouse was almost new. Five years ago, he had dragged it across two lakes on the ice from the competitor's camp where he'd snatched it. He had built a new generator shed — with someone else's lumber.

A quarter of the way up the slope behind the camp, they stopped for a breather in a small clearing. Fitch was more winded than he let on — in addition to his daypack and a folding shooting stool, he was packing the big sniper rifle in its case.

While they rested, Ritchie began to tell them what he'd learned of the bull's habits. "The big fella usually comes down to the water by late morning. But if we miss his morning walk … just a sec … listen," he paused, scanning the sky to the south. "Fuckin' yellow bird," he said, pointing toward an aircraft that was just a tiny yellow dot, high in the sky, headed southwest. He watched for a full minute before speaking again.

"It's okay. Government plane alright, but that's not our asshole game warden. That one's headed for the Soo probably. But if you hear a turboprop today anywhere nearby, you guys let me know. I've got a big bone to pick with that prick and his bitch pilot. They're the fuckers who snatched my Super Cub."

In the MNR plane ten minutes later

"Reggie's Beaver is still there," Darren Brown said over the intercom.

"Yeah!" McNabb did a fist pump. The plane could be seen from their side of the government bird this time. "Okay, after we're out of sight again, let's circle north and land on Helen Lake like Eric suggested."

"Did you remember the parachutes, guys?" Brownie asked. Not one of them was into sky diving, and that had never been an option.

"Sure would save a lot of walking." Snyder said smiling. "But those guys would probably have the last laugh … get to the top of the ridge and find the three of us hung up in the trees dangling from our chutes."

After five minutes continuing their southwesterly course, Sam began a wide, gradual turn to the north and backed off the power to begin a slow descent toward normal bush flying altitudes. After a few minutes, she came on the intercom. "You guys can shut off your oxygen now. And since the wind is still calm, we'll approach Helen Lake straight in from the northwest. I don't like doing that without making a pass to check for floating objects, but we didn't see any shoals when we flew by last week. And we risk being seen if I circle Helen Lake. It's not much more than three klicks from the south end of Helen to Loftus."

—

After ten more minutes, Sam had the turbine whispering at idle speed as she descended in a flat glide from the northwest toward the long narrow surface of Helen Lake. The Turbo Beaver settled onto the water and Sam taxied to the south end of the lake. She beached the plane there and McNabb, Brown and

Snyder got out and tied it ashore. Sam helped them offload their packs and wished them luck.

"I'll monitor the marine radio and my sat phone, guys. What channel do you want to use if you call on the VHF, Rob?" They didn't know if Ritchie had changed his camps to a new frequency after being caught.

"Let's go with sixteen, Sam. He's least likely to have chosen the calling channel. Even if the Coast Guard folks pick up our signal, it shouldn't be an issue. But to be safe, we'll just use our nicknames so they can't track us down and grumble about improper radio procedure."

"Sixteen it is. You be careful out there, Flyboy."

"Harry Mitchell says the truckload of reinforcements should be here before noon. See you, Sweetie." McNabb gave her a parting hug and kiss, then turned to Eric Snyder. "Okay, faithful guide, lead us to the camp at Loftus Lake."

While their destination was only three kilometres away straight through the bush, the route they planned to take would be more like five or six kilometres, using old logging roads and natural openings in the bush that made for easier walking.

Chapter 50

Police detachment, Elliot Lake

Rick Webb met Harry Mitchell at the Elliot Lake police detachment. They sat in a vacant office, working on mugs of bitter detachment coffee.

Mitchell had his fingers crossed that Reggie Ritchie and the sniper rifle hunter would be caught, and both go down without a lot of excitement.

There were a lot of unpredictable moving parts to McNabb's plan, and the thought lingered in the back of Mitchell's mind that someone high in the management chain might grumble that they should have just grabbed the sniper and been happy with that.

He wished McNabb hadn't mentioned the possibility of a miss. It wouldn't be an issue if the plan worked, but if things went sideways….

Regardless of what happened today — or whenever it went down — they still had Ritchie on that whole list of stolen supplies and equipment and the assault on Snyder and threats against McNabb's family, but if the team could catch him spotting moose from the air again, that would sure ice the cake.

Webb was sitting across from him, working on his laptop. They waited in standby mode in case McNabb or Williams called with updates or a request for more assistance.

One of the moving parts was coming together as planned; there was already a police crew cab with three constables and their sergeant on the road. When Ritchie's destination had been revealed, Mitchell had directed them to get up highway 129 and head in the logging road where McNabb's ground team was starting its hike.

But in the confines of the small office, the atmosphere was like waiting for a toaster to pop. And true to form, Webb jumped when his phone did ring. Call display said Larson — the Michigan DNR detective.

"Hey, Bud, what's up?" He put his phone on speaker.

"*Rick, our guy we've got embedded with the Drummond Island poacher just sent me a text. Late last evening they delivered a hunter with a Macmillan Tac-50 to the beach at the east side of Drummond and he was picked up by a Canadian registered float plane. Registration was CF-OMG.*"

"Thanks, Bud, we also got a heads-up on that last night from a sailor anchored nearby, a retired Toronto detective. An airborne team followed them out of Elliot Lake this morning, and they flew over where the outfitter landed them to hunt. The last we heard, our guys were headed through the bush on foot toward that location. Any word on who this guy is?"

"*Big wide-bodied guy with a last name of Fitch, F-I-T-C-H. That was all our man was told. But we ran his vehicle plate: Warren Fitch is from Dayton, Ohio. He's got hunting convictions in Mississippi and Alaska and he's wanted for an illegal elk hunt in Wyoming. Didn't show up for court.*

"*We haven't found anything criminal on him yet. But he's got a mean lookin' sidekick with him. We don't have a name for that one. Tell your people to be careful out there.*"

"Okay, thanks Bud. I'll pass that along to the ground troops and we'll let you know if we need your help."

"*Lookin' forward to it, Rick. We'll stand by. Catch ya later.*"

When the call ended, Webb looked over at Mitchell. "Got a name for you to run, Harry."

"I heard." His fingers were already clicking on a keyboard as he spoke.

"And I've got to pass it along to McNabb and get my comm centre people looking for any poaching history here."

Chapter 51

McNabb's team

Any of the three men could have led the way. Each had his own GPS unit and knew his way around the bush, but McNabb figured that since Snyder was more than double his age, he'd let the retired guy set the pace — a decision he began to regret after the first couple of easy kilometres along the winding logging road. Snyder set a brisk pace that kept the two younger officers hustling to keep up.

The tentative plan was to leave Constable Brown watching over Reggie's Beaver at the Loftus camp when they got there. McNabb and Snyder would head up to the ridge overlooking Nigick Lake, the single highest spot with an unobstructed view anywhere near the two lakes. It was the most likely place for a long range shot with a sniper rifle.

Snyder was pretty sure Ritchie's bull moose was staying near the lake and maybe back on the island it had been chased from the day the Super Cub was seized. Rumour had it that Ritchie was watching that moose almost daily on his flights to service his camps.

Sam would keep the yellow bird standing by on Helen Lake, ready to respond as needed for picking up the troops, moving the reinforcements, engaging in aerial pursuit or whatever else came up. Like Rob and his companions, she was equipped to spend a few days in the bush. That was nothing new to a bush plane pilot — she'd done it enough times before.

Lottie and Mae Ling were staying with Nancy Snyder for the duration. It was anticipated the project would last no more than four days if the original information was correct. So far, things happening were consistent with Smith's original report to McNabb.

After the team left, Sam climbed on top of the Turbo Beaver and set about spreading wide strips of a large green, plastic tarpaulin from side to side over the wings and from the engine cowling back over the tail. The tarp was a cull they'd found in a corner of the hangar and had been a last-minute improvisation.

It was far from a military grade camouflage job, but the bright yellow plane would not stand out to anyone in an aircraft flying by at a distance. Without proper tie-downs it would have been impossible to keep it in place if there was any significant wind, but the morning air had remained dead calm. Sam secured it using a few strips of duct tape at key locations, but not so much that she couldn't uncover it in a hurry if she was needed. And if the wind got up and blew it off first, so be it — camouflage hadn't been in the original script.

—

Ritchie's group overlooking Nigick Lake

The trail leading up to the ridge wound under towering white pines on a carpet of fallen needles, and in places, across lichen-covered bedrock. After two more rest stops, Ritchie, Fitch and Parker finally approached the top of the ridge. They emerged from a patch of stunted oak trees to walk on a ridge of bare bedrock with a scattering of glacial erratics — granite boulders — of different sizes.

Ritchie pointed off to the right. "There's the island, Warren. You can set up wherever you want. Maybe one of them big boulders would be suitable as a gun rest."

While Fitch and Parker looked for the ideal spot to set up, Ritchie glassed the island with his binoculars to see if there was any sign of the moose.

—

McNabb's team

To make the most of old logging roads and skid trails, McNabb and his companions followed a zigzag route that entailed first hiking two kilometres west on the main logging road, then two kilometres southeast down an abandoned extraction road and a couple of more kilometres down old skidder trails and along the back side of a rock ridge.

They hoped to arrive at Loftus Lake in less than half the time it would take to hike a straight line through the bush. And that was rarely a straight line, what with obstacles such as slash piles and blowdown in the old cutovers, plus creeks, ponds and cliffs to be skirted around.

As for the best laid plans — the Google Earth image they had used to lay out their route was taken before the beavers dammed up the last creek they had to cross. Now they stood looking at a pond that stretched out of sight to the left and right of them.

McNabb: "Crap. I don't remember it looking this big from the air. Barely paid attention to it when we flew by."

"Sorry, guys. I distracted us with the comment about parachutes." Brownie apologized. "We were all looking down and imagining three guys hanging from the trees."

Although the day was warming — now plus 4° C — none of them was keen on wading the hundred metres to the other side. It also looked like it might even be deep enough that they'd have to swim part of the way.

"Well, we can't stand here doing nothing," Snyder said. "The dam is going to be somewhere downstream between here and the lake. We'll cross there. That should put us right close to the camp."

"God, I hate crossing beaver dams," Brownie said. "Slightest misstep, you slip into the pond on the high side for a guaranteed a soaker or drop into a hole and land on your butt or jab your nuts on a sharpened beaver stick."

"You speaking from experience?" Snyder asked.

"Not personally. But my little brother gave himself a pediatric colonoscopy doing that when we were kids. And I got royally reamed out by our old lady when we got home. I've had a phobia about beaver dams ever since."

McNabb: "Don't worry, Brownie. I'm sure the beavers of today are much more careful about leaving sharp sticks pointing out of the breastworks than they used to be. Occupational health and safety standards, you know?"

"Didn't take you for a desk jockey, Flyboy," was Snyder's rebuttal. "Their dams these days are higher and longer and no less awkward to cross than I remember from my years on the job." He adjusted his pack and set off to lead the way south along the edge of the pond.

—

On the ridge overlooking Nigick Lake

Warren Fitch had set up the McMillan TAC-50 sniper rifle and was watching the island where Ritchie claimed the big bull moose was hanging out. He had chosen a boulder with a flat top. It was about thirty inches high and had once been a round boulder, deposited by the glaciers during the last ice age. But the other half had been delivered elsewhere, so the hemispherical natural table had some legroom underneath.

He sat on a collapsible three-legged shooting stool, and the combination of the stool and boulder table made a perfect rest for the rifle's bipod. He was ready for the show to begin.

But the bull moose had not shown himself yet. And despite Fitch's claims of being a great hunter, he was already getting impatient. It had only been an hour since they'd arrived on the spot.

Ritchie gave his head a shake and said, "Warren, that moose will show when he's ready to. Doesn't do things on our schedule. There's lots of browse for him in those hardwoods that grow right below the high pine knob … all the way around the island. He's probably working his way around the far side right now. He'll get here soon enough."

"Wish the beggar would show up right now. I want him so bad I can taste it."

Ritchie and Parker were sitting side by side in their camp chairs in a warm sunny patch, ten metres behind the impatient hunter. They looked at each other. Parker shrugged as he poured more coffee into his Thermos cup. He whispered to Ritchie, "Always the same. Got the patience of a four-year-old."

Chapter 52

McNabb's team

"Aw, shit, no," McNabb said, frustrated. He and Snyder and Brown stood, staring straight down at the near end of the beaver dam, almost fifteen metres below them. Fifteen metres down a sheer cliff. "How in hell did they do that?"

The crafty rodents had built a large dam along the lake shore right on the narrow beach for over a hundred yards, and anchored it at the near end to a notch in the base of the cliff. The dam held their pond back from draining into the lake. From where the group was standing, it looked as if the pond level was close to two metres above the lake level.

"What keeps the weight of all that water from forcing the dam down the beach into the lake?" Brown asked.

"I'm guessing," Snyder said, "that when they started work, they cut a whole lot of birch trees that were growing right along the shore. The stumps imbedded in the base of the dam will be what's keeping it anchored in place. I've seen some amazing beaver engineering in my time, but never one like this."

"Well, I guess we'll go and check out the other end of the pond," McNabb said. There was no way for them to climb down. Not anticipating doing any mountaineering, they hadn't brought any climbing ropes. "Brownie didn't want to go this way anyhow." They were all disappointed, but things like that happened in the north. Murphy's law followed good people everywhere, just waiting for the least opportune moment to throw a wrench into their plans. If anything could possibly go wrong, it probably would.

—

Police crew cab driving in the logging road

The crew cab carrying the reinforcements sent to meet Sam Williams at Helen Lake was making good time. They were headed east four kilometres after leaving highway 129. The constable driving the truck was telling his three passengers that he knew this road well. The engineered gravel haul road was designed for carrying heavy log transports at more than 60 km/h. "We brought the camper in during the summer and camped at a lake up ahead with a great sand beach. The kids had a super … *Oh shit!*"

The truck crested a small knoll at almost 70 km/h and the road ahead was gone. It wasn't where it had been two months ago, or even two days ago. He jammed his foot down on the brake pedal. And prayed.

"This is going to hurt," came from someone in the back seat.

The constable got truck stopped with less than a metre to spare.

A beaver dam somewhere upstream had given out during the heavy rain on Friday and washed out the road, taking two big steel culverts with it. It was evident that a raging torrent had done the damage and all that remained was a twenty-five-metre gap before the road resumed on the far side.

The washed-out gap was not something that a four-wheel-drive pickup could negotiate — not with a two-metre drop from the road surface to the scoured streambed. His sergeant got on the radio to call it in while the rest of them got out to relieve themselves and exchange comments about needing fresh underwear.

—

On the ridge overlooking Nigick Lake

Fitch: "Hey, Reggie, I'd normally be willing to spend all week sitting here waiting for the right critter to come along. But seeing as how I've never had a chance to bag anything with this marvel of engineering, I'd be forever grateful if you'd get airborne and send that big fella out where I can get a crack at him."

Ritchie was about to stall for more time — he was nervous about risking his remaining aircraft on another moose chase — but Fitch hadn't finished.

"And that's 'forever grateful' spelled in *big* dollar signs."

The dollar signs were very persuasive. "Alright, but on one condition."

"What condition?"

"If you see or hear *any* other aircraft, you get on that walkie talkie and call me off."

"We can do that. Parker can bird-watch while I concentrate on my moose."

"Okay, then. I'll be airborne in about twenty minutes, give or take." Ritchie left all his gear where it was and started a quick hike back down the hill. The prospect of the extra cash inspired him to walk fast. He even jogged in places where the ground was smooth enough to run safely.

—

McNabb's team

As the officers made their way upstream, the beaver pond began to narrow, and finally, at a small set of rapids, it was confined to the original stream bed. There, it was no more than four or five metres wide. Fifty metres farther upstream, they came on a scattering of random boulders in the stream, ideal stepping stones.

"Thought for a while," McNabb said as he crossed, "that if this pond stretched any farther, we were going to end up all the way back at Helen Lake … in time for lunch with Sam." He stood on the east side of the creek waiting for Brown and Snyder to join him and pulled the GPS out of his pack. He turned it on while they stopped for a five-minute rest and a drink of water.

"Now, back downstream again. According to this, we're about seven hundred metres from the camp, and it should be level walking beside the pond. There's just a small ridge to cross for the last hundred and fifty metres before the camp."

He predicted correctly — or at least, the GPS did. It was easy walking beside the pond, and the final ridge before the camp was nothing more than a gentle rise through a birch grove. They stopped no more than a hundred metres behind the camp. Would have been an easy hike if not for the sound of Ritchie's Beaver starting up.

"Crap. We're not ready yet, Reggie." McNabb looked at his GPS. "Okay, I need to scamper through the bush straight east toward Nigick. I'm just guessing here, hoping that the rumours are right … that the moose is still over there. If he's going to do some spotting, I need to get it on video. I'll never make it all the way up that ridge in time, so I'll just have to find an opening near the lake that's big enough and high enough to get a three-sixty-degree view.

The plan for Brown to wait near the camp, remained unchanged. He would be there to welcome Ritchie back — if he returned after his flight.

"Don't forget, Brownie, Randy Ritchie is out here somewhere too. Be stealthy."

"Ten-four."

"I'll head for the lake with you, Rob," Snyder suggested. "Even with video coverage, two sets of eyes testifying that we observed him spotting moose will be twice as good in court." He looked at McNabb. "Hope I'm not overstepping here."

"No, this is where I'm depending a whole lot on your experience, Eric. I've never been on the ground here."

"It's five hundred metres from here to Nigick," Snyder said, consulting his own GPS. "We'd better hustle. And I think I remember a high rock outcrop that we can watch from. It lies between here and the lake. We may not have to go all the way through." He pointed to a slight opening in the trees and took off at a fast gait. "There's an old portage trail through this way, Rob." His daily walks around Blind River kept him as fit as most men half his age and McNabb had to work to keep up.

Ritchie's Beaver was howling at full takeoff power. The echo bounced off the nearby hills. Even though the plane was headed away from Nigick as it raced southwest across Loftus to build up airspeed, it wouldn't be long before it was airborne and circling back to fly over Nigick Lake.

Eric Snyder went into speed-walking mode and McNabb broke into a jog to keep up. He'd never known a person who could speed walk over an uneven forest trail.

Chapter 53

In Ritchie's Beaver

The fear of being caught spotting moose again by the game warden made Reggie take the simple precaution of doing a bit of aerial surveillance first. And he'd brought Randy along for the flight as an extra pair of eyes.

The kid was good in the air, and he occasionally took the controls when his dad allowed him to take over. His interpersonal skills were shit, but he had the makings of a natural pilot and never had any problem with air sickness. But today, Reggie took full control of the Beaver.

Before heading for the island on Nigick Lake, he climbed to fifteen hundred feet and began to make a wide circle several miles out. He and his son scanned the sky in all directions from the forest-covered horizon to high overhead. There were no yellow Turbo Beavers in sight. No aircraft of any sort. A quick call to Parker on the walkie talkie confirmed it.

"Okay, our bonus is waiting, Randy," he shouted. "Let's get this done." Power back, flaps down a touch and turn toward the lake, which was now several miles south of him.

If he had been looking to the north at that moment, he might have picked out the shape of the Turbo Beaver as he passed near the south end of Helen Lake. Randy should have seen it, but Sam's rudimentary camouflage job worked. The contour was still that of an aircraft, but the green tarpaulin was nearly the same shade as the trees. There wasn't a flash of yellow to draw the kid's attention. Besides, Reggie told him to watch for planes in the air, not ones beached on neighbouring lakes.

As he neared Nigick on his final descent, Reggie lowered the flaps and boosted the power all the way up. Full flaps required full power if you were intending to stay airborne. And he figured the extra noise from the bellowing engine would help get the moose moving.

He cruised just off the water down the east side of the island, opposite to where Fitch was watching. He cranked up the flaps to gain speed when he was past the island and used the increased airspeed to climb and execute a tight turn before repeating with another slow pass at full power, closer to the island.

His one wingtip was only yards away from some of the treetops. At the same time, he watched for signs of the moose moving through the bush and he caught a glimpse of it heading out of the hardwoods, moving fast up onto the pine knob. He needed to keep it going or it might stop there, so he turned away from the island, completed a 270° turn and approached head on, pulling up just in time to clear the tallest pines on the knob.

He couldn't see the moose, passing right over top of it, but had flushed it out and now it was making a fast dash for the water on the west side of the island. Ritchie didn't want it to swim from the island, so he made one more pass just above the water, flaps up and engine throttled to cruise speed — much quieter now, just enough commotion to convince the moose to return to the island's narrow beach. Which it did.

—

Snyder and McNabb

Ritchie's surveillance circuit looking for unwanted aircraft, bought the COs just enough time to save the day. Rob and Eric managed to get most of the way to Nigick Lake. They missed seeing Ritchie's first pass down the island, but their view would have been blocked by the island anyhow. Eric led Rob up a rock knob in time for him to aim his camera and catch the Beaver in the middle of its tight turn to begin the second run.

The plane disappeared behind the island again, but the video caught part of the three-quarter turn and the beginnings of the head-on run toward the far side of the island. The best part was when the moose came dashing down to the water in full stride just as Reggie's plane popped over the top of the island and circled to make his final pass.

"*Gotcha*, Reggie!" McNabb exclaimed with a fist pump for emphasis. "Couldn't have done that without you, Eric. I owe you big time." He kept the camera going, aimed at the big moose.

"Hey Rob, just being here to witness the event…." A rifle report, louder than either officer had ever heard, cut off the rest of Eric's sentence. And in the same instant, they watched the big moose collapse in a heap on the island's beach. Ritchie's Beaver made one more pass — to see the results, presumably — and waggled his wings, a victory salute. McNabb caught that on video too.

"Damn. The big guy never had a chance." McNabb suddenly regretted his earlier willingness to sacrifice a moose to bring these guys down. "What a waste." But his boss had gone along with the plan, and like McNabb, he knew the risk.

"Rob, we've been waiting years to catch Teflon Reggie. You and Sam have finally made it possible. As unfortunate as the loss of that bull may be, he has just served a very noble purpose. And when all the seizures have been made and the paperwork filed with the court, the meat will be butchered and sent off to feed some needy folks." Snyder scanned the sky in the direction of Loftus Lake. They heard but couldn't see the Beaver now.

"It sounds like Reggie is circling back toward Loftus. Time to go and conduct some serious business, partner."

McNabb nodded and pulled the small FRS walkie talkie out of a pocket. "Brownie, have you got your ears on?" There was a brief delay.

"*Ten-four, Flyboy. I hear the Beaver circling and powering back. Coming home to roost, I'm guessing.*"

"Why don't you continue hiding until we meet you behind the camp. He's going to be royally pissed when we arrest him and seize his bird. I think we'll need to be three on one, or maybe three on two, depending on where the kid is."

"*Yeah, there should be enough fun to go around. Did I hear someone doing some blasting up on the ridge?*"

"Unfortunately, Ontario has one less bull moose. Would have been nice if we'd made it in time to get up on the ridge before he had a chance to shoot."

"*Yeah, but it couldn't be helped. Anyhow, Reggie's touching down now. I'll wait for you on the trail behind the camp.*"

"On our way."

—

Up on the ridge

"Hey, man, what a rush," Fitch was dancing a jig and pumping his fists and laying high-fives on his sidekick. "Did you see that big fella drop, Wayne? Perfect fucking shot. What a sweet rifle this is. Man, I'd love to do that again!"

"No mistaking the sound of that sucker, boss," Parker said, his fingers trying to dig an imaginary blockage from his ears. "You wanna wait here for Reggie to come back up? After you fired, he said something about bringing up something to celebrate. Said he could hear the shot over the sound of his engine."

"No, let's get down and find that canoe. He said it was on the beach right below us. I want to go get that rack." The man had no interest in the rest of the animal. "If Reggie wants the meat, it's all his."

The two men gathered up their gear, leaving Reggie's stuff, and started down the steep side of the ridge.

Chapter 54

Loftus Lake camp

Ritchie taxied to the dock. While he was tying up the plane, he noticed that the passenger side float was a bit low in the water. It had been leaking all summer but was getting worse as the season progressed.

"Randy, while I'm gone up the ridge, pump out those floats, will ya?"

"How do you do that?"

"What, I never showed ya? C'mon, you must have seen me do this before." Annoyed, Reggie shook his head, then took a couple minutes to get the kid set up for the job and a couple more to micro-manage, then he headed for the trail leading up to the ridge.

As he started up the trail, he remembered he'd offered the Fitch and Parker a celebratory beer. He doubled back and went into the camp. It was a simple, sixteen by twenty-four-foot plywood-sided cabin. The long side faced the lake. There were two windows on the front wall and two on the back.

There was no front porch, just a couple of worn steps up to the door. The place needed a fresh coat of stain, but it was in better shape than any of Reggie's other facilities.

Inside the camp, the front half was an open living, dining and kitchen area and there were two bedrooms at the back with curtains hanging in the doorways. In each bedroom were two steel-framed, institutional bunkbeds, one on each side of the doorway. Accommodations for eight.

He went to get the small beer cooler from his bedroom. Food coolers were out in the kitchen and available to everyone, but his beer was his own, unless he felt like sharing. And with the bonus he was expecting, he sure felt like sharing. After a celebratory beer up on the ridge, he'd lead the guys down to the shore where he'd stashed an aluminum, square stern canoe and a small outboard motor. They'd cross to the island and field dress the moose and he'd fly it back to the camp to hang when they were done.

That was the plan — until someone knocked on the door and said, "Police and Conservation Officers, Reggie. We're coming in."

"Aw, shit." He hadn't heard anyone approaching. Where was their Turbo Beaver? He grabbed an old revolver from under his mattress then turned and stood just inside the bedroom doorway with his right arm out of sight behind the curtain.

"What the fuck do you assholes want now?" he called out as the front door opened. "You guys are really pissing me off. My lawyer is filing a harassment complaint against all of you. Now get the *fuck* out of my face and *leave me alone*."

Constable Brown came in despite the angry tirade. He scanned the main room, both left and right. His pistol was still holstered, but he had his hand firmly on the grip. "We've come to discuss your most recent flight, Reg."

McNabb came through the door right behind Brown. He looked straight across the room at Ritchie. There was enough light coming from the bedroom window to see the revolver's profile through the curtain's fabric.

"*Gun!*" he shouted and drew his own pistol. Fast. But he was still behind Brown, and when Reggie fired his gun through the curtain, it hit Brown and knocked him backward into McNabb.

McNabb was still standing but got knocked off balance and was unable to return fire quickly. When Ritchie fired again. Rob felt the slap on his thigh. "Shit," was his immediate reaction to being hit. But his training kicked in. Don't give up. If you are still alive, you're not out of the fight.

He ignored his own injury long enough to fire two quick rounds at Ritchie. In the heat of the moment, he barely registered Ritchie's third shot.

McNabb's first round caught the man in the stomach and the second rushed shot was off target but knocked the revolver out of the poacher's hand and sent it skittering under one of the beds.

McNabb was about to squeeze off a third round of his own, but his brain caught up with what his eyes saw and told him that Ritchie was out of the game. So, he held fire and kept his pistol trained on the man while he bent over to check the constable.

"Brownie…."

"I'm okay," he gasped. "Got the vest. Good shooting Rob. Quick thinking. You okay?"

McNabb looked down at his thigh. "Apparently. No blood, no holes in my pants, but it smarts like hell and the sat phone is toast."

When Randy Ritchie heard the gunshots, he dropped the handpump in the lake and raced up the dock toward the camp.

Quick on his feet despite his size, he cleared the shore end of the dock as the last shot was fired and he ran up the path. Not too smart running toward a gunfight with no weapon, but then, he'd never really mastered thinking before reacting.

Eric Snyder was still outside but had been less than two metres behind McNabb when the shooting broke out. He dove to the ground to the left of the steps. That put him below floor level and out of the direct line of fire, just ducking the shot that took out McNabb's sat phone. Seconds later, he heard the pounding of heavy feet coming up the path behind him. The kid!

He sprang to his feet again, determined to stop the junior Ritchie from rushing into the camp — possibly into a firefight, or just as likely, into a physical fight.

Snyder yelled, "Police! Stay there, kid." But young Ritchie kept coming, like a charging bull moose. With the kid's speed and size, Eric knew he'd just get bowled over if he got in the way, so at the last instant, he stepped aside and palmed the boy on his bandaged nose. Not a straight-arm and not hard. Just enough to make his point and cause some pain.

The kid went down screaming like a baby.

"Hey assholes," Ritchie moaned as he lay in the doorway to the bedroom. "I'm dyin' over here. Jesus *fuck*, this hurts. Ya gotta get me to a hospital. And what did ya do to my boy? If you hurt him, I'll sue yous all for everything you got. Fuck me this hurts."

"Sue us? You shit-for-brains jerkoff." Darren Brown was on his feet and working up to a boil. "You just shot two peace officers. *You are fucking under arrest.* You *have* the right to remain silent. And I'd sure fuckin' use it if I were you. And you're right, that hurts. Fuck *me* that hurts."

"Have you got a first aid kit in this shack, Reggie?" McNabb asked and began to organize things.

"Not much of one," he groaned. "Better one in the plane. Storage compartment behind the seats."

Before heading out for the kit, McNabb pulled off his backpack and dug out a plastic evidence bag and looked at Brown. "Sure you're okay?"

"Yeah, after I dig a six-foot fucking hole for this asshole out in the yard, I'll feel much better."

"Revolver is under the bed," he handed the bag to Brown. "I'm the shooter. I'm not touching it. Take pictures first.

I know this is a crime scene and it should stay there, but we'll have to take it with us if we are flying him into town to get that leak fixed. The scene's not going to be secure, and we don't want to leave anyone alone here with the sniper rifle still on the loose."

He left to get the first aid kit from the Beaver and passed Eric Snyder who was busy in the yard, using zip ties to handcuff junior Ritchie.

Chapter 55

In the camp, Brown grabbed Ritchie the elder by the legs and dragged him, screaming in pain, out of the bedroom doorway toward the centre of the living room area. "Don't move or I'll kick you in the balls."

He went into the bedroom, knelt on the floor and used his phone to take pictures. Then he reached under the bed and lifted the revolver. "Huh. Here's the .32 you used to shoot up McNabb's truck, Reggie."

"Like fuck it is." Didn't deny shooting the truck.

"Oh, you used a different one then? Well, don't worry. Ballistics will sort that out," he said. Ritchie didn't know that the bullets in the truck were beyond testing.

"What are your hunters doing, Reggie? They coming back down here?" Brown asked as he came back out of the bedroom. He was calming down now as the adrenalin rush began to ebb. Turning professional again.

"Told them to head over to the island to dress out the kill if I didn't get back up there soon enough," Ritchie gasped out between groans. "There's a canoe stashed in the bush, below where they were sitting."

"Your friend Fitch is a convicted poacher, you know."

"I don't ask my guests about their history,"

"Big game convictions in Mississippi and Alaska. Wanted in Wyoming, too. And you flying him in and out of the country without checking in — those Homeland Security fellows over there are going to be wanting a major piece of your hide after the Canadian justice system slaps your fingers for shooting two officers and flying unwanted aliens into our country."

—

McNabb came in with the first aid kit. "How's he doing?"

"He's not bleeding a whole lot," Brown said.

"Probably some internal bleeding," McNabb said, as he plugged the hole with some gauze and slapped on a bandage.

McNabb: "Good enough for the bush, Reggie. You ready to travel?"

"You got your plane nearby?" He gasped.

"Yeah. Probably take me two hours to jog back for it … since you shot my phone. Otherwise, she'd only be about ten minutes getting here. Portable radio isn't going to transmit over that ridge."

"Two *hours*? I'm dyin' here. My guts are in knots for fuck's sake. I'll bleed out."

"No, no … internal bleeding, remember? You'll bleed in. But don't worry, the ministry just came into possession of a Beaver that's right close by. Low engine hours I understand. Kinda tired looking, but a sound bird, just the same. I guess I didn't mention we were seizing your plane. Funny how little details like that get forgotten when the excitement starts."

"*Assholes*," came out as an angry groan. "Can't do that. It's my livelihood. It's all I've got."

"Rob," Snyder called from out in the yard. "There's a deer carcass carrier out on the roof of the outhouse. I'll bring it around to the door."

The three officers carried Ritchie out of the camp and loaded him, with some difficulty, onto the strange looking contraption. They thought about releasing Randy from his restraints to help, but he was mouthing off about what he'd do to them when he got any of them alone. So he remained restrained. To get him out of the way, Brown took him out to the aircraft first, securing him to one of the seats, wrists *and* ankles, with more zip ties.

The deer carrier was basically a stretcher, mounted above a single bicycle wheel. They wobbled down to the dock, where the manoeuvring became difficult. The dock wasn't steady, nor was it wide enough for someone to walk along beside the carrier and help balance the contraption.

"Hey, watch out. You assholes almost dumped me," Ritchie cried out between groans.

McNabb: "Your cart has a flat tire, Reggie. Hard to push it in a straight line. You should take better care of your equipment."

Brown: "Not necessarily his. He probably stole it; like all the rest of the stuff he's ripped off from other camps. Right, Reggie?"

"Fuck off."

McNabb folded the rear seats out of the way on one side of the Beaver, and they got Ritchie loaded and strapped to the deck with a minimum of additional grumbling. Brown did a quick pre-flight check of the aircraft while Snyder went up to the camp and fetched their backpacks. McNabb replaced the rubber stoppers covering the float pump-out tubes and stood by to cast off once the engine started.

Chapter 56

Nigick Lake

Fitch and Parker covered the five hundred metres down to the shore with relative ease and found the canoe where Ritchie said it would be.

On the way down, Parker told his boss he thought he heard gunshots. Not rifle or shotgun shots. Sort of muffled pop, pop, pop, like you'd hear in the city when the street gangs are going at it a few blocks away. Fitch, whose ears were still ringing from his single shot with the big rifle, said he'd heard nothing.

It took only a few minutes for the little two horsepower kicker to push the canoe over to the spot where the moose lay dead on the island's gravel beach.

"Nice rack, boss."

"Mehh, not near as big as a northern moose … Alaskan, Yukon, you know. But, yeah, pretty good for Ontario."

"Here's the saw."

"Pictures first, Wayne. Me with the moose. Me with that beautiful rifle and the moose. Rifle resting on the antlers like it's on a gun rack. You know the drill." Fitch posed for half a dozen shots, wearing a smug grin. Then he went over and took the phone from Parker and reviewed the results.

"Good stuff. Here Wayne, let me get some pics of you with the moose. Can't leave out my right-hand man."

—

Leaving Loftus Lake

As soon as Constable Brown had Ritchie's Beaver airborne, McNabb used the walkie talkie they had seized with the Super Cub to call Samantha. "Sam, Sam, Sam, this is Flyboy on channel sixteen, do you read?"

Dead air for a moment, then: "*Flyboy, Sam here. Over.*"

"Roger, Sam, the sniper has a moose down and we've got Ritchie down … gut shot. The three of us are flying him down to Elliot for emergency repairs. Among other things, he shot my sat phone. Can you call for an ambulance to meet us at his dock in about twenty minutes? Then get airborne yourself and follow us down. We'll need to fly back here ASAP to deal with his guests. They are still on the loose."

"*Roger that, Flyboy. Are you guys okay?*"

"A little bruised and shaken up and a lot pissed off. I'll have a bruise on my leg for a few days, and the constable is thanking his stars for Kevlar vests and old soft-nosed ammunition."

Sam didn't respond. McNabb started to repeat his message but saw that the walkie talkie had quit. He turned it off and back on, but it died half a second later. Batteries dead. "Crap."

"Darren," he yelled at his stand-in pilot. He got his attention and pointed first at the dead portable radio and then at the door on the other side of Brown. The constable figured out the pantomime and pulled Ritchie's portable out of the map pocket and handed it over. The volume knob was already turned on, but the radio was not. Batteries again. "Double crap."

He turned to the Beaver's dash panel and realized for the first time since getting in that there was an empty space where the aviation VHF set should be. "Awe, shit!" He wouldn't be able to re-establish contact with Sam until they got close to Elliot Lake where he could use his regular cell phone.

—

It took Parker and Fitch only a few minutes to cut the antlers off the head of the moose, along with the bridging portion of the skull cap to keep the antlers joined as a set. Just as they were finishing, they heard Reggie's Beaver begin a takeoff run on Loftus Lake.

"Hey, the man's got his head screwed on right," Fitch said. "Door to door pickup and delivery. Faster than UPS."

While Parker washed the blood and bone fragments from the meat saw, Fitch stood and listened to the Beaver's snarling engine pulling it away to the south and out of earshot.

"Idiot, where's he going?" Fitch pulled the walkie talkie from Parker's backpack. "Reggie, aren't you forgetting something?"

No response.

"Reggie, where are you going? We're ready to be picked up."

No response.

"Fuck."

Chapter 57

Helen Lake

Sam didn't take more than a few seconds to figure out that the walkie talkies in Ritchie's Beaver had died. In a shoestring outfit like his, things didn't get replaced until they didn't work. She had flown for a couple of operators like his in the past. Shook her head at the memory.

She made the sat phone call to Rick Webb and relayed Rob's message, then quickly pulled the camouflage tarp strips off her own plane, bundled them up, stuffed them behind the seats and prepared to fly. Ten minutes later she was airborne and headed in a straight line for Elliot Lake.

It was good to know that Ritchie's plane had been seized. Even if the guy survived his gunshot wounds, he probably wouldn't be in business any longer. Now they had enough dirt on him, jail time and the fines alone would cripple his business. The likely permanent forfeiture of his planes, if he was convicted of his wildlife offences, would guarantee it.

—

Fitch and Parker on Nigick Lake

The sniper and his right-hand man had no intention of staying on the island to wait for Ritchie to return. The gunshots that

Parker claimed he'd heard probably quashed any chance of that happening.

They loaded their gear and the moose antlers into the canoe and decided to go back to the Loftus Lake camp. With the lakes so close together, there had to be a portage somewhere between them. They would figure out their next move when they got there. Reggie probably hadn't even left them a note if it was a shootout that Parker had heard.

Fitch was fuming. "That's the last time we ever book with Ritchie. Damned idiot."

Parker was about to start the outboard when they both heard the whine of an approaching turboprop aircraft.

"There it is, Wayne," Fitch pointed to a small dot, growing in the sky as it approached.

"Get your orange vest off boss and start waving it when we get away from the island."

"They'll never land to pick us up, Wayne. They're probably chasing after Ritchie."

"Oh, they'll stop for us, alright. Or they'll send help. It's all in the presentation. You'll see." He didn't elaborate, knowing that his idea would be vetoed outright. He started the outboard. When the canoe was several hundred metres away from the island — about halfway to the other shore — Parker leaned hard to the right and the narrow vessel rolled over. Both men were dumped into the ice-cold water.

"Fucking *idiot*," Fitch sputtered when he came back to the surface.

As the yellow aircraft got closer, Parker yelled at his livid boss, "Good fuckin' time to start waving your orange vest, Warren." Fitch was furious, but he did exactly what his fixer told him to. The Turbo Beaver came up even with the men in the water, and the pilot pulled off the power, circled, and began an immediate descent.

"See, I told you."

"Yeah, yeah … f-f-fuckin' asshole," Fitch said, already shivering. "You can forget about that raise I was going to give you. Fuckin' dump us into the drink without any warning. Jerk."

—

In the Turbo Beaver

Sam was on the phone to Webb again. "It has to be Ritchie's clients down there, Rick. I don't know how long they've been in the water, but they're going to be hypothermic by the time they reach shore if they try to swim for it. I can't just leave them there."

"*You may be right. Sam. But be careful. The big guy is a wanted poacher. Don't pick them up if you get any bad vibes off them. Leave them to chill a bit. We were going to have to go back to pick them up anyhow. The police have dibs on them too. If you do give them a ride, don't let them know you're bringing them into the arms of the law if you can avoid it.*"

"Okay Rick. Landing on Nigick now. I'll see you at Ritchie's dock." As Sam made a circuit and lined up to land, she mulled over her options for dealing with these guys. If they'd lost everything overboard, then there'd be no firearms to pose a threat. She could dig the aircraft flare gun from under her seat and load a flare and stick the gun in the side pocket of her door. Just in case. No — dumb idea. Letting off a flare inside the plane would guarantee a disastrous and fiery end for everybody aboard.

And arresting them — as if a small, unarmed deputy could do that single handed — even the suggestion of arrest would run counter to the idea that maybe they were being taken to a warm place and set free. They might not know yet that the law was after them, depending on any communications they'd had with Reggie.

No, she would have to measure their attitude when she got to them.

After she landed, Sam brought the plane to a stop alongside the swamped canoe. She feathered the prop and shut down the turbine.

"Oh, thankyou, thankyou, thankyou miss, we would have died if you hadn't come to our rescue. I'm Wayne and my boss there is Warren," the guy shivered as he reached out to grab the float.

Polite and non-threatening, Sam decided.

Parker was able to haul himself up onto the float under his own power, but Fitch was suffering from the cold dip and the big man wasn't as nimble as his assistant. It took Parker and Sam working together to heave the man up onto the float, and by then he even needed a hand up the ladder into the back of the plane.

While she got a couple of blankets from the survival kit, Parker went back down to the float and retrieved everything from the swamped canoe — moose antlers, backpacks and the McMillan rifle in its case. Good thing he'd thought to tie it all in.

"Okay Wayne, the rifle's unloaded?" Sam didn't want that monster gun going off inside her plane. She had heard the one shot clearly, from three kilometres away.

"Yup."

"Okay, wrap yourself in this, and you can sit up front beside me if you want," she said as she arranged their gear at the back of the passenger compartment. She placed the rifle case at the very back, well out of reach.

"It's about twenty minutes back to Elliot Lake. We'll get you guys properly warmed up down there." She had no intention of dealing with the canoe but went forward and prepared to start the turbine.

"Just one thing," Parker said as he settled in the seat beside her. "We're not going to Elliot Lake." Sam looked at the man and the pistol he was pointing at her. Her heart skipped a few beats.

"Oookay … where would you like me to take you?" she asked, as cool as she could manage. If she panicked, these guys could turn mean.

"We'll let you know. South for now. And turn off your radio. You won't be using it. Now, start this thing up and let's get out of here. We're fuckin' cold."

Sam's hands worked quickly over the controls, flicking various toggle switches to the "on" position. Unlike a passenger airliner, the Turbo Beaver didn't have a highjack panic button. Instead, one of the toggles, the Emergency Position Indicating Radio Beacon, or EPIRB, was normally set in the automatic position. It automatically activated on impact, in a crash situation. But it can be manually armed as well, and Sam had just armed hers, making it look like part of the start-up procedure.

After takeoff, she levelled the plane at a thousand feet above the ground and headed south. She set the power ten knots below normal cruising speed. If her EPIRB signal was raising the alarm at home, she wanted to give those in charge as much time as possible to put together a rescue plan.

Chapter 58

Police detachment, Elliot Lake

Rick Webb and Harry Mitchell were leaving the building to meet the guys in Ritchie's Beaver at the dock when Webb's phone warbled. It was the provincial comm centre.

"Webb, here."

"*Staff Sergeant, it's Will Samson at the PCC. We've been notified by the Feds of an EPIRB signal from Sam Williams's aircraft. Only, it's moving. Not static. We can't seem to raise her on either the radio or the plane's sat phone. Do you have any other way to get in touch with her to tell her she must have accidentally armed it?*"

"Oh, boy … Will, I hope you're right that it's been accidentally armed. But I've got a bad feeling about this. She was stopping to rescue a pair of poachers we're working on. There's a possibility those bastards have highjacked her. Which direction is the signal moving?"

"*Due south at the moment.*"

"If it's a highjack, those guys are probably looking for a ride back to Michigan. Advise the Feds and ask them to keep you constantly updated."

"*Better than that, they are sending me the link to her feed. I'll have her on screen in a minute or two.*"

"Okay. Following her is your priority until this is resolved. If you need more help at the centre, call someone in. I'll get back to you as soon as I've made some calls here." He disconnected and caught up with Sergeant Mitchell, who was about to start the police SUV.

"Harry, I'll ride with you. We might have a highjack going on." He explained the call he'd just received. "Let's get over to meet Brown and McNabb. I'll call my Michigan contact while you drive."

"Aw, jeez. We should have sent someone to stay with her."

"You did, Harry, but the road washed out. Not your fault. One of the uncontrollable moving parts." Webb said, then spoke at his phone. "Bud, Rick Webb here. We need all hands on deck if you can help." And he briefed Michigan DNR Detective Larson on the developing situation.

"*That's sure not good, Rick, but your timing couldn't be better. We're sitting just a few blocks from the Drummond poacher's place listening in on a wire that our embedded guy is wearing. Nothing new has happened for almost a week, so we can scoop the poacher right away for all his past sins. Then our undercover officer can substitute for him when your perps call for a rendezvous.*"

"Thanks Bud. We are really worried about our pilot. She's a very attractive woman *and* the wife of our CO McNabb. It could add an additional level of complexity to what the moose sniper is prepared to do. She'd make a high-value hostage if they find out who she is."

"*Okay we'll get on it and call you back ASAP.*"

Mitchell drove the police cruiser into the North Shore Air Service parking lot. An ambulance was waiting at the head of the ramp to Ritchie's dock, but there was no sign of the white and blue Beaver yet. Webb looked at his phone and pressed on the contact for McNabb's cell phone. He answered on the first ring.

"Rob, ETA?" he asked.

"*About five minutes. We're over Dunlop Lake.*"

"How's your fuel? We might need to borrow your seizure."

"*Looks like about half full. Easily two hours of flying time remaining, I'd guess.*"

"Okay, we'll brief you when you get here."

"*Heard from Sam yet?*"

"She called just after she was airborne. Figured she was about fifteen minutes behind you, but something came up. That's why we need Ritchie's plane."

"*Is she okay?*"

"She was still airborne the last we heard. We'll give you the whole story when you get here."

"*Okay … but I'll need another sat phone if we're going anywhere remote, Rick. Either that, or a pocket full of AA batteries for the marine portable. I feel naked, flying without a working VHF up here.*" The call disconnected.

"Constable Miller," Sergeant Mitchell called out, and when he saw his rookie approach, he said, "Bust into Ritchie's office and find us a supply of AA batteries. Exigent circumstances … it doesn't require a warrant."

"Sure, Sarge." She walked up to the building and kicked in the door. Did it with a single kick. She'd always wanted to do that. It was too bad no one else saw it happen. Everyone's attention had already turned to the rumble of Ritchie's Beaver on final approach.

Constable Brown eased the plane down toward the water, made a smooth landing and taxied to the dock. Two paramedics rolled a stretcher down the dock and waited for several constables to secure the aircraft.

Chapter 59

Darren Brown and Rob McNabb scrambled out of the pilot's front door and their supervisors wove their way through the gathering of first responders to brief them on Sam's situation.

McNabb's heart sank. Sam had been caught up in bad situations before but had lived to tell the tale. Would things work out in her favour this time? Or would her luck run out? It damned well better not.

Webb had scarcely finished speaking when his phone warbled again. It was Bud Larson on Drummond Island.

"*Things are unfolding fast here, Rick. No sooner we had our poacher in chains than your sniper called his phone. Wanted an immediate pickup, regardless of the fact it's not dark yet.*

"*Our undercover guy answered and improvised … bought us some time. Told the guy there'd be no gaps in the Homeland Security drone schedule until late evening. He added that the wind is whistling through False Detour passage right now. They'd never be able to land the plane in the rough conditions there. He told him to land at Cockburn Island until we call him back. The guy wasn't happy, but he had to accept the situation.*"

"Thanks Bud, that's great. I've got you on speaker. Our team's gathered around me on a dock on Elliot Lake. We've seized the outfitter's Beaver and … uh, standby one.

"You *are* okay lending your pilot, Harry?"

Mitchell's reply was instant. "Absolutely. I want your MNR pilot and her aircraft back, safe and sound, and I want that sniper in my cells by tonight."

"Sorry, Bud, just checking with the guys. So, yeah, we've got the police pilot at our disposal, plus CO McNabb, and his deputy, Snyder.

"Without putzing around here getting it refueled the Beaver's got enough gas for at least a couple of hours flight time. Now, do you have any suggestions what we do with this time you've bought us?"

"*Well, it's unlikely that the wind drops tonight, so let's just forget about landing them in the open water of the passage. But you've got a sheltered water landing spot at Milford Haven on St. Joe's Island. I've been there before.*

"So, have your team fly down here to Drummond, dock your seized Beaver at the Island Yacht Haven. We'll use our poacher's boat to run over to Milford and have your Turbo Beaver rendezvous with us there. That way, they'll see a boat. Not Ritchie's plane, which would be out of place, the way this is going down. The boat will take two of us and two of you. Any more than that and we'll be tripping over each other trying to hide until we get our chance to grab them."

"What do you think, guys?" Webb asked.

"I like it," McNabb said. "With the Beaver being a legitimate seizure, we'll need Eric to stay with it to maintain continuity of evidence, especially since we haven't even had a chance to search it yet. You okay with that, Eric?"

"Can do," said Snyder.

Brown nodded in agreement and added, "Yeah, and I agree with doing the takedown in Canadian waters. When we arrest these guys, we won't have to dick around with extradition proceedings."

"Will our badges work as passports when we get to Drummond?" Snyder asked, speaking toward Webb's phone.

"*Yes, sir. With our reciprocal CO powers, you'll be just like one of us.*" Larson replied. "*Don't worry, my neighbour is the local customs agent. You'll be good to go ….*"

Everyone stepped aside to let the paramedics wheel Reggie Ritchie past. He was beginning to go into shock, but still alive. Two constables led a whimpering Randy Ritchie up the dock toward their cruiser.

Constable Miller squeezed past the upbound traffic. "Found a big Costco package of AA batteries for you, Rob, but I can't get it open. You'll need a knife."

"Thanks Mary, I've got that covered," McNabb said. Then he spoke toward Webb's phone. "Detective Larson, it's Rob McNabb here. Our new-to-us plane doesn't have an aviation radio. But I assume your boat has marine VHF. We'll call you on channel 16 when we get close."

"*Ten-four, McNabb. We'll be listening.*"

"Alright, Bud," Webb said, as Brown, McNabb and Snyder climbed back aboard the Beaver. "The guys are mounting up. McNabb is in a hurry to get his wife back. I'll call you when they leave. First, I've gotta find out where the yellow bird is now. We don't want them to cross paths in midflight."

Webb ended the call then connected with the comm centre. "Will, where's our plane now?"

"*She's just east of Kynoch, Staff. Seems to be taking her time. I've done the math and she's only doing about a hundred knots over the ground. There's also quite a headwind building, the farther south she goes.*"

"Trying to buy some time, I think. Okay, she's been told by our Michigan contact to land and hold at Cockburn Island. Let us know when she stops. Wherever she ends … uh, I mean, lands." He turned to the float plane and passed along the information.

"Not sure how long you need to wait to avoid being seen by someone in the yellow bird, guys. But we don't want to leave it too long."

"Simple solution, Rick," Brown said. "We leave right now, and I'll fly toward Kynoch. They'll be way past it by the time we get there, and then we'll turn south for Drummond.

You can tell Larson, our ETA at Drummond should be about thirty minutes from our takeoff."

Webb held the Beaver against the dock by the wing strut while Brown started the engine. McNabb and Snyder were already strapped in, ready to go.

Chapter 60

In the Turbo Beaver, approaching Cockburn Island

"Where do you want me to land?" Sam asked Parker. He seemed to be the one making most of the decisions. "You want to land on the water and tie up at the marina? Or put it down on the community airstrip?"

They could see the island ahead. The docks lay right in front of the small settlement of Tolsmaville. They couldn't see the airstrip yet, but the GPS screen showed it to be inland and apparently isolated from the community.

"Land at the strip. Then if there's somewhere we can conceal this yellow eyesore, park it there. We don't want to attract attention, especially if we have to wait until tonight."

Having been given the instruction to divert to Cockburn, Sam figured that someone in Michigan — or at home — was putting together a rescue plan. Or maybe that was just wishful thinking.

From her experience at reading flying weather, she knew there was no way the wind would die down any time soon. More likely, it would continue to blow. Probably hard. Probably all night. No moon, either — the sky was already completely clouded over. There would be no moonlit landing on False Detour Passage.

So, maybe there *were* some guardian angels looking out for her. By now, the EPIRB signal probably had a whole lot of agencies on full alert — in both countries. She just had to be patient.

The island airstrip was gravel and made for a bit of a rough landing, but she got the Beaver stopped without incident next to the small, unoccupied terminal shed.

"Park it back at the other end," Parker ordered. "We're right beside a crossroads here. We stay here, someone's bound to come snooping."

Obeying his instruction, Sam pivoted the plane and taxied back to the far end of the runway. Given their growing legal problems, she needed to keep the two men at ease as much as possible. Back on Nigick Lake, the moment Parker pointed his pistol at her she had promoted the two of them, in her mind, from evil poachers to dangerous criminals. And the pistol's aim hadn't wavered since that moment. The guy was scary.

At the far end of the runway, she pivoted the Beaver once more to line up for a quick get-away, if it was called for.

"Now back it into the trees out of sight, then shut it down," Parker said. "We don't want the noise attracting attention."

"If I use reverse pitch with enough power to back up on this soft surface, we'll be heard all the way to Sault Ste. Marie. Besides, if I back into the trees, something's bound to get damaged, and you guys will end up having to swim to Michigan."

"Well then, shut the fuckin' thing down." His patience was beginning to wear thin.

She powered down the turbine and all electronics except the EPIRB. Now they had to wait for a call from the guy in Drummond village.

"Shit," Parker complained. "We must stick out like a sore thumb. Bright yellow plane against a backdrop of green pine trees. Fuck." The forest behind them was mostly cedar, but Sam wasn't about to give him a dendrology lesson.

Instead, she suggested camouflage: "There are some green tarp strips behind your boss's seat, back there. Enough to cover the wings and the top of the fuselage. The trees around us are probably blocking the wind enough that they might even stay on." Given her situation, she wasn't keen on making the plane invisible, but it was a project that could buy some time. And anyhow, the home team would know where she was by her EPIRB signal.

"You hand them up to me and I'll do the wing walking. You'd probably break something."

Fitch spoke up, shivering from the back seat, "You're being pretty goddamned cooperative for someone who's been taken hostage, missy. What's your angle. You cookin' up some trouble for us?"

"I don't need to cook up any more trouble than you've already got. As far as I'm concerned, the sooner I get you to where you want to go, the better. But when the word gets out that you are trying to get back to your side of the border, I for one, don't care to become a target for one of your Homeland Security drones."

"They won't do anything when we have you with us. Besides we are in Canadian airspace," Fitch said.

"The rules have changed since 9/11, Mr. Fitch. A lot less reluctance on the part of your government to eliminate potential threats these days. And I guess you weren't listening to the news last night … an item that sort of reinforced that policy. Your Secretary of Homeland Security was on CNN." She figured with them arriving in Elliot Lake late in the evening, they wouldn't likely have watched any news shows — would not have seen that there was no such announcement. Fingers crossed, anyhow.

"He said they've launched a big crackdown on human smuggling. No mercy on folks illegally walking, driving or flying people across the border. Our prime minister came on right after that and gave them his full approval for overlapping jurisdictions. Human smuggling's a big problem in this country too.

"My family would be real pissed if I got shot down, but in the big picture, I'd just be considered collateral damage. You guys should watch the news more often." She figured, there was no harm in spreading a bit of fake news, not if it helps the good guys. And that gave her an idea.

She unfastened her seat belt harness, popped open her door, looked at Parker and jerked a thumb toward the rear of the passenger seats.

"I'll get up on the wing. You get me those tarps." She went out the door and scrambled up the foot pegs and got on top of the wing before Parker even had his seatbelt released. She took advantage of her moment alone to take out her cell phone and send a quick text message to McNabb:

In case it helps: Advised Fitch of major HS border crackdown. CDN PM authorized US drone intercepts of unlawful transits. Second guy: Wayne Parker.

She knew they already had Fitch's name, but she wasn't sure that his right-hand man had been identified yet. As fast as her thumbs typed the message, she had barely pushed the send button and pocketed the phone when Parker emerged with the bundle of tarp strips. Now it was up to McNabb, or whoever was lining up a rescue plan, to make some use of that brief message. If they could. If it helped.

Chapter 61

In Ritchie's Beaver

"Thessalon off to the right, Rob," Brown shouted above the thunder of the engine.

"Yeah, I see that." McNabb consulted his handheld GPS and yelled back, "Fifteen minutes to Drummond village at this speed."

Ten minutes later, Brown idled the thundering engine down to a muted rumble and began his descent, and McNabb picked up Ritchie's newly revived portable marine VHF. "Larson, Larson, Larson, this is McNabb calling on sixteen, over."

"*Go ahead McNabb.*"

"Roger Larson, arriving your location in about five, over."

"*Land out front. The channel to the docks is a bit complex if you don't have nav charts. We'll be there with a shiny black fast-mover to guide you in. And we can hear you coming now.*"

"Ten-four, thanks. McNabb out." He pointed out the harbour entrance to Brown. "That little black dot out front is probably him."

After they landed and docked the Beaver, they made their introductions and sorted out their plans. Bud Larson was a tall skinny guy in his mid-fifties. His silvering hair was cut military short. He was accompanied by a short stocky undercover conservation officer who he introduced as Frenchy

Gregoire. The man was no more French than Larson was, but his ancestors had migrated from northern Ontario back in the 1800s. Frenchy was the only one who had ever met Fitch and Parker and it was he who spoke to Fitch on the phone and told them to divert to Cockburn Island.

McNabb's phone pinged. He checked. "Hey guys, it's a text from Sam." He read it to them and asked if there was any way Larson could run Parker's name through their system. Larson called his people while Rob checked with the MNR comm centre.

Two minutes later, Larson's dispatcher called back. He listened for a couple of minutes before telling the operator to email him the list, then ended the call. "Shit. This Parker guy makes sniper Fitch look like a boy scout. He's got priors for assault, attempted murder and was charged in two different states for murder. Got off, pleading self-defence. Never loses his cool … just does his bad shit when Fitch needs to get out of a jam, which is apparently not infrequent for the big boy. We gotta get going … Have to get your pilot back ASAP, McNabb."

McNabb's heart was in his throat. Sam was resourceful and had handled herself well in desperate situations before, but Fitch and Parker sounded, at the very least, as dangerous as the others she encountered before them.

The boat was a new, twenty-eight-foot day cruiser with a cuddy cabin. Electric powered, it could do close to forty knots and the battery was fully charged. Larson handed old floater coats to McNabb and Brown and headed for Milford Haven, back on the Canadian side of the border. The coats would cover their uniform jackets. They needed to resemble civilians at first glance when they met Sam's Turbo Beaver.

Snyder stayed back to watch Ritchie's Beaver.

—

In the Turbo Beaver on Cockburn Island

"Can't we get some heat in this goddamned tin can?" Warren Fitch whined from his seat in the back. He and Parker were still sitting in their wet clothes. Both were shivering. But Parker suffered in silence.

"It's an aluminum can," Sam corrected, looking over her shoulder. "And you guys don't want me to make unnecessary noise. This isn't a commercial airliner that we can just plug into an auxiliary power source and turn on the heat. I can start the turbine if you want, but that would blow our camo tarps off. Then we'd be bright yellow *and* noisy all over again. Your choice."

"Alright, leave it off then. Fuck. That guy had better get back to us real soon. I'm dyin' back here."

—

Aboard the speed boat

The whirr of the propeller driving through the water beneath them and the steady hiss of spray splashing down on the waves were the only sounds as Larson ran the boat north, toward St. Joseph Island. It was unusual to experience travelling at high speed across the water without the accompanying roar of an internal combustion engine. McNabb and Brown were both impressed.

When they first left Drummond Island, Larson ran the boat full out, but as they got farther away from the shelter of the island, the water became choppy. The detective gradually backed off the speed to minimize everyone's discomfort.

"Shouldn't take more than twenty minutes from here," Larson said. "When we get there, we'll go all the way to the far end of the inlet to wait, then follow her out as she comes in to land," he said. "It will be just Brownie and Frenchy on deck any time we are in a position for them to see us. Frenchy, because they've met him, and Brown because the pilot knows him. You and I'll hide in the cuddy, McNabb, until we duck behind them to let you off."

He picked up speed again as they passed in the lee of Harbor Island but had to ease back again out on the choppy waters until they neared St. Joe's. Another five minutes had them in the sheltered waters of Milford Haven, a narrow inlet stretching almost two kilometres into the southeast corner of the island. At full speed he raced to the head of the bay before bringing the boat to a stop.

"Okay, Frenchy, make the call."

The undercover CO pressed the last caller contact on the phone they had seized from the Drummond poacher. It was answered on the second ring.

"*What's happening?*" came from Fitch.

"Change of plans, Mr. Fitch. They've doubled up on the drone coverage. No way you could get through their increased flyovers without getting caught. Drone pilots are under orders to intercept all unauthorized air traffic. So we're going to pick you up by boat."

—

Fitch in the Turbo Beaver

"We're soaking wet and fucking near frozen and you want us to go for a boat ride?"

"*Not from there. Just a short ride from where we pick you up. Now put this on speaker. Your pilot needs to listen to my assistant's directions. He was raised on that side of the border, and he's done this stuff before.*" Frenchy handed the phone to McNabb.

"*Pilot, can you hear me?*"

"Yes," Sam replied.

"We need you to fly to Milford Haven on St. Joseph Island. From Cockburn it's just twenty-two miles at bearing 300 degrees. BUT you have to dogleg north, then west and absolutely avoid US airspace. I can't stress that enough. Approach the inlet from the northwest. When you land, you'll have a crosswind and possibly a bit of windshear but it's quiet on the surface. No need to circuit. There are no underwater obstructions, and we've just verified no floating debris. We'll meet you when you get here. You got that?"

"Roger, destination Milford Haven; avoid US airspace; straight in landing approach from the northwest. Understood." Sam was reassured to hear Rob's voice. But she kept her relief subdued. Didn't want to tip off Parker and Fitch that a rescue was in the wind. Her job now was to fly the plane, meet the boat and stay out of the way when the law came down on the bad guys — if everything went according to plan, that is. And be ready to improvise if the plan goes all to hell.

Fitch ended the call, then returned to his seat. "Well, get this thing fired up girlie. We've got to get going."

"Tarps have got to come off first," she said.

"Fuck 'em. Let 'em blow off."

"Yeah right, and we end up in the trees because one got caught in the rudder or an elevator control. The tarps are coming off before I start up. It'll only take a minute."

"Fuckin' woman. Go on, then. Do it. Watch her, Wayne. Don't let her run off."

Two minutes later, Sam had the turbine running and was going through her pre-takeoff checks. She left the tarp strips behind the plane, lying loose on the ground. A hostage wouldn't be running around folding tarps and stowing them back in the plane unless she was ordered to by her captors. She would get word to the island community about the litter after the excitement was over — if she was still alive.

Chapter 62

Milford Haven

After takeoff from Cockburn Island, Sam took the aircraft in a wide semicircle toward the north shore of the North Channel before heading west to approach St. Joseph Island at Hilton Beach.

She kept the Beaver turning in a gentle bank to the left until she was headed southeast and lined up with the long narrow inlet. The entire flight took only twenty minutes.

As she descended over the trees at the head of the bay, she could see a black speed boat sitting along the right-hand shore. It started forward as the plane glided past on its descent and was lost from sight when the Beaver's floats touched the water several hundred metres along the inlet.

Sam slowed gradually, assuming the guys in the boat would need to get into position. Using reverse thrust to stop sooner could mess up their timing — for whatever they had planned.

She caught a brief glimpse of the boat on her side. Then it veered behind the plane, out of sight for a moment before it reappeared and pulled up close to the float on her side again.

The guy at the wheel held up his hand, signaling her to stop. Another fellow beside him stood with his hands in his pockets. She didn't recognize the driver, but the other guy was Constable Darren Brown. Sweet relief to see a familiar face.

She feathered the prop and shut down the turbine. The boat and the Turbo Beaver drifted to a gradual stop. Brown and the boat captain used boat hooks to pull the boat and the aircraft together. When he was just below Sam's door, the constable put up his hand, indicating that she should stay seated. She spoke to her passengers, "There's your ride, fellas."

"Hand me our stuff, Wayne." Fitch said. He already had his door open and was on his way down to the float. Parker slipped his pistol into a shoulder holster and squeezed between the seats to go back and start passing the moose antlers, daypacks and the sniper rifle through the back door.

"Nice rack, Mr. Fitch," Brown said. "Maybe not Boone and Crockett, but pretty damned big for an Ontario set." Fitch was pleased by the compliment.

Before Frenchy brought the boat up along the pilot's side of the plane, McNabb had been let off on the tail end of the other float.

Peeking in through the back window, he saw that Parker had his back to him as he handed stuff down to Fitch, so he quietly unlatched the passenger door and opened it slowly. He was waiting for Brown and Larson to move on Fitch.

All their possessions were down in the boat, and everything was going smoothly until Parker drew his pistol and said, "What are we doing with her?" He pointed the pistol at Sam, who was still sitting in the pilot's seat.

"She can ID us, Wayne. You know what has to be done."

McNabb was near panicking and about to reach for his pistol, but Brown and Gregoire were right in the line of fire on the other side of the gunman.

He was caught in a conundrum — couldn't take a safe shot with the two officers where they were. But he had to act fast, so he chose the next weapon on his belt. He pulled the door fully open and balanced on the top rung of the boarding ladder as he drew his collapsible steel baton.

Normally an officer whips the baton forward and downward to extend it *before* engaging the subject. But there was no time for that. Parker was holding the pistol on its side like a street gangster, and it was pointed directly at Sam. He was no longer looking at the boss but had shifted his attention forward to the pilot.

"Yeah, girlie, it's time," the guy said. There was no emotion in his voice.

"Think again asshole," Rob yelled as he leaned into the cabin and whipped the baton down hard. The extendible sections snapped open as Parker started to turn toward him, and the pistol went off just a microsecond before the steel baton smashed the back of his hand. The pistol dropped to the cabin deck and the outlaw let out an agonized roar.

"Coming through," McNabb yelled and threw himself at the shooter, catching him broadside. Brown and Gregoire shoved Fitch to the deck at the back of the boat just as Parker and McNabb burst out of the Beaver's doorway and fell into the speedboat's cockpit. McNabb landed on top of Parker — a padded landing of sorts. Parker smacked down hard on the boat's deck, winded and temporarily immobilized.

Brown and Gregoire wrestled with Fitch. The big man was out of shape but still had the strength of a bull. It took both officers to subdue him and get him in cuffs.

Bud Larson bolted out of the boat's cuddy cabin like a rodeo bronco released from the chute. He grabbed Parker and helped Rob roll him over and cuff him too.

"You are under arrest," McNabb started, but went no further than that. "Sam!" He had to check on Sam and he left Larson to guard the shooter while he scrambled back into the aircraft. The gunshot had him terrified. "Kill him if he moves," he yelled to Larson.

The rapid action scene replayed through his mind as he hurried up the ladder. Parker's gun had been pointed at Sam when it went off. As soon as he got in the back door, he looked forward. "Sam!" She was sitting in her seat. Facing forward. Not moving. "Sam?" Still didn't move. "No, no, please God, no."

Chapter 63

Rob stumbled over two rows of seats to move up beside his wife. Her face had gone white, and a stream of blood was running down her cheek. But she blinked. She was alive. She turned her eyes toward him without moving her head, but instead, lifted her hand to show him the aviation headset she'd been wearing. The ear-muff piece on the right side was a shattered collection of plastic and wires. And there was a bullet hole in the Plexiglas windshield in front of her.

Sam started shaking and McNabb was lost for words. He reached down to her waist and worked the release to free her from the four-way seatbelt harness; they immediately embraced, both shaking — both in tears.

Brown climbed into the back of the Beaver to check on them before going back down to the speed boat. Fitch and Parker were cuffed and secured, sitting on the cockpit deck.

Brown started into the police caution. "You are under arrest for a big list of charges including but not limited to attempted murder, highjack commercial aircraft, unlawful entry into Canada, unlawfully hunt moose, leave flesh suitable for food to spoil, possess prohibited weapon. Do you wish to say anything in answer to the charges…." The constable continued until he completed the caution. And when he finished, Frenchy caught his attention.

"Pilot get hit?"

"No… but a very near miss and a minor cut caused by flying debris. She's had a bad scare though. They've both had a bad scare and are pretty shaken up. They've experienced more than their share of shooting events before this. More than the average cop or CO does in their whole career. It's bound to take a toll on them."

"I saw some liquid courage stored down in the cabin. Do you think it might help?" Frenchy asked.

"See what you can find … but not too stiff. We need to get Sam back in the air, both for her own good, as well as our need to get those two locked up."

Brown climbed back into the Beaver to find Sam comforting McNabb, who was now the one most in distress. He sat in the co-pilot's seat, choked up and in tears, his mind crowded with dark thoughts, sure that he'd almost gotten Sam shot. If she'd been killed, how would he tell their daughters? The near loss of Sam, the love of his life, his "sweetie," left him numb. He barely took in what she was saying.

"I thought he shot my ear off, but he didn't. And I was sure he'd burst my ear drum, but my hearing is starting to return." She held a wad of Kleenex tissues to her cheek.

"I should have waited a second after I yelled at him, Sam. Then he would have turned more toward me. I could have gotten you killed.

"No, Robbie, you saved me. He was going to shoot me. I heard him say 'It's time.' I could hear it in his voice."

"If anything, Rob," Brown said from the back door, "when you yelled at him, I saw him turn his head toward you, but his hand barely moved when the gun went off. With self-control like that, he'd have just as easily shot at you, then reacquired his original target. She might not have been so lucky if you hadn't reacted as quickly as you did. And your fast action with the baton guaranteed he wasn't going to fire another round."

Frenchy emerged from the speedboat's cuddy cabin and made his way forward on the Beaver's float. He opened the pilot's door, "Coffee, anyone? For the lady," he handed Sam a mug of coffee and followed it with one for McNabb. "Hi Sam, I'm Lucien Gregoire. Everyone calls me Frenchy … not Lucy. *Never* Lucy. And my partner back there, in charge of the villains, is my boss, Bud Larson. I'm sure glad we got these guys. Close call for sure, but we're all still standing.

"Too fucking close," Sam said, and she waved the shattered headset at him. "Thanks, Lucien. Thanks for coming to the rescue. This dangerous shit is getting to be a habit with McNabb and me."

"Maybe you should fly for an airline instead."

"Ha! No effing way. Sitting and watching one of those big birds do almost everything for itself would *bore* me to death."

"So, the coffee is fresh from my Thermos, but it is reinforced with a little something creamy from the galley."

She sniffed the mug. "Baileys? I probably shouldn't drink before I fly those two assholes back to Elliot Lake … but you did say it was coffee, right?"

"Ah, oui Madame … that's about all the French I know … all of the polite French, anyhow. Yes, I did say coffee."

"Thanks Frenchy." She took a sip and grinned. "Yeah, that'll work. Here, Rob guzzle this down." She gave her man a one-armed hug as he took the second mug. "We've got work to do before we get airborne again. When you drain that, get me the duct tape from the tool kit."

McNabb took a tentative sip. Gasped at the first swallow. "Good stuff," he managed to get out.

"I gave you a double, Rob. Maybe a bit more than double," Frenchy said, grinning. The boosted coffee, combined with Sam's call to action snapped him out of his dark thoughts. He came back to the present and got out of his seat. "Duct tape coming right up."

Minutes later, Sam stuck a small square of the durable adhesive on the inside of the windshield over the bullet hole.

Then she stood in the doorway and leaned out over the windshield where she placed matching piece on the outside. "That'll keep the draft out until we get it replaced," she said.

While Sam was patching, McNabb placed the shattered headset in an evidence bag and moved a headset from one of the back seats up to the pilot's plugin. Then he joined Brown and the Michigan COs in the boat. The constable was planning the next steps.

"Okay, we've got two planes and two bad guys to get back to Elliot Lake. I want Parker and Fitch to be accompanied by at least two officers other than myself. I can't guard and fly at the same time. And we don't want to take them into Michigan either. One option is for me to catch a boat ride over to Drummond with you guys and fly Eric back here."

"No need for that, Brownie," Bud Larson interrupted. "Frenchy and I will help McNabb escort these two. Now that we're involved, we'll have to give statements to the police here anyhow. You take the boat back to Drummond and fly the other plane directly home. I'll call my neighbourhood customs agent, and he'll secure the boat for us. All we need is a place to crash for the night up there, and a ride home after all the paperwork is finished."

McNabb: "Lots of accommodations available up our way, and Rick Webb can drive you back tomorrow. He'll need to hang around for the debriefing anyhow. Does that work for you, Brownie?"

"Sounds like a plan. And, Rob, you need to call our bosses while I'm out joy riding with this fancy boat. They're probably tearing their hair out by now, wondering what's happening down here."

"I'll call them as soon as we're airborne."

McNabb was back to his organized self. He called out to the waiting passengers. "Elliot Lake flight number one now boarding. Criminals, get your sorry asses in here.

"Mister Fitch, welcome aboard. I will be your personal attendant. Try anything stupid and I'll break *your* fucking knuckles too." McNabb wasn't going to trust himself near Parker. The urge to kill the guy was still strong, so the two Michigan officers would guard Fitch's murderous henchman during the flight.

When everyone was aboard the yellow bird, Brown untied the lines and hopped into the speed boat. Sam fired up the turbine and the constable blasted out of the inlet alone on the electric boat.

McNabb phoned Rick Webb, who put his phone on speaker and listened to the highlights along with Sergeant Mitchell.

"*That's great, Rob. You two are going to need some time off after all this is settled. You can have as much as you need.*"

"Wasn't just Sam and me, Rick. It was a team effort. Really impressive, considering that most of us have never worked or trained with each other before."

"*True enough, but you and Sam have both accumulated enough terror points to cause lesser men and women to cry out in their sleep … or worse. Anyhow, we'll deal with all that when we debrief.*

"Rick, before we debrief, we have to drop our prisoners in Elliot, then get back up to Nigick Lake before dark to gut that moose. I'd hate to see it spoil. Sam says these assholes just took the antlers and were going to let the rest go to waste."

"Already taken care of Rob. There's a Dr. Gordon Tribe, a retired coroner from Sudbury standing by on the scene as we speak. He was flying over with his grandsons in his own floatplane. They saw the swamped canoe and called it in expecting to have to initiate a search and rescue mission. Long story short, we briefed them on the situation, and they are with the moose now.

"If you agree, he'll open it up, do the forensic stuff, collecting and recording evidence as he goes. He says the three of them'll hang the carcass and camp there for the night."

"Sounds good, but … is he for real? I'd sure hate to screw up our evidence because we fell for a scam of some sort."

"*Harry knows the guy. Handled a couple of forensic exams he needed done a few years back. Couldn't ask for better.*"

"Okay. Give him the go-ahead, then. We'll fly up for the moose tomorrow morning and I'll look forward to meeting the good doctor."

"*Will do. By the way, Teflon Reggie is alive and recovering from surgery. The surgeon said your name came up as he was going under. The poacher can't stand your guts, but he was impressed that you are the first guy to get the better of him. You've earned his grudging respect, the medical team said.*"

"Again, team effort, Rick. Not just me. Have you got transport arranged for these two terrorists when we land?"

"*We'll meet you at the airport and haul them to the lockup.*"

"And more comfortable accommodations for our Michigan heroes?"

"*Ten-four.*"

Chapter 64

Monday, October 31, 0830 – Nigick Lake

It was -5° C, clear and not a breath of wind. A lacey film of frost decorated the trees along the shore as Sam Williams taxied the Turbo Beaver toward the beach where Warren Fitch's moose was now suspended under a crude tripod of spruce poles.

A cream-coloured Cessna 180 was backed up to the beach, and Sam backed the government aircraft in beside it. Two boys in their middle teens and a tall white-haired man in his late sixties stood on the beach waiting to greet the ministry folks. The teens waded in to ease the Beaver's floats close to the stony shoreline.

"Doctor Tribe, I presume?" McNabb said as he stepped ashore. "I'm Conservation Officer Rob McNabb and this is my wife and pilot and deputy CO, Samantha Williams."

"Good to meet you, Rob and Samantha. I'm Gord and these are my grandsons Steve and Pete. I understand from your staff sergeant that you folks had a pretty harrowing time of it yesterday. I'd have thought they'd give you a few days off after that."

"We're the entire MNR enforcement team here, Gord, and we need to wrap this up first. Then we get to do the peer support interviews and take some time off. We sure appreciate you guys stopping to secure the seizure for us. We didn't get through locking up our poachers and de-briefing management until late last night."

"We would have quartered this big fellow for you, but we were just on a sight-seeing tour, and we didn't have a meat saw with us."

"Got that covered. We brought a Sawzall," Rob said. "Did you find anything of forensic value?"

"Great big entrance wound … about .50 calibre according to my plastic navigation ruler."

"That fits. Good evidence. The guy was using a .50 cal. sniper rifle," McNabb said.

Tribe continued: "We took pictures as we progressed. I'll email them to you. The exit wound wasn't much larger, so the bullet had to be a full metal jacket, and it didn't hit a rib on the way in or out. Slim odds of that happening. The only sign of the bullet is a copper streak Steve found on this rock over here. Ricochet mark I'd suggest. Got pictures of that, too."

"So his bullet is hiding somewhere on the island," Sam said.

"Yeah, finding it would be a lost cause."

"Well, fortunately, their egos got the better of them and they took a bunch of trophy pictures on their phones," McNabb said, smiling. "Them with the moose. The rifle resting across the moose's antlers, the moose, the hunter and the rifle. Both guys."

"And we'll compare DNA on this carcass with the antlers we seized," Sam added.

"If you guys bring me the head and antlers, I'll match the saw cuts. Positive ID on tool marks gives you one more piece of confirming evidence in case a judge or juror is from the dark ages and thinks DNA is just a bunch of hokus pokus."

"I appreciate that. We'll get them to you right away Gord." They exchanged business cards and McNabb looked across at the other shore. "After we get this fellow quartered and loaded, I'd like to hike up to the ridge where the shot came from. It would be helpful if I could find an empty shell casing. It wasn't in any of their packs when we searched them last night. Probably needle-in-a-haystack odds, but you never know. And there might be other useful evidence there too."

The canoe that Fitch and Parker had abandoned was now drained and beached beside the Cessna. "We left the outboard in the water," Peter said. "My shop teacher said that the internal parts on a submerged outboard can start to rust soon after they are hauled out of the water. It's better to leave it submerged until you are ready to dry it out and start it up. I think Steve and I can get it started while you cut up the moose."

"Go for it, then, young fellow," McNabb gave him the green light, and half an hour later, with the last moose parts loaded aboard the Beaver — everything except the gut pile — the boys got the tiny outboard running.

"We had to drain some of the gas to pour off the water in the tank, but it looks like there's almost a litre of gas left."

"That will get me over and back with plenty to spare, Peter. Thanks. These tiny motors run pretty much on fumes."

"Do you want help looking for stuff up there?"

"What say you, Grandpa?" McNabb asked. "Are you in a hurry to leave?"

"I think we can spare a couple of hours, boys. Then I can break camp and stow things in the plane the way *I* want, instead of the jumble you guys made of packing when we left home."

—

1040 – High on the ridge overlooking Nigick Lake

Finding the general location of the shooting spot was easy. They topped the ridge close to where Reggie Ritchie had left his camp chair and daypack. McNabb scouted for a spot with the best view of the exact location the moose had gone down. That was a bit trickier and it took a few minutes, but he spotted three marks left by a three-legged stool in the dried moss. It had been set up next to a large hemispherical boulder. That gave Fitch's watch stand away. But there was no sign of the brass casing lying around.

"Might have to bring in a detector dog to find it, boys."

Before he could say anymore, the youngest Tribe boy called out, "Found it!" The kid was lying on his belly, looking under the gun rest boulder.

"Don't touch it, Steve."

"Nope, but we'll need a long skinny stick to get behind it to roll it out." When Fitch had ejected the empty brass casing, it must have bounced off an adjacent rock and rolled into where it got wedged in the tiny space.

When they fished it out of hiding, McNabb showed the boys faint fingerprints on the big brass casing. "Betcha at least one of those prints will match our poacher." He took out his phone and took pictures of the poacher's watch stand location before heading back down to the lake.

"That was fun. I think I'd like to be a CO, Rob," Steve said, and he quizzed McNabb on career possibilities all the way back down to the lake.

Fifteen minutes later they returned to the island beach. Grandpa Tribe and Sam had the Cessna loaded and ready to go. They lashed the canoe to the Turbo Beaver, and both planes left within minutes of each other.

Epilogue

Bail court by video link: Elliot Lake, Blind River and Sault Ste Marie

Warren Fitch and Wayne Parker sat with their handcuffs chained to the table in front of them. They faced a camera in a drab interview room in the Blind River police detachment. Senior Constable Archie McEwen stood guard, towering over them.

Reggie Ritchie stared at another camera and monitor while propped up in his hospital bed in Elliot Lake. Ritchie's lawyer, Thornton J. Greene agreed to act for the Americans as well as Ritchie, and he watched all three clients on a monitor from the relative comfort of the courtroom in Sault Ste. Marie. Presiding over the hearing was Provincial Court Judge Diane Chenoweth. She was in the Soo, substituting for another judge.

Officers McNabb, Williams, Brown and Snyder all watched the proceedings on a split screen monitor in the Blind River detachment squad room. There was no camera aimed at them. They were strictly spectators. It took the system a moment for their screen to connect and they missed the court clerk's call to order and the introductions, but it came to life in time to hear the clerk read out the lists of charges against the three defendants. Long lists. They watched the judge's unchanging neutral expression as she listened to the clerk.

"The Crown's position on bail?" Judge Chenoweth asked when the clerk was finished.

McNabb's heart stopped when the crown attorney's face came on screen. "Ohhhh God help us! Mark Wilson … he's the incompetent rent-a-crown who dumped the whole aircraft seizure hearing in my lap that day in court. We are truly screwed, guys."

The four of them sat forward in their seats and held their collective breath.

"Your Honour," Wilson began. "The crown's position is that pretrial release for these defendants is absolutely out of the question. All three of these men are parties to a serious poaching conspiracy that involved using an aircraft to hunt.

"Even more serious than that were their attempts to evade capture, which resulted in two peace officers being shot and a third officer shot at, but missed fortunately… even then, by only the narrowest of margins. And she sustained minor facial injuries in the incident. Not only are the defendants charged with attempted murder, but there are also serious firearms offences, plus illegal entry into the country and a raft of major provincial offences under the Fish and Wildlife Conservation Act.

"Now, specific to Fitch and Parker: these two men are residents of Ohio and are currently on the lam from the law in the Wyoming State, wanted for failing to appear at trial for poaching offences in that jurisdiction. If they feel free to evade the law in their own country, the court *must* recognize that if released, it is highly doubtful that they would voluntarily return to face justice here.

"As for Mr. Ritchie, earlier this month, he was charged with using an aircraft to hunt, and the first of his two aircraft was seized by the officers on that occasion. During his apprehension he assaulted a peace officer and was arrested but released on his own recognizance the following morning.

"Apparently, he found it difficult to adhere to his bail conditions, for during the intervening time, he coerced an employee into engaging in a series of escalating harassing events at the home of Officers McNabb and Williams. The events ranged from minor mischief to outright vandalism as well as sending threatening social media posts to their teenaged daughter.

"Not only do the criminal code offences permit incarceration, but the Fish and Wildlife Conservation Act also provides for up to two years in jail upon conviction, as well as stiff fines and permanent forfeiture of unlawfully used equipment. That, Your Honour, is how serious these offences are considered in the world of natural resources law enforcement."

McNabb said to his fellow officers: "Well, I stand corrected, guys. Our Mr. Wilson appears to have sharpened his game."

"I heard Harry and Rick talking to him on the phone last night, after the rest of you left," Brown said. "He apologized profusely for his first wildlife court caper and promised to be prepared today."

"I'm thinking he must have stayed up all night studying," Rob replied.

They watched Wilson sit down and the camera returned to the judge. "Mr. Greene, does the defense have anything to say on bail?"

"Yes, Your Honour," Greene said, as the camera focussed on him. "Remand in custody would only project an aura of unfairness, particularly for Messrs. Fitch and Ritchie. These men have businesses to run.

"Mr. Ritchie can't just be locked up for months while awaiting his trial. He tells me he still has nine parties out in remote camps, inaccessible by any means other than by air. Surely the court is not going to leave those hapless hunters languishing in the wilderness all winter."

"Excuse me, Your Honour …"

"Yes, Mister Wilson?"

"Sorry to interrupt, Mister Greene. Your Honour, defendant Ritchie's second aircraft was seized as a result of yesterday's poaching activities. Even if he were not lying seriously injured in a hospital bed after engaging two peace officers in a losing gunfight, he would still have no means of fetching his nine parties of hunters back to civilization.

"Therefore, the staff at Natural Resources have already arranged with two of the defendant's competitors to fly these parties out."

"Your Honour, I most strenuously object," Greene bellowed. "By seizing my client's aircraft and then allowing his competitors to scoop up his guests, the government people have as much as put the man out of business, even before he's had a chance to defend himself against these frivolous and vexatious charges in court. This officer McNabb has had it in for Mr. Ritchie ever since he arrived in the area earlier this month. He's been harassing my client at every turn. I *insist* that these ridiculous charges be dismissed."

"Mr. Greene," Judge Chenoweth sent the man a searing look over her half glasses. "We are here to discuss bail, not to entertain pre-trial motions, not to hold a trial, not to contest a sentencing of parties not yet convicted. Please sit down, sir.

"The defendants Ritchie, Fitch and Parker are remanded in custody for trial. Counsel will attend at Blind River court one week from today prepared to agree on an expedient trial date. We are adjourned."

Smiles broke out in the detachment squad room. "Alright!" McNabb did a celebratory fist pump as the monitor screen went blank. "We're winning. Just gotta get through a trial now."

"You guys shouldn't have any trouble winning there either," Brown said. "She will probably move your wildlife charges up to be tried alongside of the criminal matters in a case this complex. That's been done before."

"What about Ritchie, the younger?" Sam asked.

Eric Snyder had the answer for that. "He's still on the hook for assaulting Mae Ling and young Mitchell. As for yesterday, my perception, as he raced toward me like an out-of-control locomotive, was that he was in a panic to see his dad and I was simply in his way. He got his nose rebroken, and I came out of it unscathed. I suggested that he not be charged with the additional assault, and Harry agreed. The kid has arrived at a fork in life's road. Let's hope he chooses wisely."

"He's back with his mother in Blind River," Brown added. "And I understand he's under her version of house arrest."

Sam looked at Rob. "Ready to go, Flyboy?"

"Yeah." He stood and looked at the others. "Thanks for everything, guys. I really mean it. We make a great team. But now, we'll be incommunicado for three weeks. We're off to critical incident counselling first. And then we're taking a big time out with the phones turned off while we do some needed renos to our new home. Sam's dad is driving up with the funds and the knowhow to help us put new siding on the house before the snow flies.

"While we are off, the air service is lending you a pilot and the yellow bird, Brownie, to gather up Reggie's stolen goods before freeze-up. I'll be available for court any time after we return to duty."

Afterword

In Ontario, Conservation officers protect our natural resources from misuse and abuse by thoughtless or greedy people.

These officers, numbering around two hundred, form the thin green line of folks who enforce the twenty-seven laws and regulations that protect our lands and waters and the creatures that dwell thereon from harm. Some of those regulations — particularly those regarding firearms, snowmobiles, ATVs, boats and alcohol — also protect the safety of those enjoying the great outdoors.

Conservation officers frequently work alone in remote locations and must be their own detectives, crime scene investigators and court officers. Above all, a CO must be a proficient juggler, able to handle any number of cases simultaneously, each case being at various stages of completion.

It is a rewarding career choice for those who have the determination and drive to succeed.

About the Author

David Ferguson's career as a conservation officer (CO) with the Ontario Ministry of Natural Resources (MNR) spans almost thirty years and began in eastern Ontario as a deputy CO when he was hired as a fish hatchery technician in 1970. He became a full-fledged CO in the MNR's former Moosonee District in 1975.

He served in that capacity, making his way south, first to Elliot Lake and then Minden, from where he retired in 1999. During his career, he came into contact with thousands of people. By far, the greatest number were law abiding folks. Of those he encountered breaking the law, many would politely accept their fate, causing no problems for the officer. But there were also some of the kind of people you didn't turn your back on — men of the sort who are also known to the police.

David retired with his mental warehouse full of memories that could be fictitiously woven into the fabric of his stories. His believable characters are composites of the many people he has met over a lifetime. The places he has lived, worked and travelled, provide the realistic settings for his fictional stories. This is his fifth such book.

He lives with his wife Pat in northern Ontario.

www.ingramcontent.com/pod-product-compliance
Lightning Source LLC
Chambersburg PA
CBHW070220260626
47160CB00002B/616

9780993952258